HEART
OF THE MATTER

Visit us at www.boldstrokesbooks.com

Acclaim for *House of Clouds*

"...impressive first novel...wonderful characters, intrigue, history, and superb writing." — *JustAboutWrite*

"KI Thompson's historical romance, *House of Clouds*, envelops the reader in the drama of the Civil War and the intense passion of a woman's love story. Thompson shares her gift for vivid description with fascinating detail to make her characters and their struggles come alive. This novel offers the reader an opportunity to enjoy a good story that is both well-written and captivating." — Diane S. Isaacs, PhD in African American Studies, Professor, George Washington University Honors Program

"KI Thompson has ventured into well-trodden ground—the American Civil War—and made it fresh and fascinating all over again...It has the inevitability of a well-structured novel and the emotional delight of a troubadour's tale one wants to hear again and again. Welcome, Ms. Thompson, to the ranks of the writers. I look forward to your next book." — Ann Bannon, author of *The Beebo Brinker Chronicles*

By the Author

House of Clouds
Heart of the Matter

HEART
OF THE MATTER

by

KI Thompson

2008

HEART OF THE MATTER

ISBN 10: 1-60282-010-4
ISBN 13: 978-1-60282-010-4

THIS TRADE PAPERBACK ORIGINAL IS PUBLISHED BY
BOLD STROKES BOOKS, INC.
NEW YORK, USA

FIRST EDITION: APRIL 2008

CREDITS
EDITORS: SHELLEY THRASHER AND STACIA SEAMAN
PRODUCTION DESIGN: STACIA SEAMAN
COVER DESIGN BY SHERI (GRAPHICARTIST2020@HOTMAIL.COM)

Acknowledgments

My grateful thanks go to Len Barot for continuing to publish my work. You, and all the BSB authors, inspire me every day.

My deep appreciation also goes to my editor, Shelley Thrasher, whose patient guidance keeps me headed in the right direction. To Jennifer Knight, whose insights are tremendously invaluable, and to Stacia Seaman, who never misses a beat.

Thank you to Sheri, for creating such a lovely cover without much input. Not only do you have artistic talent, but you're a mind reader, too.

As always, my love and thanks go to Kathi for her unequivocal support and encouragement.

And finally, to readers everywhere who still love the feel of a book in their hands. Thank you.

Dedication

For Kathi: for knowing my heart.

CHAPTER ONE

A nd we're away."
　　Kate Foster looked up from the camera whose light had just blinked off and yanked out her earpiece. Abruptly rising from her chair, she jerked the microphone from her jacket as well. "What the hell happened with the video, Mike?"

Even without the microphone, Kate made herself heard through the glass panels of the Channel 5 sound booth. Some people claimed they could hear her on the floor below as well, which secretly pleased her.

"There was an error on the clip number," Mike Spencer, her producer on the evening news program, replied. His voice sounded tinny and hollow over the speakers in the newsroom. "The numbers were transposed, and when someone caught it, there wasn't enough time to get it on air. Sorry about that, Kate."

"Jesus Christ." Kate shoved a hand through her dark, shoulder-length waves. "Let's get it right next time, people. This isn't some Mickey Mouse operation in a third-rate market. This is DC, for cryin' out loud. We're supposed to be the best."

An intern about to cross her path paused, then detoured to the back wall. The room hushed as Kate hurled the mike and earpiece onto the console in front of her. Grabbing her notes, she started to stalk out of the room, then stopped and took a deep breath. The politically correct thing to do was to soothe everyone's ego, but God, she hated that crap.

"Okay, everybody." She kept her voice subdued. "I know we've all worked hard to turn this program around, and the ratings show it. But the little things make a difference, and we didn't achieve what we have because we let them get away from us. Let's try harder, because the guys over at Channel 2 are dying to knock us off our pedestal."

She strode out the door, but before it closed behind her, the room returned to its normal buzz of activity. She shook her head and continued down the hallway. *Christ.* Today it was the video on the three-alarm fire in the South Capitol area, yesterday the inane comments by a moron reporter. She was almost to her office when she heard footsteps behind her.

"Kate, do you have a minute?" Mike Spencer caught up to her.

"Sure, Mike." Kate stopped and waited for him.

She had an idea what was coming. After lengthy negotiations between the station's lawyers and her lawyers, they had finally been able to hash out a contract acceptable to both sides. Management wanted Kate to sign it, something she had been putting off.

Since Kate had come on board two years ago, Channel 5 had risen from the bottom to number one in the ratings. She was their star quarterback, and they knew it. Kate loved a challenge and had told them she could turn the place around. And she had.

Now the rush that success always gave her was fading, and she was once again searching for the high that went with it. Why was she so dissatisfied with her progress so soon? She wanted more, but she couldn't quite determine what the more could be.

She followed Mike into his office where she was surprised to see Sheila Dalton, chief programming officer, already waiting for them. They were obviously attempting to nail her down and get her to sign. Kate sat on the plush leather sofa and laid her arm across the top, knowing that her body language connoted expansive self-assurance. Mike closed the door behind them and poured three tumblers of scotch.

"Hello, Kate." Sheila smiled warmly.

"Hi, Sheila." Kate returned the smile and took the glass from Mike. "I didn't expect to see you here."

"Well, everyone seems satisfied with the contract, but you still need to sign it. We just didn't want to let it go any longer."

Kate nodded and took a sip. As the single malt burned its way down to her belly, she almost closed her eyes in ecstasy. There was nothing like a good scotch at the end of the day, and Mike always kept her brand in his office. It was a small thing, really, but she appreciated it.

His thoughtfulness had made her feel welcome ever since she joined the station, and she remembered how they had fawned over her. She was the new kid on the block, the award-winning investigative journalist everyone wanted. It was all bullshit, but she had played the game, knowing they needed her more than she needed them.

"I don't have to tell you, Kate, that we are very pleased with the turnaround Channel 5 has made in the past two years," Sheila began. "And any fool can see the direct correlation between our rapid rise in the ratings and your arrival in the anchor chair. Our audience loves you, in almost every age and race category we've polled. We see nothing but a bright future, and we want you to play a major part in Channel 5's growth."

Sheila removed the contract from a leather portfolio and slid it across the glass coffee table. "Everything's in order. Just put your Jane Hancock on the last page."

Kate placed her drink on the table and picked up the contract, scanning to see everything she had asked for. She should feel ecstatic, but she yearned for more and realized what it might be. She laid the contract down. "Very generous, thank you. But I want to add one more thing."

Sheila glanced warily at Mike, obviously surprised at this unexpected turn of events.

"I want more time out in the field, special assignments, that sort of thing," Kate explained. "At least once a month, schedule permitting, of course."

"We just got you into the anchor chair and now you want out?" Sheila grinned nervously.

Kate leaned forward, wanting to impress upon her boss the importance of her request. "I need to be out there," she gestured vaguely toward the wall, "to keep fresh, to keep my finger on the pulse of the city. Our audience is smart enough to know when the person sitting in front of the camera is feeding them a line of bull or knows what the hell they're talking about. And that will keep us number one, Sheila. If I become stagnant in that chair, those ratings will drop like a lead balloon."

Sheila walked over to the window, the night sky lit up by the adjoining office buildings. After staring outside for a moment, she turned back.

"I need to take this upstairs," she murmured. "I'll have to get back to you, Kate."

"Great. Thanks, Sheila." Kate rose and extended her hand. "Once you know for sure, I'll be happy to sign."

That would give them something to think about.

Kate left Mike's office and strode down the hallway to her own office, where she deposited her notes and picked up copy for tomorrow's broadcast. Glancing at it, she grabbed the phone and punched in a number.

"Jerry, what's this shit on my desk? This isn't what I wrote. Who's editing my work?" She paused, listening to the response. "Well, fuck that. Tell her if she touches my copy again she'll be working the night shift at some single-watt in rural North Dakota."

After slamming the phone down, she left her office and took the elevator to the parking garage. She climbed into her Porsche Boxster and sank into the seat with relish. "It's good to be me," she said aloud.

Kate was right on her career track from where it had begun ten years earlier after grad school. All those years of hard work, first as an intern at the *Chicago Tribune*, then as an award-winning reporter for the *Washington Post*, had culminated in turning around this station.

After making the transition from print journalism to television,

Kate found being on air a challenge compared to her routine at the *Post*. Anything could go wrong in front of the camera, and it frequently did. She had to stay alert throughout every show and prided herself on making each one appear to come off flawlessly, despite the behind-the-scenes glitches.

No wonder Channel 5 had been at the bottom of the ratings, with as many screwups as they'd had. Without her, they'd still be seeing the backside of Channel 7, a station that really sucked. She'd had to step on quite a few fingers and toes in the process and knew what they called her behind her back at the station, but she didn't care. The thrill of success was worth alienating a few lazy employees.

She flipped open her cell phone and pressed the number five, holding it down until it connected.

"Hey, girl. So did you sign already?" Dean Parker, her agent, inquired jokingly.

"Almost."

"Almost?" He sobered immediately. "What do you mean, 'almost'?"

Kate sighed. "Don't worry, Dean, you'll get your cut. I decided I want special assignments written into the contract, but I don't think they'll object. It's a deal breaker and they know it."

"But, Kate," he was clearly exasperated, "I thought everyone had agreed to all the stipulations."

He was beginning to annoy her. "Everyone but me. Don't worry. They'll give it to me. They don't have a choice."

"We should celebrate, then." His mood readily shifted. "Champagne and all that. We need to talk anyway, about your future."

"I'll have to take a rain check." Kate glanced at her watch and turned the key in the ignition, revving the Porsche to life. "I've got a hot date tonight and have to get home first. But let's talk this Tuesday over dinner."

Kate said good-bye and flipped her cell phone shut. She still had time to shower and change and make the quick commute to Chevy Chase to pick up her date. The Beltway at this hour would be fairly calm and, absent any traffic accidents, she would be there in an hour. *What was her name again? Pamela, no, Paula, that's right.* They had met at a dinner party last week and the chemistry had been instantaneous. Kate hoped to get lucky, especially now that she had something to celebrate.

She pulled out of the parking garage and waited for a break in the traffic before turning onto the street. While she idled, she glanced up at the fifty-foot poster of herself plastered to the side of the Channel 5 building. Her arms folded confidently across her chest, she gazed out at the city with a look of piercing intelligence. She acknowledged that physically she wasn't the typical female news anchor. She was brunette instead of blond, her face chiseled and strong rather than feminine and muted.

But she didn't really care, and neither did her audience, from all accounts. Fans frequently e-mailed her, saying how relieved they were that someone finally delivered the news honestly, with integrity, in-depth analysis, and understanding. She had worked grueling hours to reach this point in her career, and her efforts were paying off.

As the first raindrops fell she turned right and headed home. Tonight was definitely looking up.

❖

Ellen Webster pressed the mute button on the TV remote and placed it on the end table beside the couch. The image of the striking newswoman still burned in her mind, though no longer on the screen, and she sighed. Kate Foster was every lesbian's fantasy, and Ellen was no exception. Worse, Kate was Ellen's next-door neighbor, and she had the pleasure, and pain, of seeing her more frequently than most. The condo building off Dupont Circle had only four units, two downstairs and two up, where Ellen and Kate lived, so they had regular contact.

Of course, Kate was way out of her league. Handsome, in an androgynous sort of way, slender and athletic, she was too glamorous to ever notice someone like Ellen. Kate had a powerful magnetism onscreen and off, and she oozed sex in both contexts. All

Ellen had ever managed to say to her was "hello" or "nice weather we're having."

She got up off the couch and trudged into the kitchen to take out the leftover Chinese from the night before. After dumping the contents onto a plate, she covered it with plastic, shoved it into the microwave, and punched in a few minutes. As she poured herself a glass of wine, General Beauregard, her brown tabby, jumped up onto the counter and pressed into her.

"Hey, Beau." She petted him gently. "Are you hungry, my little pumpkin, hmm?"

A loud motor was his only response and she opened a can of cat food, emptying half of it into his bowl on the floor. He leapt down and devoured his dinner.

"My God, you'd think you hadn't eaten in days instead of this morning."

The ping of the microwave interrupted her conversation, and she carried her meal and wine to the living room where a stack of papers waited. Normally her teaching assistant would grade these undergraduate papers, but Jenny was busy trying to finish her own graduate work by the close of the spring semester. Besides, Ellen loved to read the papers of the American history survey class she taught to freshmen and sophomores. Hopefully a few of them would go on to advanced study in American history, her area of expertise, and she might spot them early on.

She ate a forkful of Kung Pao chicken and picked up the paper on top of the stack. After a while, her thoughts drifted back to Kate and she wondered if the newscaster would arrive home at her usual hour. Ellen glanced at the time on the DVD player and saw it was almost seven thirty, when Kate usually returned to change and leave again. She always looked devastating and Ellen assumed she went out on dates. Maybe she could glimpse her through the peephole in her door.

"Oh, geez, get a grip," she chastised herself.

Having polished off the Chinese and downed the remnants of her wine, Ellen took the remaining papers into her bedroom. She placed the stack on her nightstand and was about to undress when her doorbell rang. Surprised at the late-night intrusion, she hurried to her door and peered through the peephole.

She momentarily froze, stunned to see her handsome neighbor on the other side, then quickly threw open the door. "Hi," she exclaimed a little too brightly.

"Good evening," Kate said. "You had a package sitting outside your door."

Ellen glanced down to see a small box that Kate held. "Oh! Yes. Thanks for letting me know." She took it from Kate and waited expectantly; for what, she didn't know.

"Well, good night." Kate backed away and headed to her condo.

Ellen stood in the doorway, still holding the package and wishing she could think of something to say. Should she invite her in for a drink? No, too obvious. A cup of coffee? *Shit, I used the last of it this morning.*

The sound of Kate's door closing jarred her from her thoughts. It was too late now. Sighing, she retreated into her condo and shut the door, leaning back against it. She closed her eyes and thumped her head back and forth against the door. *Stupid, stupid, stupid.*

General Beauregard rubbed against her shins and meowed. He could always make her feel better and she bent down to pet him. She glanced at the package, recognizing the return address. A colleague at Princeton had sent her an advance copy of his latest biography of Lincoln. He wanted to know what she thought of it, and she was curious to see what he could possibly say that was new about the beloved president.

Scooping up Beau in one arm, the box clamped to her side with the other, she returned to her bedroom and tossed both on the bed. She undressed, turning on her closet light to grab her nightgown off the hook just inside. As she stood naked in front of the full-length mirror on the back of the door, she frowned at the image.

She had gained more weight this year. Her breasts were full and heavy, her hips round, and her belly further from flat than ever. Her skin, however, was still smooth and unwrinkled, belying her forty-two years, and she could still find her hipbones—after a bit of searching. She was what her mother would politely call a "full-figured" girl. Her sister, Joan, would simply say "fat."

She sighed unhappily at the thought of her thin, petite sister. Joan was married to an orthopedic surgeon in Baltimore and had two kids and a dog. She had exactly the kind of life their parents had envisioned for both of them, but only Joan had managed to achieve. She seemed to have it all, but still found an inordinate amount of time to criticize Ellen—about her single status as well as her weight. Ellen always tried to convince her she was a lesbian and would never change, but Joan simply ignored her. She could get nothing but women because of her weight, Joan argued, and if she got into shape some great guy would snatch her up.

Ellen surveyed her figure in the mirror again. She knew this wasn't the body someone of Kate Foster's caliber would ever find attractive, let alone sexy. She imagined the tall, willowy blondes Kate probably went for, draping themselves over her arm at a gala function. Ellen chuckled at the thought of taking her to a faculty party with everyone dressed in their tweeds and cheap suits, discussing the unglamorous topics of their latest research.

She jerked the nightgown over her head, concealing from view the body she no longer recognized. Inside, she still felt like the twenty-five-year-old grad student she had once been, lithe and athletic. Nearly twenty years of research sitting in front of a computer or cocooned in books had taken their toll. As had the countless years of pizza and beer—quick and easy take-out—with other PhD candidates in her department to get them through their program. Once she could have eaten like that and more because back then she would always play tennis or jog. But with her workload and now the impending sabbatical, which would mean more research sitting in museums and libraries, she saw her future predictably unfold in increased clothing sizes. She silently vowed that this year, this sabbatical, she would make time for exercise and eating right.

❖

Kate drove along the inner loop of the Beltway, cursing the idiots who couldn't drive in good weather, let alone when a little rain fell. Glancing at her watch for the umpteenth time, she swore again. She would be later than she thought, but at least she had called ahead and told Paula she would be there as quickly as she could. Paula's obvious disappointment had only made Kate more anxious. Paula was clearly not a patient woman, and Kate didn't want her to change her mind. She never liked to hurry a seduction, and the mere thought of what she would do to the willowy blonde caused her heart to flutter.

A large semi passed her on the left, spraying water onto the Porsche's windshield. Kate flipped the wiper switch to high and watched as the truck driver signaled to switch back into the lane in front of her. She slowed to let him in, conceding that big trucks always had the right-of-way when it came to little Porsches. She never wanted to try to prove who was stronger, although if the traffic had been lighter she would have definitely proved to him who was faster.

The taillights flashing bloody red first alerted Kate that something wasn't quite right about the truck. And the quiet, proverbial lull before the storm really struck her; she saw everything as if standing outside herself. The semi jackknifed onto its side and a white SUV careened out of control to avoid hitting it, rolling over and smashing into the concrete highway divider. Another car collided with the SUV, a dark sedan of some sort.

Intellectually she knew that all of this occurred instantaneously, but everything moved in slow motion. By the time the events registered, it was too late for her brakes. She crushed the pedal nevertheless, a reflex, nothing more, because she intuited that her reaction would be useless.

She endlessly slid on the wet pavement as metal crunched and glass shattered. Then all went black.

Chapter Two

Ellen nodded as students dropped their midterm exams on the lectern and filed out of the classroom. She told them all to have a pleasant weekend and that she would post grades on her office door. Once they had left, she gathered up the papers and headed for her office, making her way down the hall to the history department, located in Georgetown University's Intercultural Center.

Ellen, a tenured professor of American history, specialized in the nineteenth century, specifically the Civil War. She was one of many professors in the department but the only one leaving on sabbatical this year, courtesy of NEH and Guggenheim Foundation grants. Ellen had received her PhD from the University of Virginia and had been fortunate to be born and raised in the cradle of the Civil War. Working at Georgetown let her remain in the area so that even without her approaching sabbatical, she could visit many of the sites she had frequented since childhood.

Ellen walked into her office and put the stack of exams on her desk. She stuck a Post-it Note on the answer key, asking her assistant Jenny Nelson to get them back to her as soon as possible, then finished tidying up her office. Not much was out of place; she merely had to attend to last-minute paperwork.

She had filed the last of her work when a light tap on the door drew her attention. Linda Cohen, professor of medieval studies, stood expectantly at her door. Plump and vivacious, Linda was Ellen's colleague and closest friend. Despite her constant dishevelment and seeming lack of interest in her outward appearance, Linda possessed a brilliant mind and a quick sense of humor.

"School's out for the week, teacher. Are we ready to party?" Linda danced a little jig of excitement. "And you have no reason to say no this time, missy. There's nothing left for you to do until Monday. Tonight it's all about you and the possibility of meeting Ms. Right. What do you say to Italian first, then Rosie's?"

Ellen groaned. She hated going to the bar but couldn't think of a good reason to avoid it this time. She disliked the dating scene, disliked the social pretense of making small talk, all the while knowing that some stranger merely wanted to get her home in bed or, worse still, wasn't interested in her at all. She sighed. "Italian sounds fine."

"Wonderful. How about Janice and I meet you at Al Tiramisu at seven?"

Ellen nodded. She might as well go, but she couldn't help shake her head at her friends' deviousness. Linda and her partner Janice knew Italian was her favorite.

❖

Ellen rummaged through her closet trying to find something fashionable that still fit. Disappointed to find that one of her favorite blouses refused to button, she flung it to the floor with disgust. General Beauregard sniffed it curiously, then stepped on it, making a delicate pastry of it with his paws. Finally settling on a pair of black slacks and tan blouse, she again faced herself in the mirror.

"Well, it'll just have to do."

If no one liked her for who she was, then screw them. She made a face in the mirror at her false bravado and grabbed a black sweater off a hanger. It had been unusually warm that day but she knew the evening would be cool and, besides, the black sweater tied strategically over her shoulders also managed to hide her imperfections. She picked up her purse off the kitchen table, opened her front door, and nearly collided with someone in the hall.

"Oh. I beg your pardon," Ellen exclaimed, reaching out to steady the slight figure.

At first she thought she'd grasped the arm of a stranger, but she was appalled to find herself staring at Kate Foster. She almost didn't recognize her. An ugly red gash crossed her cheek diagonally from the left bridge of her nose down to the lower tip of her left ear. The stitches stood out like black spiders, frayed and angry, giving Kate's face a singularly crawling effect. Ellen couldn't speak, the pain in her heart almost unbearable. Her throat constricted and hot tears rushed to her eyes.

"Oh, Kate," she whispered.

Without thinking, she reached up to touch Kate's cheek. Flinching visibly, Kate jerked her arm from Ellen's grasp and lowered her head, keeping the left side of her face out of sight. Before Ellen could think of something to say, Kate stumbled to her condo and slammed the door behind her. Ellen stood where she was, aching to comfort her.

When she had first heard of Kate's accident, she couldn't believe it. But the newscaster had been certain it was indeed Channel 5's anchor who had been involved in a six-car pileup on the Beltway. Not knowing what else to do, Ellen had sent Kate flowers in the hospital. She had thought about visiting her, but didn't want to intrude. After all, they barely knew each other, and Kate probably didn't even know her name. Since then Ellen had kept a close eye at the peephole, hoping to glimpse her returning home. She hadn't expected to run into her so soon.

My God, her face.

Her mind was filled with images of Kate—Kate, striding purposefully into her condo that night, only to emerge in a stunning outfit with a look of anticipation. Kate eight days later, almost unrecognizable, the hollow eyes, the gaunt cheeks.

Ellen withdrew a tissue from her purse and dabbed the corner of her eyes. Though her makeup was light, she didn't want to smear her mascara, an indication to Linda and Janice that she'd been crying. The subject was too raw right now for discussion. She took the elevator down to the first floor and headed for the restaurant a few blocks away. She barely registered the traffic on Connecticut Avenue or the already crowded sidewalk around Dupont Circle filled with Friday-night diners. When she reached Al Tiramisu, she spotted her friends at a table against the wall. The lights were dim, thank goodness, and she forced a smile as she approached. Linda and Janice greeted her with the usual jokes and teasing, like this was just another day.

But it wasn't just another day, and she was more disturbed than she cared to admit. Seeing what Kate had been through, her life changed instantly by events outside her control, had stirred Ellen. Tragedies like the auto accident weren't supposed to happen to someone like Kate. She was strong and vibrant, a constant on the television screen, almost a member of each viewer's family. If a life-changing event like that could affect someone like Kate, what would Ellen do if it happened to her? Her life was rather dull and mundane compared to Kate's. She loved teaching, but her personal life had become routine, practically nonexistent. She had avoided intimate relationships most of her adult life, not because she didn't want one, but because no one would be attracted to what she had become physically. If her life suddenly ended, she would never experience the one thing missing from her life—love.

❖

When Kate flipped the light switch inside her door she noticed the silence first. The condo felt cavernous, as if her voice would echo endlessly if she called out. After a week of constantly being poked and prodded, and hearing machines hiss and beep, she found it odd to hear the stillness again. She tossed her keys onto the chest in her entryway and limped to her bedroom, stripping off her clothes as she went. The suit she had worn on her way to Paula's that night had been cut away from her body and was completely unsalvageable, with the exception of her shoes. Recalling Paula brought back an unpleasant memory. She had never even called. Then again, why would she? It wasn't as though they knew each other that well. Still, that no one outside of work had bothered to find out how she was doing irked her.

When she had learned she would be released today, she didn't know what to do about clothes. She had no one to call for the favor—no family, no friends. Her agent was in Miami for a few days, and even if he was home she wasn't sure she would ask him. As a last resort, she asked a candy striper to buy her a set of GWU sweats and socks at the hospital gift shop. She was glad to have worn the strange clothes only a few hours. Like everything else at the hospital, the sweats felt foreign and out of place.

Turning the shower faucets on, she stepped in quickly, letting the hot water cascade over her. She placed the palms of her hands on the cool tiles in front of her and bent her head so the spray hit the back of her neck and spread down her back. It felt so good to finally shower at home in her bathroom. At the moment her place felt slightly unfamiliar, but at least she was alone and back in control of her life. She had known the first thing she would do when she arrived home was shower, so she had the hospital staff tape plastic covers over all the places with stitches to keep them from getting wet. Everywhere, that is, except for her face.

As she stood there in a daze, letting the water wash away the antiseptic smell of the hospital, her mind drifted, as it had so often the past few days, and she tried to remember what had happened. She could only recall driving to Paula's that night and then waking up in the hospital the next day. She should recall something about the accident, but she couldn't access the memory. She only knew she was lucky to be alive.

She switched off the faucets and stepped out of the shower, grabbed a towel, and dried off. Glancing into the mirror, she could see a faint image of herself and, hesitating briefly, rubbed a clear spot with her towel. She gazed at herself dispassionately, observing with interest the purple and yellow bruises marking her chest and arms. She avoided looking above the neck for a moment, fascinated by the stitches that traced a line down her left arm from the elbow to her wrist. She guessed somehow she had turned the wheel of the

Porsche hard to the right and impacted the truck on the left side of the car. But that was only speculation. She'd have to examine the damage to her car at some point and file an insurance claim.

Steeling herself for the inevitable, she peered curiously at her face, and as had happened the last day or two when she did, it shocked her. Her fingers found their way to the scar, tracing with a delicate touch the jagged, stiff ends of the stitches. She felt strange. It was still her face—her eyes, her nose, and mouth—but she seemed to look at it for the first time. Kate had never spent hours in the bathroom primping and fussing with her appearance. The only time anyone paid any attention to it was when the makeup artist prepped her before going on camera, and that was a necessary evil. As far back as she could remember, it was simply her face, neither pretty nor ugly. Women called her handsome and were apparently attracted to the firm jaw and sharp planes.

But now she examined it for what it had gotten her so far in life. The camera loved her, enhancing and magnifying all the positive qualities and giving her a toughness that came across the television screen. People had trusted her and looked to her for reassurance. Now they would stare at her in horror.

❖

"Hello. Earth to Ellen." Linda waved a hand in front of Ellen.

Snapping out of her reverie, she managed to refocus on Linda and Janice.

"Where have you been all night?" Linda asked. "You're a million miles away."

"Sorry, guys. I've been preoccupied." Ellen sipped her white wine.

"Oh, no, you are not allowed to think about your research tonight." Janice loved to admonish her. "Tonight is all about having fun."

"Exactly," Linda agreed. "Surely someone out there looks promising."

Ellen scanned the dance floor and tried to look interested.

Rosie's was crowded, as usual, and the cigarette smoke made her eyes burn and water. She hated the thought of getting home and taking a whiff of her clothes and hair after being in such a place. General Beauregard always refused to come near her until she showered and changed. But she had to at least make a show of enjoying herself, if for no other reason than to please Linda and Janice. After all, they tried so hard to get her out to places like this, to meet people—rather, to meet a woman.

She could hardly concentrate, though, since running into Kate in the hallway. She couldn't take her mind off her and was angry at herself for having behaved so badly. Kate had been through a horrific experience, which Ellen had made worse by reacting to her face as though she had seen a three-headed monster. *What must she think of me?*

"Hey, what about the redhead in leather, over there by the bar?" Linda pointed to what Ellen could only describe as an Amazon.

Easily six feet tall, loud and apparently tipsy, the woman was cackling uproariously at some joke being told by a shorter woman in her party. When she slapped her companion on the back and shouted to the bartender for another round of tequila, Ellen instantly disliked her.

"Uh, I really don't think she's my type," she said delicately.

"She's breathing, isn't she?"

"Linda." Janice poked her in the side. "Don't be mean."

"I'm only kidding." Linda pouted. "So what *is* your type, Ellen? What do you look for in a woman?"

That was a good question. Ellen actually didn't know and had never examined why she was attracted to someone. Somehow she knew when she was interested in a woman simply because of the way she made her feel when they were together. Looks had never been the most important aspect of a person, although when Ellen looked at Kate Foster her toes curled. The slash across Kate's cheek flashed bright red into her consciousness.

"Janice? Hi."

"Sandra? Well, hello."

A dishwater blonde stopped at their table and hugged Janice

around the neck. Ellen noted how her impish face lit up when she smiled and that her tasteful attire was understated but elegant.

"Sandra, you remember my partner, Linda?"

"It's been a while," Linda said as they shook hands.

"Too long." Sandra's glance had already shifted to Ellen.

"Ellen, I'd like you to meet a colleague of mine," Janice said. "Sandra Powell, Ellen Webster. Sandra works with me on Senator Teasdale's staff, and Ellen is in the history department at GU with Linda."

Sandra's grip was firm and warm, yet Ellen couldn't drop her hand fast enough. She cringed reflexively into the smallest size she could manage as Sandra regarded her more closely. She understood that everyone habitually inspected someone that way; she often did it herself, but she was always uncomfortable when someone appraised her body. Whenever she met a woman whom she found even marginally attractive, she always chided herself for not having begun her diet sooner.

"Won't you join us?" Janice asked.

"I'd love to, but I was on my way out. I'm here with friends and they're getting the car now."

The veil of invisibility that so often came over Ellen descended quickly. For no reason, she felt rejected. A woman she thought attractive had glanced her way and found her wanting. If she was interested in Ellen, she could have found an excuse to stay, taken a cab home or, hell, Ellen would have driven her home. She fixed her eyes on the dance floor again, pretending to be interested in what was going on in the writhing mass of bodies, pretending this woman's brief entry into her life had no significance whatsoever.

"Maybe next time," Sandra was saying. "It was nice meeting you, Ellen."

"Hmm? Oh, yes, nice to meet you too, Sandra." She watched Sandra cut her way through the crowd to the front door.

"It's a shame she had to leave." Janice sighed. "I'd completely forgotten she and Cheryl had broken up. She'd be perfect for you, Ellen. She's smart, funny, attractive, and sexy as hell, don't you think?"

"Oh, I suppose."

It was a game she often played with herself. Reject before being rejected. It was the only sane thing to do, especially in Sandra's case. Ellen had to admit her heart rate had picked up a bit upon seeing the sparkling blue eyes, the tiny dimples, and trim figure. But when she saw Sandra was obviously not interested in her, all her systems had shut down and her defenses had gone up. Her heart was safe and relatively undamaged from the encounter. Not for the first time she wondered why she ever allowed Linda and Janice to talk her into coming to these things—to try to give her hope.

"You suppose?" Linda asked. "Geez, don't you think your standards are a bit high? What's wrong with Sandra?"

"Nothing," Ellen exclaimed defensively. "She's obviously not interested, so why bother?"

"Not interested?" Linda's eyebrows shot up. "What makes you think that? She was barely here a minute."

"Exactly my point," Ellen declared triumphantly. "If she was interested, she wouldn't have left."

"Oh, Ellen, come on." Janice chortled. "You're reading too much into it. She was on her way to the door before she even ran into me. But I'll tell you what, I'll sound her out next week at work, see what she thinks of you."

"No. Don't you dare." Ellen was embarrassed at the prospect. She could only imagine what a sorry figure she would present to Sandra. She had to have her friends get her a date because she couldn't get one on her own. Oh, yeah, that would make her even more appealing.

"Don't worry, I'll be discreet." Janice sipped her Cosmopolitan. "She'll never know."

"God." Ellen dropped her head into her hands.

❖

Ellen stepped off the elevator into the hallway and shoved her key into the lock. It was a little after eleven, and she was looking forward to washing the cigarette smell off and climbing into bed with Beau. But when she heard a muffled crash from Kate's condo, she rushed down the hall, her pulse accelerating with each step.

Tapping briefly, she called out, "Kate, are you all right?"

Silence. She couldn't hear anyone move or speak. If Kate had somehow injured herself and was unconscious, nobody would know about it—at least she didn't think anyone else was inside. She felt the heat rise to her face, wondering if perhaps Kate wasn't alone. But if that was the case, why didn't anyone answer the door? She knocked a little more forcefully now, sure that anyone inside could hear her.

When there was still no response, she tried one last time. "Kate, if you're okay in there you'd better let me know. Otherwise I'm calling the police or an ambulance, or something, to break this door down."

After a few more minutes of silence, Ellen could barely make out the shuffled sounds of footsteps approaching the door.

"I'm okay."

Ellen sighed with relief. "Can I do anything to help?" She pressed her ear to the door, trying to hear Kate on the other side.

"No." Kate's voice sounded more distant than it was.

"Are you sure?" Ellen persisted. "If you need anything, I'm right down the hall. I'd be happy to help any way I can. If you need me to run errands, I can do that, or—"

"I said no." Kate's voice was a little stronger. "Now go away."

Stung, Ellen muttered, "Sorry I disturbed you."

Beau came running as soon as she was back home again, rubbing his sleek body against her legs and purring. She picked him up and kissed him, scratching behind his ears as she walked into the bedroom. But as soon as he caught the scent of cigarettes, he extended his front legs into her chest, pushing against her and writhing to get away.

"All right, I know, I'm going to shower as fast as I can."

She was in and out in five minutes, threw an oversized T-shirt over her head, and crawled into bed, followed quickly by Beau, who curled up immediately between her legs. She picked up the Lincoln biography, but put it back down again after a few minutes when she couldn't concentrate. Thoughts of Kate kept running through her mind. She felt sorry for her, for what she must be going through, and it bothered her that she couldn't help. It bothered her even more that no one else seemed to be helping her.

She turned off the bedside lamp and slid under the covers, momentarily unsettling Beau. Determined to stop thinking about her neighbor, she steered her mind to Sandra Powell. Maybe she'd been too quick to dismiss her. She was definitely attractive, but it seemed she hadn't been interested in her. Oh, well, Janice would feel her out next week, whether Ellen liked it or not. If Sandra was interested, she'd find out soon.

As Ellen drifted off, Kate's face replaced Sandra's. The gash was no longer there, and Kate's lips were sensuously close to her own. Even in her dream she felt herself get wet, just as their lips connected.

Chapter Three

The harsh jangle of Kate's bedside phone jarred her from her drug-induced sleep. Though her ears registered the sound, her brain didn't engage for another few seconds. She was home, in her own bed, and it was almost noon. Finally aware of her surroundings she picked up the phone.

"Hello?" Her first word of the day came out dry and broken.

"Kate? Are you sleeping? Hey, sorry, I'll call back later."

It was her agent. He had visited her in the hospital the day after her accident when her face had still been bandaged, and he hadn't been back to see her. He blamed his reluctance on a deep aversion to hospitals and being out of town, but Kate knew better.

She cleared her throat and sat up. "No, it's okay. What's up, Dean?"

"Not much. I lobbed a call into the station last Wednesday to let them know I'd seen you and you were recovering rapidly, ready to get back to work and all that, right?"

"Yeah, right."

Kate had received a huge bouquet of roses from the station, followed quickly by visits from both Mike and Sheila. None of her visitors had seen her without the bandage, and she had kept it that way. The only person who had seen her without it besides medical staff was her neighbor.

The woman's intrusion last night annoyed her. She had probably wanted her to open her door so she could stare at her wound again and had already spread the news all over town that the thing looked hideous. Kate imagined her standing before a barrage of cameras and reporters, lights flashing as she revealed all the gory details.

"They asked me if I knew when that might be, Kate. Not that anybody's pressuring you." Dean backpedaled quickly. "They don't want Bob Stelling sitting in the chair too long. They think their ratings drop a point a day while that guy stumbles around his copy."

"Bob reads every word from the TelePrompTer. If that thing broke down, he'd be lost."

"Which is why they're asking me when you might return. They're afraid a news event will break and viewers will change the channel in droves when they realize Bob can't speak extemporaneously."

Kate threw the covers off and got up unsteadily. Her left leg was throbbing but she managed to hobble to the large mirror above her dresser. The disfigurement startled her—she was surprised to see it was still there—and her fingers went to it of their own accord. It reminded her of strip mining in an otherwise pristine landscape, a shock to the eye and a jolt to her heart. It mesmerized her.

She knew her voice was devoid of emotion when she spoke. "Tell them I'll call them as soon as I feel up to it."

"Uh, Monday, Tuesday…any idea when?"

"Tomorrow, okay?" She was getting irritated again and her voice rose in pitch.

"Okay, okay, I'll let 'em know. They'll be happy to hear from you." He paused awkwardly. "Well, I'll let you get back to sleep. I know you're still recovering, and everyone wants you to get well soon."

Sure you do, Kate thought, knowing everyone was losing money by the day.

"Oh, and uh, Kate, if you need anything, let me know."

It was an afterthought, an offer made out of obligation rather than kindness, and Kate recognized it for what it was.

"Thanks, Dean, I'm fine."

"Great, just great." She heard his relief. "Okay then, I'll talk to you later."

She hung up and continued to stare at her face, her eyes never having left it. Then she returned to the bed and sat down, trying to think, but she had no idea what her next steps would be. Before long she would have to decide about work, but she couldn't go back on air like this. Her brain still felt jumbled, as though she was trying to see through a thick fog, and she shook her head to try to clear it.

Her stomach rumbled loudly and she realized that, unable to stomach the midday meal the hospital staff called food, she hadn't eaten since yesterday morning. She limped to the kitchen, her left leg still tender and sore, but thankfully not broken. Her hip and thigh were blossoming into an array of interesting colors, but those would disappear eventually. Opening the refrigerator, she saw the leftovers of a meal she no longer remembered eating, several bottles of condiments, a bottle of chardonnay, a few bottles of beer, and a chunk of molding Brie. The freezer was no better so she searched the pantry.

A jar half filled with peanut butter caught her eye so she grabbed it, some saltines, and a spoon. She slid a beer from the refrigerator to wash it all down. She always ate out, never having the time or inclination to cook, so she rarely shopped for food. She would have to get to the grocery and restock soon, though. The thought stopped her cold. No way would she be able to go out in public. Her face was too recognizable. People would stare and point.

Her stomach queasy at the thought, she pushed the food away, picked up the remote, and turned to Channel 5 for the midday news. Bob Stelling tried to make an off-the-cuff remark about the weather and failed miserably. The meteorologist helped him out with a quick change of topic, heading into the weather outlook for the next five days.

"Christ," Kate muttered.

Taking a long pull on her beer, she clicked to their competitor on Channel 2. The anchor was reporting about a shooting incident in Southeast DC. She was good, Kate admitted, but too young and inexperienced. With the right mentoring she could make it to the big time. She also had a nice pair of breasts and a face that wasn't hard to look at.

Kate grinned. But she slowly let the grin fade when she realized she would no longer be chasing younger women like that—or older women, for that matter. The accident had affected more than her career. No one would be attracted to this face anymore.

❖

Ellen pushed the shopping cart down the produce aisle, selecting the makings for salads as well as the freshest fruit she could find. She was determined to get a head start on her diet before the spring semester was over so she could work on it full-time during her year-long sabbatical. She also planned to begin a regular exercise regimen and would have no excuse not to when her time was her own. Each day she would walk, building up strength and speed as her body grew used to the exercise. She wanted to look and feel great by the time she returned to school.

She fondled a cucumber, hesitating before putting it in the cart. Thoughts of Kate filled her mind and she giggled. She moved on to the dairy aisle. Ellen was a little worried about her attractive neighbor, whom she hadn't seen all day. Of course she might have missed her comings and goings, but she didn't think so. She also hadn't seen anyone else there, which depressed her even more than not seeing Kate.

If Kate hadn't left and no one had visited her, she probably needed groceries. She might not be well enough to leave or perhaps didn't want to because she didn't want anyone to see her. Kate had told her to go away, but she would eventually have to either come out or have groceries brought in.

Ellen picked up the rest of the things on her list, then set about choosing some things for Kate. She didn't want to overwhelm the poor woman, so she bought only a few toiletries and items she knew Kate liked. Once when they were both heading for the trash, Ellen saw empty Diet Pepsi cans and a frozen pizza box in Kate's garbage. So she grabbed a twelve-pack of the soda and a couple of frozen pizzas. But she also decided to make something for her, something she could get several meals out of and have the pizza just in case. Ellen's mother would be proud of her domestic felicity.

Once inside the building, she pushed her collapsible cart out of the elevator and entered her condo, dropping her purse and keys on the credenza. Beau jumped up on the counter where he knew he wasn't supposed to be, but grocery days always meant a treat, and he constantly got in Ellen's way until she gave it to him. Sure enough, with a Pavlovian response, she dug through a grocery bag and opened a can of Pounce cat snacks. As she put the rest of the groceries away, she set out all the ingredients for making lasagna. People always told her how great her lasagna was, and she wanted to show Kate she cared.

By six thirty that evening, the lasagna was done and she carried it and the rest of the groceries next door. She took a deep breath, uncertain of the reception she was about to receive, and knocked firmly on the door. Like the first time, there was no immediate response, so she knocked again.

"Kate, it's me, Ellen...your neighbor. I brought you something to eat and a few groceries. I thought you might be able to use them."

She stood quietly, straining to hear any sound from within. For a moment, she thought she heard a slight movement, but wasn't sure if it was Kate or the sound of her own heart beating. When she didn't hear any acknowledgment, she tried another tack.

"Kate, I'll tell you what. I'm going to leave these here and when you feel like it, you can come get them. I'll be next door if you need anything." She propped the grocery bags against the door and set the lasagna on the dish towel she had carried it with.

"Oh, and I should tell you I made lasagna. So you might consider eating it while it's hot. It tastes best that way. Although, come to think of it, it's pretty good cold, too. I like it the next day right out of the refrigerator after it's had time—"

Ellen shut her mouth so hard her teeth clicked together and she almost bit her tongue. What the hell was she doing? "Anyway...um, if you need anything, you know where to find me."

❖

Kate watched through the peephole as Ellen—so that was her name—retreated and closed her door. What a busybody. Kate couldn't believe it. Who was this woman who thought she could randomly intrude where she was neither invited nor wanted? And groceries. Who the hell did she think she was?

She was angry and embarrassed by what appeared to be nothing less than charity. *I'm Kate Foster, for Christ's sake.* She was not some socially and economically deprived person who needed help from the outside. She was perfectly capable of taking care of herself. If she wanted help she could afford to hire it. If her inquisitive neighbor had any idea how much money she made, perhaps she would understand that simple fact.

Still…Kate contemplated what the grocery bags might contain. Admittedly, earlier that day she had been wondering about this dilemma—needing groceries and not being able to venture outside.

Kate leaned against the door, debating whether she should open it. Lasagna. She loved lasagna, but only if it was made the right way with ricotta cheese and a good béchamel sauce. *No. I don't need anybody's help.* Kate limped as fast as her leg allowed into the living room again. She'd been watching an old Audrey Hepburn movie, *Wait Until Dark*, and she flopped onto the sofa and focused on the television screen again.

But after a few minutes in which she hadn't absorbed anything in the movie, she got back up and strolled leisurely into the kitchen. After looking into the refrigerator door for the tenth time that day, still expecting to see something she hadn't seen before, she closed it.

Damn. She'd eaten the rest of the peanut butter for dinner, along with a can of sardines, and the bottle of chardonnay was half gone as well. All that remained were two bottles of beer, some spices and condiments, coffee, and a little sugar. She leaned her head against the refrigerator, a lump in her throat. How had everything changed so quickly?

"Ah, screw it."

She returned to the front door and opened it. After picking up the groceries in one hand while juggling the still-warm lasagna in the other, she kicked the door closed and put everything on the kitchen counter. The lasagna smelled heavenly, and she had to stop herself from taking a fork and digging into the large aluminum container. The frozen pizzas and Diet Pepsi delighted her, the microwavable popcorn surprised her, and the toilet paper and toothpaste, among other things, embarrassed her.

She shoved the pizzas into the freezer, then scooped a large piece of lasagna onto a plate. The first bite was ecstasy, and she held it on her tongue to savor the full panoply of ricotta, oregano, and béchamel.

After finding a bottle of cabernet on the wine rack, she filled a glass and took it and her plate back to the couch and the movie. Just this once she would accept assistance. But only because she was still recovering. One thing Kate had learned covering news stories was that people had a basic need to play Good Samaritan. What harm would it do to allow Ellen to indulge herself for a day or two? Kate would soon be back on her feet and in control again.

God, I suppose now I have to give her a thank-you note or something. She took the last bite of lasagna, finished the glass of wine, and sat back on the sofa completely satisfied. By the time Richard Crenna returned to kill Audrey Hepburn, Kate's eyelids drooped heavily and she felt herself drifting off.

❖

Around eight o'clock Ellen couldn't stand the suspense anymore. She quietly cracked her front door open and peered into the hallway. *Yes.* She pumped her fist and skipped back into her living room. General Beauregard eyed her suspiciously from his comfortable spot on the couch.

"She took them, General. She took them, and right now Kate Foster is eating my lasagna."

He watched her dance around the room for a few seconds, then slowly closed his eyes and went back to sleep. Kate's acceptance of her offering only confirmed she had needed the groceries in the first place. *She must not have anyone to turn to right now.* A woman who had been severely injured, lived alone, and refused to come out into the world might be suffering from more than just a physical trauma.

Well, Ellen would have to take it one step at a time. Kate was too proud to accept any help beyond groceries, and she'd resisted even those. Now Kate had enough to eat for at least a few days, but Ellen would get her to give her a list of things she needed. How she would do that she hadn't figured out yet.

She poured herself a glass of wine and went into the bathroom to fill the tub. When it was the perfect temperature, she climbed in and soaked, letting the warm water soothe and relax her. Maybe Kate could use a nice hot bath. She made a mental note to add a jar of bath salts to her grocery list. Thoughts of Kate and bubble baths drifted sensually into Ellen's mind and she closed her eyes.

"Oh, Ellen, yes, please take me, fill me, I need you so much."

"Shh, it's all right, Kate. I'll give you that and so much more."

She kissed Kate, gently but firmly, her tongue pushing against her lips until she was allowed entrance.

Ellen's nipples tightened and a dull ache asserted itself between her legs. The mere thought of Kate touching her, of feeling her skin against Kate's skin always turned her on. She could easily imagine the strong, athletic body and the power of her lovemaking.

But in her fantasy world, Ellen also possessed a firm, slender figure—womanly, of course, but much thinner than she was in reality. Kate would be enthralled with her body, caressing her everywhere and admiring the suppleness of her skin and the tautness of her stomach. Ellen's body was flawless and she fondled herself as Kate entered her, filling her and loving her until nothing was left but the lingering traces of her orgasm and the tepid feel of bathwater against her skin.

CHAPTER FOUR

Ellen sat at her desk in her office, reading her graduate students' papers. Some of them were terrific, including one from Jenny Nelson that dealt with the impact of religion on the Civil War. Her teaching assistant was incredibly bright and inquisitive, and Ellen loved having her in the program. Jenny planned to spend the summer working with her on her research, and Ellen looked forward to being out in the field with her. While she thoroughly enjoyed research, she welcomed company. She already spent too much time alone.

Hearing a light rap on the door frame, she looked up and saw Linda, her sweater buttoned in the wrong buttonholes, expectantly waiting.

"Hey, girl, how about lunch? I'm starving."

"You look like the Cheshire cat," Ellen said. "What's up?"

"Come on, I'll tell you."

They walked to a nearby deli. Over Reuben sandwiches and potato salad, a meal Ellen swore she would not have on her diet, Linda shared the news.

"Janice ran into Sandra Powell on her way to the Capitol yesterday. They chatted for a while and, according to Janice, Sandra asked about you. Janice did *not* bring you up, she swears it. It came totally from Sandra."

"Really? She really asked about *me*?"

"Yup."

"Well, exactly what did she say?" Ellen put her fork down.

"She simply asked about you, and Janice told her you were single, you taught at Georgetown, and you were a good person. Then she gave her your phone number."

"*What?* You're kidding."

"I'm deadly serious. You know Janice wouldn't give it out to just any wacko. She's known Sandra for years."

Ellen was stunned. She couldn't believe anyone as attractive as Sandra Powell would be interested in her. She looked down at her half-eaten sandwich and the pile of potato salad, angry at herself. This was one more example of her willpower failing miserably. After all the money she spent on healthy food at home, she could never resist temptation when she ate out with friends. Sure, she could have ordered a salad at the deli, but what fun was that?

"Anyway, I suppose she'll call you, although Janice didn't know when," Linda said blithely. "Relax. I'm sure it'll be soon. And remember, little Miss Nobody-Could-Possibly-Find-Me-Attractive, if things don't work out, she'd make a great friend. And I'm not saying that because you're not attractive. Frankly, I don't see how you can say that about yourself. You're a knockout, kiddo. I mean if you don't hit it off, it's not the end of the world. So no pressure, okay?"

Ellen nodded absently, her mind already racing. What would she wear? Should she buy a new outfit, despite her determination not to spend any money on new clothes when she had a closet full of perfectly good ones at home? But she couldn't possibly get into anything other than work clothes, and she didn't want to wear them. If she and Sandra went out, she wanted to look stunning. Besides, she didn't have a great outfit for special occasions that wasn't at least two sizes old. One new outfit would do for now.

Ellen got home around four thirty that afternoon and immediately started making a salad for dinner. Then she chopped vegetables and fruit to snack on when she had the craving. It was a warm, sunny day, and she decided to eat out on the deck off her living room at the small wrought-iron table.

She had barely managed to carry her iced tea out through the French doors when General Beauregard darted after her. "Beau! You know you're not supposed to be out here." She took a step toward him, but he skittered to the other side of the deck. Crouching and inching forward, she made kissing and cooing noises to coax him back toward the open door. He looked up at the railing and she could see his little brain working.

"No, no, General PGT Beauregard. Don't even think about jumping up—"

Too late. In one graceful leap from his curled position he was up on the railing, apparently quite pleased with himself.

Ellen panicked and glanced over the deck to the first floor below. It was a long way down. "Please, honey, please, don't move. Let Mama get you and take you back in the house. I'll give you some tuna. You know how much you love tuna."

Beau eyed the deck across the way—Kate's deck, at least four feet from hers.

"Oh, no, no, not that, please. Not that, Beau. Oh, God, please don't try it."

Of course that was tantamount to a dare.

❖

Kate lay on the couch, reading a lesbian romance about a blind pianist who had lost the will to make music and the assistant who inspired her to get it back. The French doors to the deck were open and a cool breeze ruffled her hair. She was completely engrossed when a punch to her stomach knocked the air out of her.

She shouted, "What the fuck?" and leapt off the couch.

A rather good-sized brown tabby, whose ears were lying flat at the moment, looked back at her serenely.

"Where the hell did you come from?"

A knock on the door surprised her, but she had a good idea who it might be.

"Kate, it's Ellen," Ellen shouted from the hallway. "My cat jumped across our decks and is somewhere inside your house."

"Shit." Kate ran a hand through her tangled hair. She walked over to the French doors and closed them, then picked the cat up off the arm of her couch and carried it to the entryway. She hesitated, unwilling to face her neighbor, but wanting to get rid of the cat. Maybe if she simply stuck the animal out and dropped it into her arms that would be good enough.

"It's okay, Kate. I understand you might not want to come out, but if you'd just give Beau to me I'd be grateful."

Kate stood reluctantly, annoyed at her temerity. She never used to be this way, uncertain and withdrawn. She invariably attacked any situation with confidence. Being in an accident that left her disfigured was no reason to hide. So why couldn't she open the door? Her neighbor had already seen her face, already expressed her horror. What difference did it make now? Taking a deep breath, she turned the handle and held the cat out.

Ellen took Beau and held on tight, relieved to have him back in one piece. She gazed up at Kate. The jagged line was still a striking contrast to her smooth complexion, but it wasn't as red and inflamed now. However, all Ellen could see was Kate's wounded dark eyes staring defiantly at her. She felt Kate's pain, and her seclusion appalled her.

"Thank you so much," Ellen said. "I'm sorry if he bothered you. He's never done that before."

Kate didn't respond and Ellen saw her wary look. Making Kate realize she only wanted to help was going to be tough.

"Do you have what you need? I'm making another run to the grocery store soon. If you want anything else, why not make a list and I'll be happy to shop for you."

"Why?"

Ellen was surprised by Kate's bluntness, but pleased that at least she responded. "Because that's what neighbors do for each other. I merely figured it was convenient, my living next door and all. It's no trouble."

Ellen watched several emotions fly across Kate's face, from annoyance and relief to anger and defeat. She wanted to touch her, to make her understand her motives. If she could soothe some of what Kate was going through, she would be satisfied. But would Kate let her? Would she let anyone help her?

"I owe you money," Kate muttered.

"No, that's okay—"

"I have money," Kate spat angrily.

"Of course. I'm sorry, I didn't mean…" Ellen took a deep breath, then started again. "It was about thirty dollars."

Kate disappeared and when she returned, she held out the cash. Grudgingly, she said, "I'll make a list."

❖

A carton half full of Häagen-Dazs coffee ice cream beckoned her seductively. Ellen took it out and set it on the counter. She put a spoonful into a small dish for Beau, who attacked it with relish. Not even thinking of getting a bowl for herself, she dug right into the carton and scooped out a mouthful, savoring the smooth, creamy texture on her tongue.

"Oh, God, that's good." She closed her eyes.

The phone rang and she raced to pick it up. Kate had her number and maybe she needed something. "Hello?"

"Hello, Ellen?"

It didn't sound like Kate. Her voice was deep and sexy.

"Yes?"

"Hi, Ellen, this is Sandra Powell. We met last week at Rosie's?"

Ellen put the carton down on the counter. It was closer to two weeks, but who was counting. Her heart did a little happy dance and she tried to calm it with deep breaths. "Why, yes, of course I remember you, Sandra. How are you?"

"Good, thanks. Listen, I hope you don't mind, but I managed to finagle your phone number out of Janice."

"Yes, I mean, no, I don't mind." Ellen forced herself to drop her voice a notch. It had strayed too high in pitch.

"Great. Well, good, I'm glad, because I don't normally do this sort of thing. At Rosie's that night, it was a little hectic and I was with other people. Otherwise I would have joined you all. But I couldn't stay and… God, I'm rambling, aren't I?"

Ellen giggled. She loved self-deprecating humor. It made her feel more at ease.

"You're making perfect sense, Sandra. Why don't you just tell me why you're calling?"

She heard a long sigh on the other end of the phone.

"Well, I have two tickets to the symphony this Saturday and thought you might like to go. I usually take my mother, who doesn't get out much these days, but she's in Tampa visiting her sister and won't be back until the end of the month. I don't enjoy going alone and I hate to waste them. Are you interested?"

A thrill ran up Ellen's spine. "I'd love to."

"Wonderful. Uh, would you care to make that dinner beforehand as well?"

"I'd love to, but I'm afraid I can't. How about a drink instead?"

"Sounds perfect."

Ellen gave Sandra her address and hung up the phone. "All right."

She took one last spoonful of ice cream and put the container back in the freezer. This Sunday didn't give her much time. She would have to go shopping, and she needed someone with her to give her a second opinion.

Picking up the phone again, she dialed Linda and Janice's number. After an inordinate amount of screaming from the other end, Ellen finally got Linda to calm down enough to agree to go with her the next day.

But after she hung up, all her insecurities rushed back. She was too fat, not pretty enough, not interesting enough. Frustrated before she even began, she retreated to her bedroom to bury herself in a book.

❖

"Let me see." Linda entered the dressing room and her eyes grew wide. "Hubba, hubba, honey. You're too hot to touch. Sandra is going to have a hard time keeping her hands off you."

Ellen grimaced. "You don't think it's too…revealing?"

She glanced uneasily at herself in the full-length mirror of the dressing room. The black cocktail dress she'd selected, the only color that she would even think of wearing, seemed to emphasize her every flaw. The spaghetti straps exaggerated her fleshy shoulders, and the plunging neckline left practically nothing to the imagination. Frowning, she studied her reflection more closely, trying to uncover the thin woman she had once been. Where had she gone? More important, how would she ever get her back? The curtain rustled and the clerk peeked in.

"How are we doing in here? Oh my, but you look absolutely lovely."

"I'm not so sure about this." Ellen tried to hitch up the bodice. Breast spillage impeded the taut fabric. "Maybe I should try a larger size."

"Are you kidding?" Linda made an impatient, huffy sound. "This is a perfect fit. As a matter of fact, you could pull these straps down a bit more." She tugged the straps of the dress, exposing more cleavage than Ellen wanted to know about.

Annoyed, she grasped the dress and poked her breasts back where they belonged. Out of sight. She caught an odd look that passed between her friend and the clerk, and demanded, "Just tell me the truth, for heaven's sake. You don't have to soften the blow. I know what I look like."

Not surprisingly, the clerk chickened out. Mumbling something about other customers, she vanished behind the curtains, leaving Linda to break the bad news. But Linda didn't answer right away. She walked around Ellen, looking her slowly up and down, no doubt trying to come up with a tactful comment.

"God, I wish I had shoulders like yours," Linda finally said. "You look stunning. That dress lays on you like a second skin. And look." She lifted Ellen's hair, holding it on top of her head. "We'll put this up properly and expose your neck and shoulders more."

"I don't know…" Ellen felt as though she should put a sweater on to cover her upper arms and hips.

"Buy it," Linda said. "If you don't, I'll buy it for you."

Ellen sighed. Maybe when she got home she could work on it and somehow find a way so that it didn't make her look so big. Once Linda had left the dressing room, Ellen changed into her clothes and hung the dress on its hanger. As she shoved the curtain aside, a very thin young woman strode past with a dress over her arm. Ellen followed them out.

"I'd guess you're a size two?" the sales clerk inquired, heading for the petite section.

"Puh-leeze," the young woman whined in a high-pitched voice. "I'd have to gain twenty pounds to fit into a size two. I'm a zero, but if you don't have this in my size, I can go to the Juniors section. I'd simply drown in a two."

Ellen sidled up to the cash register where her clerk took the black dress and her credit card. She envied the thin girl being able to choose anything in the store knowing that it would look good on her. A size zero. How did any adult woman stay that small? She would never have to get a dress altered to hide her flaws.

"Wouldn't you just love to be that thin and find clothes so easily?" Ellen remarked to the clerk.

The clerk glanced up from her register and followed Ellen's gaze. "Are you talking about *her*?" She seemed incredulous. "I shouldn't make personal comments about customers, but she's made us crazy for the past two hours. Nothing but complaints."

Ellen couldn't imagine what a woman like that would find to complain about.

"She says everything makes her feet and hands look big," the clerk said as she wrapped tissue around the dress. "Like it's our fault she's a skeleton. Actually, a skeleton would have more fat, and more color for that matter."

"You don't think she's pretty?"

The clerk laughed with patent incredulity. "I'd much rather have your figure and those great legs of yours. My boyfriend drools over women like you."

Ellen would have attributed the comments to customer relations, but the clerk actually seemed serious. Surprised, she tried to find the right words to accept the compliment. She wondered what beautiful women normally said at times like these. No doubt they took flattery for granted. "Thank you." She glanced around furtively for Linda, who waved from the lingerie department and strode over. Ellen noticed a splotch on the front of her GU sweatshirt, evidence of the lunch they'd shared earlier.

Linda held up a lacy teddy with faux leopard spots. "I think you should add this to your purchase."

Ellen merely stared and shook her head. "Over my dead body."

CHAPTER FIVE

Kate finished processing the insurance forms for short-term disability, but delayed e-mailing them to her secretary. She had begun to think she might exceed the time limitations and roll into long-term. Perhaps she should talk to her agent before she started sending in the paperwork. She glanced at her watch. Ellen would be getting back shortly with the few items she'd asked her to pick up. She also wondered if her neighbor would continue to do her shopping. Surely the kindness limit would wear off and she would want to get back to her life. But she insisted it was no trouble, and Kate did nothing to dissuade her.

Kate set her laptop aside and returned to her other boring activity, channel surfing without absorbing anything. Normally, she hated killing time this way and rarely watched television, except for her own news program, and that was a matter of quality control. In her business no one could afford to drop the ball on image and presentation. To keep herself in good shape, she usually ran several times a week, but she hadn't been out jogging in quite some time. Her body felt flaccid and weak, a state she detested.

She couldn't recall letting so much time pass without running since high school. She could almost hear her father's voice admonishing her to get up off her ass and get outside and train. Weather conditions made no difference. Rain, a blizzard, subzero temperatures, he'd still made sure she was up an hour before getting ready for school so she could run. And she knew the feel of his belt on her backside if she didn't. Track was supposed to be her ticket to college, since they couldn't afford the tuition. She had been thrilled to disappoint him by being accepted to Northwestern on an academic scholarship.

She didn't stop training, and her first experience with a woman was with a senior on the track team at Northwestern. Merely the thought of telling her father that his insistence on her running led her to a lesbian affair made her feel better.

The doorbell intruded on Kate's recollections and she crossed the room expectantly. She was actually excited to see Ellen, not just because she was in need of entertaining, but she enjoyed the sympathy and concern Ellen expressed for her welfare. She got the sense that Ellen actually cared about her, and in fact was the only person who seemed to feel that way. The thought that someone she hardly knew was her only friend depressed her. Could her life be any more pathetic than it already was?

When she opened the door, she was stunned to come face-to-face with her producer, Mike Spencer. They froze instantly, she from the unexpected visit and he, she suspected, from seeing for the first time the results of her accident. Shame and anger burned her cheeks. She looked everywhere but directly into his eyes.

She didn't know what to do, but it was too late to turn away. He had already seen her scar. Mike held a large floral bouquet in his arms but made no move to give it to her.

"Well, is that for me or what?" she snarled, wishing she could evaporate.

"Wha…oh, yeah, yeah, this is for you, Kate." He held it out to her stiffly, his eyes never leaving her face.

The awkwardness was palpable, neither of them saying a word for several moments. All the while anger boiled inside Kate, bubbling until she wanted to scream at him.

"I…I just wanted to stop by…and see how you were doing," he mumbled.

"Well, now that you've *seen* me, you can go back and tell everyone how I'm doing."

Without another word Kate stepped back inside and closed the door. She had difficulty breathing and gasped repeatedly, inhaling as much oxygen as she could. After a moment, she heard the elevator open and close and knew he was gone.

She looked down at the flowers and began to giggle. A small chuckle at first, which grew until she was hysterical. A catch seized her throat, and her amusement was replaced by sobs she couldn't control. She wept bitterly, sitting on the cool tiles in her hall. She cried until she had no tears left and then put the flowers on the dining-room table and poured herself a drink.

She was working on her third scotch and had begun to calm down after her tirade, but she felt hollow inside. Now everyone at the station would know. She could only guess what the fallout would be, but she knew it wouldn't be good. As if in answer to her question, the phone rang. She glanced at the caller ID; it was her agent's number.

"Fuck." She picked up the receiver. "Hello, Dean."

"Hey, Kate. How're you doing?"

"Great," she said, knowing her tone suggested otherwise.

"I just got a call from the station's attorneys, and they would like to meet with you."

"Call Phillip," Kate said, referring to her attorney. "He can handle it."

"They specifically asked for you to be present."

"Well, tell them I'm still recovering. They'll have to meet without me."

"Kate, they probably need for you to sign your contract. You never did, you know."

She snorted. "Dean, I'll tell you right now that signing the contract is the furthest thing from their minds."

There was a pause on the other end. "What do you mean?"

Wishing she didn't have to talk about this but knowing it was no use, she sighed. "Go to the meeting for me, will you, Dean? You and Phillip. See what they have to say and call me back." She hung up without waiting for a response.

She picked up the bottle of scotch from the coffee table and poured another long shot into her glass. This was it, the end of her career. After everything she had achieved and after all her hard work, it had come to this. Were it not her own life, she would almost laugh at the absurdity. All the plans she had made, the benchmarks she had set for herself—she had achieved them on schedule. And they had disappeared in the blink of an eye on a rainy night on the Capital Beltway.

If she had only been early, or five minutes later, she would have missed the accident entirely. Three people had died and six walked away. She was in the heart of the collision, where the deaths had occurred. She shouldn't have been one of the survivors, but here she was. Surviving, yes, but for what? To watch her career—no, her life—go down the shit chute?

When the doorbell rang again, she dragged herself over and greeted her next unwanted visitor.

"Hi, Kate." Ellen juggled several bags and didn't look up immediately. "They were out of Tide so I got you Cheer. I hope that's okay. And since there was a sale on the bagels I—"

"Just give me the fucking groceries, will you?"

Kate tore the bags out of Ellen's arms and slammed the door.

Ellen's ears rang with the sound echoing down the hallway. She stared at the wood-grain surface inches from her face, wondering what she'd done wrong. *It was the Tide, had to be. No, Kate wouldn't get all bent out of shape over detergent...would she?*

Ellen felt dazed as she stumbled down the hall. General Beauregard ran to her as soon as she stepped inside, rubbing against her as usual. She picked him up and hugged him to her chest, agonizing over what she'd done to cause Kate's outburst. She examined every word repeatedly, including the discussion they'd had earlier that day about what Kate needed. No matter how many times she revisited each scene, she was still mystified as to what had set Kate off.

"Come on, PGT." She kissed Beau on the top of his head. "You and I need a treat to make us feel better."

She went into the kitchen, dropped him on the counter, and tried to decide what she felt like eating. The refrigerator revealed a take-out box of fettuccine Alfredo from the lunch she'd shared with Linda when they were shopping on Wednesday. Her stomach grumbled and she contemplated making a salad to go along with the pasta. But as she removed the carton from the refrigerator, she thought of the sexy new black dress hanging in her closet. Images assaulted her mind. She could see herself in that dressing room mirror, pale flesh in all directions. Her date with Sandra was in two days and she had done nothing to improve her condition. Her stomach coiled again, this time with unease, not appetite. Tossing the takeout into the trash, she decided today would be salad only.

She washed some lettuce and set out the carrots, cucumber, and tomato, but as she began to chop, her flimsy enthusiasm waned. She couldn't help but think about Kate's behavior. Maybe she was angry about Ellen's intrusion into her life and just wanted to be left alone. If so, she could have raised the topic politely. There was no reason to curse and slam the door in her face. Ellen had done nothing to warrant that type of conduct, and the more she thought about it, the more the outburst upset her. She couldn't believe how out of proportion Kate's reaction had been. She'd agreed to their arrangement, even putting grocery lists together for specific items she would need. If she wanted to stop, all she had to do was say so. Whatever Ellen's imagined faux pas, she certainly didn't deserve such rude, unfair treatment. She was only trying to help. *How dare Kate speak to me that way?*

She tossed the knife onto the chopping board, wiped her hands on the kitchen towel, and located a notepad and pen. Angrily, she jotted a brief note.

Kate,

> *I'm sorry about the tough time you're having, but I'm not your punching bag. If you'd like some groceries again and think you can show basic courtesy, give me a call. I won't knock on your door in the future unless invited. I hope you feel better soon.*

Ellen

She ripped the page off the notepad, folded it in half, and marched out of her condo. Striding down the hall, she discovered that her eyes were prickling. She had allowed herself to imagine a friendship, even picturing the two of them going out occasionally once Kate was better. She had envisioned evenings together at the theater or out at dinner, behaving like close, caring neighbors. Admittedly, she had also fantasized that their relationship might evolve with time. Even if the thoughts were unrealistic, she couldn't help wishing Kate saw her as more than just a neighbor. Ever since Ellen first began watching her on TV, Kate had drawn a powerful physical and emotional response from her. Now that they were in contact more often, it was self-delusional to pretend she felt nothing. And she did not indulge in self-delusion.

She paused at Kate's door, her emotions in a muddle. For a split second she almost knocked, then recalled Kate's face contorted with anger, those penetrating green eyes blazing contemptuously. Hurt engulfed her like an acid tide, eating away at her self-confidence. With a bitter sigh, she crouched and shoved the note under Kate's door, then escaped quickly along the hallway.

Her heart was still pounding erratically ten minutes later when she poured herself a glass of wine and deposited her freshly made salad on the table. She pondered the meal and decided that she wasn't hungry after all. Doubt crawled from her throat to her gut. She had acted rashly toward a woman who had been through a terrible ordeal. How could she be so insensitive to Kate's plight? Her frustration was a natural reaction to a situation beyond her control. It was bound to spill over sometime, misdirected at whoever happened to be there.

Ellen wished she'd waited to calm down before delivering that note. She wondered if Kate had noticed it yet. Maybe she was watching television, or sleeping. Ellen tried to think of a way to get the note back. If she slid a coat hanger under Kate's door, perhaps she could hook it. How could she have done such a stupid thing? What would her mother think of her lack of manners? Ellen cringed.

The thought also pulled her up short. Her mother's birthday

party was in two days and she hadn't even looked for a gift. She was responsible for the dessert as well, so she'd better stop at Marvelous Market after work tomorrow. She picked up her fork and stabbed a slice of cucumber. To hell with Kate. She needed to focus on Sandra and on looking good for their date. If it meant eating nothing but rabbit food from now on, so be it.

CHAPTER SIX

Ellen pulled into the driveway of the brownstone in Alexandria, Virginia, and parked behind her sister's minivan. Her parents had lived in this house her entire life, and she and her sister Joan had grown up here in rooms filled with Webster family history. Ellen always loved to visit, even when she had to endure Joan's company as well. Today was their mother's birthday and, like all other family occasions, they celebrated it together.

She picked up her present and a pastry box from the passenger seat and got out of the car, admiring the tulips sprinkled brightly around the house. The sound of Joan's two whining children assaulted her at the front door. Each insisted on handing Grandma her present, and they almost had a crying fit until Joan told them they could both carry it to her.

Ellen couldn't stand her niece and nephew, the annoying little gnats. She swatted them away whenever they came near her, which was only when they wanted something. After the kids ran out the back door, Joan turned to the counter and scowled at Ellen.

"Well, I thought you'd never get here," Joan said, exasperated as usual.

Ellen glanced at her watch. "I thought we were supposed to be here at one."

"Yes, of course, but there's so much preparation beforehand. I could have used some help."

"Joan, Mother's seventy-two years old today and can't stand a fuss. She enjoys a simple, quiet meal and family, that's all."

"That's easy for you to say. You just show up, enjoy yourself, and then leave. I do all the work."

"You know that's not true. Mother does most of the work because she enjoys it, and I'll be here to clean up. Where are she and Dad?"

Joan nodded toward the back door. "They're on the patio. Dad decided to grill the steaks outside since it's so nice today. I made a salad and the baked potatoes are in the oven."

"Here's dessert." Ellen placed the pastry box on the counter.

"What is it?"

"Bostocks, of course. Mom's favorite." Ellen lifted the lid so Joan could see.

"Oh, Ellen, you know she shouldn't be eating that. She has to watch her cholesterol."

"One bostock on her birthday won't kill her. At her age she deserves to have some fun." Ellen wiped a bit of almond cream from the side of the box with her finger and popped it into her mouth.

"Yeah, right. You just enjoy having an excuse to eat that junk yourself. Have you gained more weight since the last time I saw you?" Joan gazed at her and frowned.

Ellen's cheeks burned. "Leave it alone, Joan." She was in no mood to argue with her sister over this ongoing theme.

Joan raised her hands in protest. "Fine, fine. If you want to ruin your body, that's up to you."

"Thank you."

"With summer not that far away I thought you'd want to look decent. You can't go to the club like *that*." Joan made a sweeping gesture toward Ellen's belly and hips. "No man there would look twice at you."

Ellen clenched her fists and struggled to control her temper. "Joan, you know I don't give a damn about men. How many times do I have to tell you that?"

"Oh, that's right, you like *women*." Joan emphasized the last word as though it were obscene. "Whatever. Go have your fun, get it out of your system. One of these days, though, you'll wish you'd stayed in shape. The older you get, the less likely a man will find you attractive."

Ellen closed her eyes and took a deep breath. Her sister's determined denial always amazed her. No matter how many times they had this conversation, it was as though she spoke to the dead. She wondered why she even bothered to engage her at all. Picking up the pitcher of iced tea, she headed for the door.

"I'll be right there with the salad and the potatoes," Joan trilled after her.

Barbara Webster sat at the glass umbrella table, sipping a vodka gimlet as she watched her husband at the grill. The sound of sizzling steaks and the delicious aroma reached Ellen the moment she stepped outside, calling to mind various cookouts in their backyard since her childhood. She immediately relaxed. But it would take a stiff drink to help her forget Joan's nasty remarks.

"I hope you have more of those," she said, pointing to her mother's gimlet.

"Help yourself." Her mother pushed a pitcher toward her. "Are you and Joan at it again?"

Ellen poured herself a glass. "She just won't leave it alone."

"I'll talk to her," Barbara offered.

"No, Mom, you know that won't do any good. She's always been this way. She won't accept me for who I am, and she insists that her way of life is the be-all and end-all. I've had it with her."

"She just wants you to be happy," her mother said.

"She wants me to be like her, that's all. Well, I can't, and I'm not going to try and convince her of it any longer. I'm happy with my life the way it is, and she's going to have to get used to it."

"Are you happy?"

Ellen paused. She loved her work, and her mother knew that, but that wasn't what her mother was asking about. Her parents had been very careful about inquiring into any relationships she might be involved in. She knew they didn't want to add to any pressure she had already placed upon herself, but they were still concerned for her well-being.

"I have a date tonight." She hoped this announcement would placate them, at least for a while.

"Really?" Barbara glanced to her husband. "Do we know her? Where did you two meet?"

"Meet who?" Joan came out of the house carrying two bowls.

Ellen ignored her. "She's a friend of Linda's and Janice's. All I know is that she's an attorney and works with Janice on Senator Teasdale's staff. She asked me to the symphony tonight."

"How lovely." Barbara squeezed her arm. "Have a good time."

"Oh, Ellen, no." Joan put the two bowls on the table. Her children ran up beside her and grabbed a potato from the bowl, fighting over who got the biggest one.

"Don't start, Joan. I'm warning you." Ellen got up, taking her drink with her, and escaped into the house. She was still unsure of her feelings about Kate, as well as Sandra, and she felt dangerously near the edge of her ability to control her emotions. Once inside, she strolled toward her old bedroom, which contained many of the mementos of her childhood—her record collection, the various plaques and awards demonstrating her academic successes, and several photo albums. It was familiar and safe, and she often retreated there when she was going through uncertainty in her life. She sat on the bed and flipped through her high-school yearbook.

Images from the varsity tennis team screamed back at her. There she was, in her tennis whites and letter sweater, racket held casually across her chest. At five foot seven, she had weighed one hundred and ten pounds, and could fly across the court to reach any shot her opponent could smash her way. With her abilities, the team had gone to state, only to lose in the finals, but it was the first time her high school had ever been there. They were the dream team.

A few pages further on, she paused at a photo from her junior prom. She looked so marvelously thin; it didn't seem possible that her body would ever fit the clothes she now wore. Her hipbones were clearly prominent beneath her clinging dress and her face was angled and sharp. Ellen sighed. She had rarely eaten much of anything back then, knowing that the boys from the men's team ogled the girls during practice. One poor teammate who had struggled with weight all her life was the target of their cruel teasing. Ellen helped defend her against the boys, but the comments served as a reminder to keep her own weight down.

God, one hundred and ten pounds. She couldn't believe it had been twenty-five years since she'd weighed that much. Forty pounds. Forty pounds she had gained since that time. Just the thought of it made her cringe with self-loathing.

"You know, I can always find you here when you're upset." Her mother walked in and sat next to her on the bed.

Ellen remained silent, not knowing how to explain to her mother what she was going through, because she didn't quite understand it herself. It was all too new and complex for her to sort out on her own.

"What's up, honey?" She ran her hand through Ellen's hair and then slowly rubbed her back, the way she did when Ellen was a little girl. The familiar touch still soothed her.

"Oh, I don't know. A little jittery about going out with someone, I guess. I haven't exactly been the social butterfly of late. And my next-door neighbor is absolutely infuriating me at the moment."

"What happened?"

"I brought her groceries the other day and she yelled at me and slammed the door in my face. I can't think of any reason for her to do that and it's driving me crazy."

"Why, the ungrateful wretch." Barbara stopped rubbing her back. "I'd tell her where she could get off in no uncertain terms."

"Well, it's not that easy." Ellen backpedaled, surprised by her mother's vehement comment. "She was in a terrible car accident and refuses to go out. I think she's just lashing out because of her situation, not because of me."

"Why on earth are you the one doing all this for her? Doesn't she have family who can help her?"

"I guess not. I haven't seen anyone. Maybe she won't let them. It seems like she's closed herself off from people."

"Why are you so interested in this neighbor of yours? Why is she your responsibility?" Her mother's scrutiny was intent and unwavering.

Afraid of what her face might reveal, Ellen looked away. "I don't know, Mom. She's all alone, and she needs me. She has no one else. I know there's a good person inside of her and she just needs help until she can get back on her feet."

"It seems you know more about her than the woman you have a date with tonight." Her mother had a thoughtful expression on her face. "You know, this reminds me of the time when you were a little girl and you brought a baby bird into the house to care for when it fell out of its nest. Eventually you had to let it go, once it was strong enough to be back among its kind. You were heartbroken."

Ellen had completely forgotten the event, but it came rushing back. At the time, she thought the bird would remain her pet. Letting it go felt like a betrayal. For months she wondered if it survived. Picturing it weak or dead, she felt responsible and couldn't forgive herself for abandoning the poor creature to the wild to take its chances.

Her mother stood. "Be careful you don't find yourself caring for another baby bird, Ellen."

For a long while after her mother left the room, Ellen remained on the bed. She felt more confused than ever and knew she'd have to sort things out with Kate soon. The tension between them couldn't go on forever. The whole thing was ridiculous. They were both adults and should be able to talk about the unfortunate incident. Kate was her neighbor and perhaps becoming her friend as well. Ellen didn't need to let unrealistic daydreams get in the way of helping Kate during a rough period in her life. Kate needed someone, and Ellen was possibly the only person who could give practical support. She'd have to put aside her fantasies and focus on Kate's needs instead.

❖

Kate had just finished lunch when the phone rang. She debated answering, seeing on the caller ID that it was her agent, but knew he would only call back. She needed to deal with this situation.

"Hi, Dean," she said with little enthusiasm.

"Kate."

He paused, and she knew he didn't have good news. She braced herself, knowing what was coming but wishing somehow she could stop him.

"Kate..."

After a few more moments of hesitation, Kate couldn't stand it anymore. "Just spit it out, Dean," she snapped. "You don't need to sugarcoat it."

"Sorry...the station wants to buy out your contract. It seems like a pretty good deal, and as your agent, I would advise you to take it."

He knew. He didn't ask why, so Mike must have told him. She could imagine them all sitting around the conference table, discussing her life. "Poor Kate," they'd probably said, and then went about deciding what was best for the station, and for her, of course. In a single morning, they had determined her fate, before the inevitable lunch at an upscale Washington restaurant. She was furious she was so helpless, but she had no choice. Her anchor days were through.

"Send the paperwork over," she said flatly. "I'll look at it, and if it's in order I'll sign it."

"Kate, I've been calling some stations out West and—"

"Well, stop right now," Kate interrupted angrily. "I'm not interested in doing anything, either here or out West."

"But, Kate—"

"I said, forget it. Send me the paperwork tonight. I'll get it back to you in the morning."

She jabbed the Off button and flung the phone across the room. She swore she wouldn't answer it again, especially if it was Dean calling. Glancing at her watch, she strode to the bar off the kitchen and poured a scotch. It was too early in the afternoon for one, but she didn't care. She needed it.

The first sip was strong and harsh, but after that, the taste was smoother. A couple of hours of channel surfing and several drinks later, she realized she had emptied the bottle. *I better add that to my grocery list. Speaking of groceries.* She glanced at her watch again; it was almost five o'clock. Normally Ellen would be home by now and would bring the items Kate was waiting for or come collect her list for the next day. But that wasn't going to happen.

Kate read the note she'd found slipped under her door the day before. The ultimatum was clear: *Call Ellen and apologize or go screw yourself and get your own groceries.*

Nothing on her list was urgent; she had enough food to get by. But the scotch was a different matter. Kate inspected her last bottle and chewed at her lip. She had enough to last her five or six hours; then she would have to leave the condo so she could stock up. She shuddered. The very thought of leaving her sanctuary to go out in public and be seen made her ill. Only a few people knew of her predicament and mercifully had kept it to themselves, so far. If she were to go out, some fan might surreptitiously photograph her with their cell phone and her damaged face would be plastered all over the news.

The more she thought about her situation, the angrier she got. *Fuck them.* What did it matter anymore if people knew what she was hiding? Her career was in the trash and there was no use pretending otherwise. If someone took her photograph and it wound up on the news, she'd merely get a head start on the station by beating them to the announcement. What was she going to do, otherwise? Stay in her condo for the rest of her life? The idea was absurd and infuriating. If she was going to get on with her life, she had to start now by getting her own damn groceries. It was unlike her to be such a wimp over something so stupid. She just had to buck up and take the hard knocks, as her father always said.

❖

The symphony had definitely been the high point of the evening. The upscale bar had been rather awkward and unsettling, mostly due to Ellen's insecurities about the dress as well as feeling uncomfortable on her first date in a while. She had forgotten how to talk to someone in an interesting, flirtatious manner. Her every word sounded superficial and trite. Thankfully their time at the Kennedy Center had preempted further conversation and she could relax somewhat until their ride home.

They were lucky to get a cab after only a ten-minute wait, but inched along due to the emerging crowd and traffic. Sandra attempted to fill in the silence with the details of her work, and Ellen tried to appear interested, but the specifics of passing legislation didn't appeal to her and her mind wandered.

"I'm sorry. I must be a dreadful bore, going on and on about my work."

"No, of course not," Ellen quickly reassured her, guilty that Sandra had obviously noticed her disinterest.

"First dates can be rather awkward," Sandra said. "You'd think at my age I'd be a lot smoother."

Her sigh sounded so wistful that Ellen almost touched her in apology. "I've had a really nice time tonight. The wine was lovely, the music enchanting, and the company both. Thank you so much for an enjoyable evening."

"Thanks for being so kind and for putting up with me."

The cab stopped at the curb in front of Ellen's building and Ellen reached for the door handle. "Thank you again for such a wonderful time."

"Here, let me at least walk you to your door."

As Sandra asked the driver to wait, Ellen climbed out, her heart racing. She hoped Sandra wasn't expecting anything more than a kiss good night.

❖

Kate drew the hooded sweatshirt over her head and pushed her arms through the sleeves. She stood in front of the mirror and saw a gangster in a B-movie. *If I was the guy in the liquor store, I'd think I was being held up.* She tugged at the sides, covering her face as much as possible. The shadowy look only made her seem more threatening, but she didn't care.

While the irritating stitches had now been removed, the resulting white skin, speckled with dots where the stitches had been, made the damage look worse. Her arm had a similar scar, but under a sleeve it didn't matter. The doctors had mentioned plastic surgery, if she was interested. She had seen the results of the cosmetic surgeon's art firsthand. Several colleagues had gone under the knife, trying to extend the warranty on their time in front of the camera. But the wind-tunnel effect turned her off and the possible complications gave her pause. Still, she might look into her options. Improvement would probably come too late to save her career, but at least she wouldn't be humiliated every time she showed her face in public.

She grabbed her keys and wallet and headed for the door when muffled conversation in the hallway made her stop and peer through the peephole. Ellen stood at her door talking with another woman. Kate couldn't quite make out what they were saying, but Ellen seemed to be asking the woman in. The woman shook her head and said something, an excuse of some kind, Kate supposed. Then the woman put her arms around Ellen's waist. Kate was surprised and grinned when she realized what she was about to witness. Sure enough, the woman brought her lips to Ellen's and they kissed.

"Well, I'll be damned." She let out a low whistle. It was a gentle, unhurried kiss, but not terribly passionate. It was definitely not the kind of kiss Kate would ever waste her time with, but she didn't know what kind of woman Ellen was interested in.

When the two separated, Kate studied Ellen with interest. She certainly looked good tonight; the dress she wore revealed a deep cleavage. Kate considered herself a breast woman and was surprised she had never noticed Ellen's. Then again, she did have other things to think about of late. She watched the woman return to the elevator and Ellen retreat to her condo.

Her mind flew to the angry note Ellen had left, and the lewd thoughts she'd just conjured up about her neighbor disappeared. In their place grew the determination to become independent once more and, for now, to replenish her damn scotch. She yanked her door open and was halfway down the hall when a heavy pounding in her chest made her stop. Her feet quite simply refused to carry her forward, and her breath came in short, labored pants. She stumbled sideways toward the wall and leaned against it, frantically trying to slow her breathing. The hallway seemed too narrow and stretched out indefinitely, and for a brief, panicky moment, she thought she wouldn't make it back.

Glancing at Ellen's door directly in front of her, she thought of knocking, but her pride wouldn't allow it. Instead, in one huge burst of adrenaline, she literally scurried to her condo and, once inside, collapsed onto the couch. Shaking and nauseous, she closed her eyes and listened to the pulse hammering in her ears. Okay, so maybe she still needed a little help. Two weeks of isolation was nothing. Hell, her bruises had yet to completely disappear.

Her eyes filled with tears. One thing was clear. If she was going to survive, she couldn't manage without help. She would have to apologize to Ellen. Not only would the people who knew her be shocked at what she had become, Kate no longer recognized herself.

Chapter Seven

Ellen absentmindedly placed her keys on the credenza and pondered that kiss from Sandra at her door—had it been only a week ago? She liked Sandra. They had a lot in common: a love of foreign films, fine dining, and a passion for politics, although in DC that was almost mandatory. Part of her was relieved Sandra had begged off that night, yet another part was disappointed.

She retraced everything she had said and done that night and couldn't come up with a single misstep. Sandra seemed to enjoy her company as much as she had enjoyed Sandra's. But the little voice inside her head insinuated itself into her consciousness—*Sandra likes you, but not in that way.* Ellen went into her bedroom and stood in front of the full-length mirror. If only she wasn't so heavy, if only she'd met Sandra ten years ago when she was a size four. Sandra would definitely have stepped in for a nightcap then, early meeting or not.

She kicked off her shoes and changed into a sleep shirt. She was determined to plow through several chapters of her friend's book on Lincoln, but once in bed, she read the same paragraph over and over. Finally, in exasperation, she put the book down, turned off the light, and snuggled deep into her pillows. She went through her mental checklist of things to do the next day, automatically including shopping for Kate before remembering that thankless task was no longer part of her routine. Knowing how Kate resisted leaving her condo, Ellen was surprised. She had expected a phone call by now, and perhaps a weak apology, but not complete silence. Had Kate found someone else to do her running around?

Simply the thought of Kate aroused her and she closed her eyes to conjure up an image of her. Strangely, when she thought of Kate, or dreamed of her, the scar never figured in. She saw only the dark hair and eyes, the firm jaw and full lips and the way she walked. The entire package was too damn sexy, and the woman wasn't even trying.

As usual, Ellen's body reacted in all the right ways. She withdrew her vibrator from her nightstand drawer and turned it on low. It felt exquisite when she rested it near her clit, but not directly on it. She liked to tease herself first, draw the orgasm up slowly while she massaged her breasts and nipples. She fantasized Kate leaning into her at the door and kissing her, kissing her passionately, then ravishing her.

Kate was undressing her and grazing her way down her breasts, her stomach, and then between her legs. Ellen moved the vibrator directly onto her clit, flipped the switch to high, and pinching her nipples felt the rolling approach of the orgasm. It started at her clit, then worked its way up her belly and into her chest until she rocked hard, its force lifting her upper body off the bed.

Ellen fell back onto the pillows and simultaneously switched the vibrator to low. It continued to draw out the last echoes of her orgasm until she went limp and turned it off. She sighed contentedly, wishing for someone to cuddle and talk with in the aftermath of lovemaking. Perhaps Sandra? She wouldn't know for sure for a while, but Sandra was certainly the nearest potential she had found in a long time. What would making love with her be like? She was warm, witty, and funny. Ellen felt comfortable around her in public, but how would she feel in private, and naked?

❖

Ellen climbed out of the tub and grabbed the phone she'd left by the sink. She'd been expecting Sandra to call all week and was trying not to read anything into the silence.

"Hello?" She dried her hair with one hand while holding the phone with the other.

"Hi, Ellen, it's Kate."

Ellen slowly let the towel drop to her side.

"Listen, about the way I acted last week," Kate continued in the kind of tone newsreaders used when they tried to convey sincerity while remaining detached, "well, all I can say is, it must have been the pain pills. Too much, too little, I don't know. Anyway, I wanted to tell you I'm sorry. I shouldn't have said what I did. That wasn't right."

Ellen was unaware she'd been holding her breath. When she finally drew in a gulp of air, she didn't know if she would laugh or cry. "Oh, Kate. I'm so sorry I left that note. You didn't deserve that. I was insensitive."

"No, no, you were absolutely right," Kate said. "I wouldn't have been half as nice as you were if someone had been so rude to me. People have told me my temper would get me into trouble. After all you've done for me, there was no excuse. I'm sorry if I caused you pain."

"Like I said, it's nothing, really. And I'm happy to help, if there's anything I can do. As a matter of fact, I was about to run out and I know you could probably use some things, right?"

There was a pause on the other end.

"Well..." Kate began.

"Tell me what you need." Ellen went in search of a pen and paper.

❖

Ellen pushed her cart into the kitchen. It was heavier when half of the groceries were Kate's. Yet she enjoyed shopping for her, enjoyed picking out exactly the right things when Kate wasn't sure what she wanted. She frowned when she thought about the amount of alcohol Kate had been consuming lately.

And she wondered when Kate would get out of her funk and back to real life. The scar was healing well, but half of her face was permanently disfigured. Ellen saw only how handsome she was, although she could imagine how Kate must feel. As she put away her groceries, she had an idea and began to prepare dinner—for two.

After knocking on Kate's door, she waited a few minutes until it opened. "Hi, Kate. This time you got everything on your wish list."

"Ellen." Kate nodded. "Thanks." She took the grocery bags out of Ellen's arms and began to retreat.

"Uh, listen, Kate," Ellen continued. "I was wondering, if you weren't busy tonight, I…that is, I meant, if you were interested in doing something different…"

Kate stared at her, then finally said, "Tell me what you want, Ellen. As you so astutely observed, I have no pressing engagements at the moment."

Ellen knew she had turned red. How stupid could those stammered comments be? She had completely started off on the wrong foot.

"Sorry, Kate. I thought you might like to have dinner…with me…at my place, tonight."

Kate appeared dumbstruck but, with a surprised expression, finally said, "So what are we having?"

Ellen was delighted.

❖

Kate couldn't recall the last time someone had offered to make dinner for her—that is, without an ulterior motive. Those times she seldom wound up eating the meal. She entered Ellen's condo with trepidation. It was strange after nearly three weeks to be somewhere else. And while the two were laid out the same, Ellen's clearly had the feminine touch hers lacked. It was warm and inviting, and Kate relaxed despite her apprehension.

After she had closed the door on Ellen earlier, she immediately began to have second thoughts. Ellen had already become too entrenched in her life, and if it weren't for the convenience of her shopping, Kate would end the relationship. But for now, she needed her.

"Here, I brought this." She handed Ellen a bottle of scotch.

"Oh, thanks." The unusual gift seemed to surprise her. Wine would be the more common choice, but she accepted the bottle and placed it on the counter.

The confusion that played across Ellen's face made Kate chuckle. "You're not a scotch drinker, are you?"

"Well…" Ellen obviously didn't know what to say.

"I didn't think you were. I thought I'd bring my own, just in case." Kate took the glass Ellen offered and removed the foil from the new bottle. Unable to go out and get it herself, she had searched the phone book for a liquor store that delivered.

"PGT, you know you aren't supposed to be up here." Ellen shooed the cat off the counter and he leapt down, then rubbed against Kate's legs.

"Didn't you call him Beau before?"

Ellen chuckled. "Yes, Beau, PGT, General Beauregard, and a host of others."

"Who's General Beauregard and what does PGT stand for?" Kate petted him on the head.

"General Pierre Gustave Toutant Beauregard was a Confederate general during the Civil War. I've always loved that name."

"Are you a history buff?"

"Sort of. I teach history at Georgetown."

Kate lifted her eyebrows, impressed. She opened the bottle and poured each of them a drink. She could smell the sauce on the stove and looked forward to tasting it, having grown tired of frozen pizzas and instant meals. Dining in a restaurant was her usual routine, but a home-cooked meal was a treat. She watched as Ellen moved about the kitchen, tasting the sauce, adding a pinch of oregano, tossing the salad. For some reason the mundane activities made her feel more at ease. Thinking of seeing her last week, Kate gazed at Ellen's chest, then looked away quickly when Ellen glanced up, hoping she hadn't noticed.

When Ellen put the bowl of salad on the table and began to hum the old Temptations song "Just My Imagination," Kate felt safe.

"Hey, do you mind if I turn on the television for a second?" she asked. "I want to catch the basketball scores."

"Of course not. Dinner won't be ready for another fifteen minutes."

Channel 2 came on and as Kate was about to switch to the Sports Channel, a picture of Bob Stelling in the upper right-hand corner of the screen stopped her.

"…when Channel 5 announced today that they will be replacing Kate Foster with long-time midday anchor Bob Stelling. If you recall, Kate Foster, Channel 5's evening news anchor, suffered injuries in the multicar accident on the Beltway three weeks ago, resulting in the deaths of three people. Ms. Foster is still recovering at home but, according to sources at Channel 5, she has resigned from the station to pursue other interests. Next up, the weather forecast with—"

Kate turned off the television, and the water boiling on the stove was the only sound. Ellen kept glancing her way but didn't say anything for a few minutes.

"Kate—"

"That smells wonderful." Kate took a large gulp of her scotch, then placed her glass on the table. "Can I help?"

She tried to act nonchalant, hoping Ellen couldn't see her pain. Kate certainly didn't want to discuss either her so-called resignation or her future plans.

CHAPTER EIGHT

Ellen crossed campus on her way to the IC building and watched as a group of students played Hackey Sack on the lawn. It was a sunny, warm April day, and both students and faculty were infused with anticipation of the end of the semester. Ellen was looking forward to her sabbatical and the freedom to pursue her specific interests, but she would miss her students and the camaraderie of the faculty. At least she would be working with Jenny, whose bubbly enthusiasm she enjoyed. In a few weeks, they would drive down to Richmond to begin their research and fan out from there into the Virginia countryside.

Thinking of how long they might be away from home gave Ellen pause. *Kate.* Taking care of her had been so much a part of her routine the last two months that she had completely forgotten about how her absence would impact Kate's life. She always paid her downstairs neighbor's ten-year-old daughter, Kelly, to take care of Beau when she was away. And while Ellen didn't anticipate being gone for extended periods of time, she didn't want to have to come home if her research detained her elsewhere.

Who would take care of Kate while she was away? Kate would probably never feel comfortable with a substitute. Perhaps if she supplied her with enough groceries to last for weeks at a time Kate would be okay until she returned.

She entered her building, still pondering the ramifications, and ran into Jenny walking down the hallway from the opposite direction.

"Hi, Professor Webster. I've got those graded quizzes right here." She patted the backpack half slung over her shoulder.

"Good, bring them into my office. I have something else for you."

Once there, Ellen pulled out a tentative itinerary of her research objectives and handed it to Jenny. "I know you probably can't be gone for too long, but I'm hoping at least in the initial stages you can be on the road with me for several weeks. Two sets of eyes are better than one, and besides, your typing skills are much better than mine."

"I'm free for the summer," Jenny said. "I've been looking forward to this almost as much as you have, so I'm around for as long as you need me. Some of your research will coincide nicely with my thesis."

"Absolutely," Ellen said. "And if you need any help along the way, feel free to ask. You'll also be able to access the libraries and museums we visit."

"Awesome. I've never been to some of these places, and certainly not behind the scenes in their archives. I can't wait."

Ellen was excited in the face of such zeal. Jenny was sharp, detail oriented, and a joy to be around. "When's your last exam?"

"The ninth, then I'm free."

"Let's see." Ellen peered at her desk calendar. "That's a Wednesday. How about we plan on taking off a week from that Saturday, the nineteenth of May, say around ten a.m.?"

"Sounds great." Jenny stood to leave. "I'll drop by your house with bags in tow, okay?"

"Perfect. Thanks a lot, Jenny. I'm really glad to have you along."

"Wouldn't miss it for the world." Jenny slung her backpack over her shoulder again. "See you then."

She waved as she left the office and Ellen glanced at her watch. She needed to pick up her dry cleaning, then swing by Lambda Rising bookstore to purchase a couple of books Kate had asked for. Her pulse quickened, the question of Kate's sexual preference finally confirmed. *I knew it.*

Thoughts about what to do about Kate while she was on sabbatical still loomed large. She needed to discuss the situation with her tonight and work out a plan. Ellen would give Kate her cell number. If only Kate would get a grip on her life and figure out what she was going to do next. She couldn't stay inside forever. She was too intelligent, had too much to give to wind up a shut-in.

But Ellen wasn't sure she was the person to tell Kate that. She'd known her only a couple of months, and they never spoke about anything personal. The phone rang and she picked it up.

"Hi, Ellen."

It was Sandra, and a little thrill crawled up Ellen's spine.

"So I'll pick you up around seven?"

"Sounds good," Ellen replied. "Have you decided where you want to go?"

"I was thinking of Zaytinya's. Have you been there?"

"Yes, right across from the National Portrait Gallery. I love it. See you at seven."

Ellen picked up her purse and headed across campus to the parking lot. She ran her errands, dropped the books on her table when she got home, and hung the dry cleaning in her closet. After stripping off her work clothes, she jumped into the shower and was out and dressed by six thirty. *Now Kate.*

When Kate opened her door, Ellen handed her the books she'd requested. "Kate, do you have a minute?"

Kate hesitated. Judging from Ellen's attire, she was obviously dressed for something other than work, and Kate wondered if she was going out with that woman. Ellen was very striking, she realized, ash blond hair, hazel eyes, a voluptuous figure, and a perfume that made Kate a little weak in the knees. It had been too long since she'd been with a woman, and the slightest provocation sent her into a tailspin.

"Uh, yeah, sure…" She stood at the door for a second, debating whether to let Ellen in. Why did she care what Ellen thought of her place? She could live any way she wanted, even if it was a little messy now and then. "Do you want to come in?"

Though Ellen was pleased to see Kate at least trying to be

civilized, she wasn't quite prepared for the dirty dishes that littered the counter, along with empty food boxes and bottles of alcohol. The drapes and blinds were drawn, the only light coming from a single lamp in the living room, which gave it a claustrophobic, incarcerated feel. The difference between their two condos amazed her.

"I wasn't expecting company," Kate said sarcastically.

Ellen changed the subject, ashamed to be caught so obviously snooping. "I had to tell you about something that's coming up for me so you can prepare for it."

"I'm not sure I like the sound of that," Kate muttered.

"In a few weeks I begin my sabbatical. I'll be doing a lot of research, in Virginia mostly, but other places as well. I may be gone for several weeks at a time, with occasional stops back here. So…"

Ellen was unsure what to say next. She watched Kate carefully and could sense her reaction as what she was telling her began to sink in. Kate looked panicky, and Ellen wanted to put her arms around her and tell her everything would be all right.

Kate's gut slowly knotted. The pressure began to build until she realized she needed more air and took a deep breath to steady herself. Her legs felt heavy as she walked into the dining room and stared at the floor. It had been a while since her last panic attack, and she struggled to control herself. What would she do, with time stretching in front of her and nothing to fill it with but emptiness?

"I figured we could stock you up on a lot of extra stuff," Ellen continued. "You have my cell-phone number. You can call me anytime if you need anything or if you want to talk."

"It's okay," Kate said, her voice quivering a little. Her hands shook and she shoved them into her pockets to still them. "I'll be fine. I'm not your responsibility."

"Kate. Maybe it's time you thought about getting out a little. You could start with the grocery store, that's all, and—"

"Thanks for your suggestion," Kate snapped. "I'm sorry for the inconvenience I've put you through."

"That's not what I meant at all—"

"I understand that you have your life to live and that I must be an impediment to your daily activities. I assure you I will find alternative methods of getting what I need. Thank you for the books and for all you've done."

"Now wait just a minute. I don't mind doing your errands and shopping. I do them when I have to do my own, so it's absolutely no imposition. All I'm saying, Kate, is that you can't hide forever. Sooner or later you're going to have to move on with your life. I hate to see an intelligent woman drink herself to death and ruin what, by all accounts, is a brilliant mind."

Kate stared at her, surprised by the unexpected outburst. Up until then, Ellen had appeared calm and easygoing. But Ellen had no business telling her what to do.

"Thanks for sharing," Kate snarled. "I'll take it under advisement."

Ellen closed her eyes. "Look, Kate, I'm sorry. I shouldn't have said that. I'm just worried about you. I don't want to leave you alone here with no one to turn to, for any reason, let alone an emergency. I want to be sure you'll be all right."

Kate shoved her hand through her hair and sighed. She knew Ellen was simply looking out for her, even knew some of what she said was true. But she wasn't ready to face reality, not yet. "Thanks, Ellen," she said halfheartedly. "I appreciate your concern, really I do. But I need some time to think, okay?"

Ellen nodded, unable to speak because of the lump in her throat. She had to touch Kate, had to let her know her intentions were well-meaning. She placed her hand on Kate's arm and a shock wave rippled through her body. "Let me help, Kate. You know you can talk to me, if you want. I'm a good listener."

Kate glanced down at the hand on her arm. "Thanks, I'll let you know."

It was all Ellen could hope for.

"So, hot date?" Kate winked.

It seemed all Ellen ever did around Kate was either apologize or blush. Once again, surprised at the accuracy of Kate's comment, she felt heat fly to her face.

"I see," Kate said. "So who's the lucky lady?"

Surprised again by Kate's seeming knowledge of her life, Ellen wasn't quite sure what to say. Clearly she had somehow figured out Ellen was a lesbian, and knowing that made Ellen inexplicably shy.

"Sandra is a Capitol Hill attorney. We met two months ago through mutual friends and we've been on a couple of dates." Glancing down at her watch, she was surprised to see it was almost seven. "Well, I better go."

"Have a good time," Kate murmured.

Ellen stepped out into the hallway just in time to see Sandra about to exit the elevator. She heard the door close quickly behind her and moved toward the elevator while Sandra held the door aside, waiting for her.

Kate watched through the peephole as Sandra kissed Ellen briefly just as the doors closed.

"What kind of lame-ass kiss is that?" she shouted through the door. These two had been out a couple of times, according to Ellen, and that woman greeted her like that? Ellen looked fantastic tonight, she was smart and interesting, and by all rights anyone should be proud to have her on her arm. Clearly this Sandra person didn't appreciate what she had.

Kate strode over to the bar and reached for the scotch. But she hesitated, then picked up the vodka instead and poured a shot, mixing it with tonic and a slice of lime. Ellen's comment about her drinking made her think that perhaps she ought to slow down. Instead of the straight scotch, a mixed drink seemed less potent. And since Ellen was so interested in talking about personal issues, Kate thought they might have to discuss her choice of women.

❖

Zaytinya, an all-glass, modern building both inside and out, served a blend of Mediterranean cuisines. A large modern sculpture out front contrasted sharply with the neoclassical architecture of the National Portrait Gallery across the street. They strolled to the bar while they waited for a table, and Sandra ordered two white wines and an appetizer. Ellen had been to the restaurant previously and enjoyed it, but was surprised Sandra had suggested dining there. The place was rather noisy and crowded, not particularly conducive to conversation and especially not for romance. But she was happy to be out on a date with Sandra, and when they were seated at their table, the effects of the wine relaxed her.

"Since the dishes are so small, I usually order several and we share. Is that okay with you?" Sandra asked.

"That's fine, although I have to tell you, the olive-oil ice cream for dessert, while unusual, isn't something I'd have again."

"Oh, well, I usually don't have dessert. Trying to watch the figure and all that." Sandra winked.

Surely Sandra hadn't meant it the way Ellen took it, but she felt stung. Was it a subtle jab at her weight or merely an innocent remark?

After the waitress took their order, Sandra asked, "You enjoy teaching?"

"Oh, absolutely. I can't imagine doing anything else. Not only am I able to teach what I love, but I get to engage students in what had previously been a dull subject for them. When I see one get excited over the Gettysburg Address, I'm thrilled."

"Part of that, I imagine, is due to their having a wonderful instructor."

Sandra's compliment pleased Ellen. "Thank you. I do try. I want them to see history as I do, full of interesting people and events that have relevance to their lives today. I wish all students could appreciate the significance of the past."

"My son is a history major," Sandra announced.

"I didn't know you had a son."

"I was married years ago, but discovered soon after that I was a lesbian. By then, I'd had Jeremy and he spent most of his time back and forth between me and his father. His life hasn't always been easy." Sandra toyed with her wineglass, seeming lost in thought.

"Divorce is difficult on everyone, more so with children." Ellen tried to soothe her.

"Yes."

"Where does he go to school?"

"He was a sophomore at Brown, but was academically suspended because of his grades. His mind wasn't on school last year because a close friend of his passed away. I'm trying to get him back in, but it hasn't been easy."

"Perhaps if you speak with his dean, that would help," Ellen suggested.

"I tried, but it was no use. His dean has something personal against Jeremy. I could see it written all over his face."

"Well, what about having him apply to another school?"

"That's where we are right now. I finally persuaded him to go to a school closer to home so I can keep an eye on him. As a matter of fact, he applied to Georgetown not long ago. But I'm not sure he'll be accepted."

Surprised again, Ellen sat back in her chair as the waitress brought their dishes and took the opportunity to collect her thoughts. "Why didn't you tell me sooner?"

Sandra shrugged. "It slipped my mind. Besides, I couldn't ask you to help. You don't even know him."

"But I know you," Ellen replied, taking Sandra's hand. "I'd be happy to put in a good word for him in Admissions, if you like."

Sandra beamed. She lifted Ellen's hand to her lips and kissed it briefly. "I can't tell you how much that means to me," she murmured, "and to Jeremy. He'll be thrilled."

Ellen felt a little thrill herself as Sandra's warm lips on her hand stirred that place inside her that yearned to be touched. "It's my pleasure, really."

"Oh, but you're leaving on sabbatical in a few weeks."

"No problem. I'll stop by Admissions next week. I know an advisor there I can talk to, so don't worry about it."

❖

Kate sat in front of the television, finally calm after her brief panic attack. She still lingered over her doubts about what she would do with Ellen gone for weeks at a time, maybe more. But the lack of supplies didn't bother her as much as their connection. She could always stock up, but she relied on Ellen more than she realized, and the loss of her, albeit temporarily, scared her.

The phone rang and she glanced at the caller ID. It was Dean again, but she wasn't in the mood. She let it roll over to voicemail and returned her attention to a movie she was only half watching. The digital clock on the DVD player showed 9:30 and she yawned more from boredom than fatigue. Having nothing else to do, however, she turned off the television and prepared for bed.

As she brushed her teeth, she examined her face in the mirror. The redness had completely disappeared, but the scar still stood out in her mind like a great chasm, splitting one side of her face from the other. She couldn't cover it, short of wearing a mask. She snorted derisively. Maybe she could be like the Phantom of the Opera, terrifying women by taking her mask off. However, she couldn't sing.

She decided to have a nightcap and read in bed for a while, so she returned to the bar off the kitchen to pour herself a glass of port. When the elevator pinged she looked toward the door and automatically headed to the peephole, though she was annoyed at herself for having become such a busybody. She chalked it up to boredom, but it also rankled that Ellen was out on a date with a woman while she sat at home alone. Of course Ellen had every right to do as she pleased, and living vicariously through someone else's sex life gave Kate a cheap thrill; that is, if Ellen was having sex with this woman yet.

Squinting through the small hole, she had a distorted view of the hall just outside Ellen's door. Sure enough, there was Ellen with that woman, *what was her name,* stepping out of the elevator. Ellen unlocked her door and turned to her. *Say no, say no.* But to Kate's extreme disappointment, the slender blonde followed her. "Well, I guess that answers that," Kate uttered disgustedly.

Port in hand, she wandered back to her bedroom and crawled in bed. She hoped to take her mind off what was going on next door by reading. If she was lucky, the book wouldn't have much sex in it and she could simply go to sleep. Three pages later, she realized her luck had run out.

She tossed the book aside, went into her office, and scanned her e-mail for anything interesting. Lately nothing had been even remotely enticing and tonight was no exception. She was reaching over to turn off her monitor when a light from outside reflected against the row of awards lining the shelf in front of her.

The one she was most proud of, her Pulitzer for the work she did at the *Washington Post*, sat prominently up front. She gazed at it a long time. The night she won, she could have had anything she wanted, and she had planned so much as a result.

Disgusted with the empty promises the awards now represented, Kate fled the office to find refuge in bed, burying herself so far down in the covers only the top of her head was exposed. She had enough money for quite some time, but was angry Ellen had thrown a monkey wrench into the plan. Her impending departure caused a tightness in Kate's chest that threatened to set off another panic attack. What if something happened while Ellen was gone? What if she fell and injured herself or became sick and couldn't get help? She shoved the thoughts aside and prayed for sleep.

CHAPTER NINE

Something jolted Ellen awake and in her confusion she picked up the phone. When it dawned on her that a car alarm was causing the noise, she lay back on the pillows and tried to calm her speeding heart. The alarm alternated between high-pitched wailing and sporadic honking, and she suddenly knew why she'd never purchased a gun.

She glanced over to the other side of the bed, finding it empty, and realized she had also heard the shower running. A slight tension in her belly made her get up and slip on her bathrobe. She immediately went to the mirror and gazed at herself. Her hair looked as though a rabid animal had been let loose in it and she grabbed her brush, quickly coaxing the tangled mass back into place.

As she headed for the kitchen to make coffee, she noticed the remnants of last night's encounter in the living room: empty glasses, articles of clothing strewn about the floor, sofa cushions askew. She straightened everything and gathered the clothing, placing it where her bathrobe had lain. The water shut off and she slipped quietly back to the kitchen, scooping coffee into the coffeepot.

Last night had been a bit awkward, to say the least. As soon as Sandra had started kissing her, Ellen had tried to relax. It had been a very long time since she had been with someone, and being with Sandra, while not unexpected, still came as a surprise. Once Sandra began to unbutton Ellen's blouse, Ellen knew she somehow needed to turn off her brain. But she thought only whether Sandra would find her body a turn-on or a turn-off.

So Ellen had taken charge and became the top, a role she never truly felt comfortable in. However, focusing on Sandra's needs had allowed her to relax, and she thought Sandra had wound up enjoying herself—so much so that Sandra had fallen asleep soon after. Ellen felt a bit frustrated, but at least Sandra hadn't seen her completely naked. She wished she could feel less insecure about her body, but this way, Sandra enjoyed herself and perhaps with their next tryst Ellen would be more at ease. If there was a next time. Their varied schedules didn't allow for frequent dates, and for now, she was okay with that.

This time the phone did ring and Ellen picked it up.

"Ellen, Mother has her doctor's appointment this afternoon and Taylor has come down with some sort of bug and I can't leave her. Can you take Mom?"

Joan sounded harassed and out of breath, as though she was in a hurry.

"When is her appointment?"

"Three."

"Yes, I can make that. I just have to give a quiz this morning."

"Good, and don't forget that tomorrow night is the dinner party Mom and Dad are throwing. Dress nicely. Several eligible men from Dad's office will be there."

"Good morning," Sandra whispered in Ellen's ear, kissing her lightly on the lobe.

"Good morning," Ellen squeaked, forgetting she was on the phone.

"Who's that? Is someone there?" Joan demanded.

"Uh, yes, a…a friend." Ellen didn't think fast enough to say it was the television, but then, why should she have to hide from her sister?

"A *friend*?" Joan repeated. "Oh, my God, Ellen. Tell me you don't have some woman there. Lord, is that what you do, bring strange women home with you?"

Ellen controlled her temper for the sake of Sandra, if not for Joan. "I can't talk right now, Joan, but I haven't forgotten about tomorrow night. Mom and Dad, you and Robert, me, and several eligible men—what else do I need to know?"

"Other women will be there, too, but Robert can't make it. He's attending a conference in New York."

Joan's husband lived the life of most surgeons, constantly working and constantly unavailable. Ellen had difficulty recalling when she had seen him last.

Ellen gazed at Sandra and on a whim said, "I'm bringing a date."

"You are?" Joan spluttered. "Who?"

"Her name is Sandra."

Sandra's eyebrows shot up and a slow grin spread across her face. Ellen hoped that meant she would go.

"What? Ellen, what are you talking about? What do you mean?"

"Gotta go," Sandra mouthed and pointed at her watch.

"Listen, Joan, I'll call you later." Ellen hung up. "I'm sorry about that. Look, I've made some coffee. Won't you stay and have a cup?"

Sandra shook her head. "Some other time, perhaps." She grinned. "Have another girl on the line, do you?"

Ellen felt the blood rush to her cheeks. "No, that was my sister. She has a knack for calling at the worst moments."

"So I guess I'm going to a party, hmm?" Sandra's eyes sparkled.

"I hope that's okay?"

"I'd be glad to. Well, thanks for last night, I enjoyed it. And thanks for your help with Jeremy. I really can't tell you how much I appreciate it."

"Not a problem, really," Ellen reassured her.

"I'll talk to you later."

Sandra leaned forward and pecked Ellen on the lips, opened the door, and was gone.

Ellen stood bewildered, her arms still hanging in the air from trying to wrap her arms around Sandra but instead finding empty space. She stood there a few seconds longer wondering what to make of that interaction. Sandra said she'd enjoyed herself. *That was good, right?* She didn't want to ponder the question for long. She poured herself a cup of coffee and took it into the bathroom with her. After a few thoughtful sips, she turned on the shower and stepped in.

❖

Kate heard the front door close and ran to the peephole. It was that *woman*, leaving Ellen's condo, at seven thirty in the fucking morning. Didn't Ellen have to go to work? What did that woman do again? Attorney, wasn't it? Probably some ambulance chaser. Kate pulled away from the door, annoyed. She didn't know why; she couldn't care less what Ellen did, as long as it didn't interfere with their arrangement.

Of course, something was already interfering with their arrangement. Ellen's sabbatical would begin soon and Kate had done her best to ignore it. However, she'd need to face up to it sooner or later. She needed to decide how she would make do while Ellen was away. She went into her office and looked at the notepad by her computer keyboard, double-checking for the hundredth time that Ellen's cell-phone number was there, just in case.

The phone rang and she looked at the caller ID. *Give it up, Dean.* The phone rang several more times before the answering machine kicked in. No way in hell would she consider a job in some place like Kansas. She'd just as soon collect empty bottles along the highway and return them for a deposit.

She sighed. It was going to be another long day, but she'd better touch base with Ellen before it was too late. Ellen must have a lot to do before she left, and Kate didn't want to wait until the last minute to have her tasks done. She picked up the phone and, as she began to dial, hesitated. Thinking better of the phone, she walked into the living room, out the front door, and into the hallway. After knocking on Ellen's door, she folded her arms across her chest and stood waiting.

Ellen opened the door, clearly surprised to see her. "Kate. Is something wrong?"

"Hi, Ellen. No, nothing's wrong. I imagine you're on your way to work, but I wanted to make sure we could talk later when you get home, about...well, you know."

Ellen stared blankly at her for a moment. "Oh. You mean about my leaving and all?"

"Yes, I—"

The elevator pinged, freezing Kate in mid-sentence. She turned to look just as the doors slid open and out stepped Ellen's friend. She slowed after a few steps, watching Ellen and Kate at the door, and when she noticed Kate's face, she stopped walking entirely. Kate could see her staring at the scar, her eyes fixed on her face and not her eyes. Angrier than she'd been in a while, Kate stared back coldly.

"Sandra." Ellen could sense the angry waves emanating off Kate. "Did you forget something?"

"Uh, yes...I think I left my car keys on your credenza."

Ellen reached back inside, picked them up, and handed them to her. She wasn't certain whether to introduce her to Kate. The awkwardness was thick and she wished Sandra wouldn't stare so openly at Kate. If she didn't introduce them, though, the situation would be even more awkward.

"Sandra, this is my neighbor, Kate."

Sandra murmured a polite hello and Kate simply nodded.

Ellen felt oddly as though she had been caught doing something she wasn't supposed to, but she couldn't think of anything else to say. Sandra helped her out by saying good-bye and took the stairs rather than wait for the elevator.

"Sandra," Kate said.

"Sorry?" Ellen asked.

"Oh, nothing," Kate replied. "So, I take it all went well last night?" She tried to seem lighthearted and upbeat, but the grin twisted into a smirk. At least someone's life was moving forward.

Ellen blushed. "Yes, thanks. I have to get ready for work, but how about having dinner with me tonight and we can talk about it? Talk about what we need to do while I'm away, that is."

This time Kate really did smile. She found Ellen very attractive when she was embarrassed. Especially when her face flushed and she stumbled around her words. "Fine, I'll see you then."

Kate returned to her condo and closed the door. Either Ellen didn't have a good time last night or she was very good at hiding her feelings.

❖

As the last student left the classroom, Ellen collected all the term papers and headed for her office. She glanced at her watch and knew Jenny would be dropping by in about an hour. It was Ellen's last class before finals week and the weight was beginning to lift from her shoulders at the thought of getting on the road soon. She was looking forward to walking the battlefields of Virginia again, hearing the cannon, smelling the gunpowder, if only in her mind.

Often she felt she had been born in the wrong time period. The present always left her feeling a little out of place and unsure of herself. The past felt more like home, like where she belonged. She was completely at ease among those relics, which was why she probably excelled at research.

She fumbled for her keys to her office just as Linda Cohen came out of hers and asked, "Last class over?"

"Yes, thank God. I'm waiting for Jenny now."

"Well, my last class isn't until one. Do you have time for a quick bite?"

"I brought lunch, but there's plenty. Come on in."

They sat at Ellen's desk and munched carrot and celery sticks, Melba toast, tuna fish, and fruit.

"If I'd known you'd brought rabbit food, I would've suggested going out." Linda examined a celery stick suspiciously.

"And therein lies my problem," Ellen complained, patting her stomach. "We go out to eat and I always wind up getting something bad for me."

"You don't call this stuff bad?" Linda asked incredulously. "Unless, of course…you're getting in shape for Ms. Powell."

Ellen waved the comment away without answering. She was hoping Linda wouldn't pursue the subject, but she knew better.

"Come on, dish. You had dinner with her last night…and then?"

Try as she might, Ellen couldn't help but expose all she felt on her face. She had never been a good liar, which got her into more trouble than she cared to remember.

"You slept with her. You dog."

"Shh." Ellen always tried to be cautious when students were around. "Not so loud."

"How was it?" Linda lowered her voice and grabbed a bunch of grapes.

"It was…nice." Ellen winced, knowing that wasn't exactly the word she was searching for.

"Nice? Nice?" Linda sat back in her chair, a disappointed frown on her face.

"Well, it was," Ellen insisted. "But…oh, I don't know. Maybe it's been so long I was scared more than anything else."

"Scared? Scared of what? Look, Ellen, you're out of practice, that's all. But honey, it's like riding a bike. You just get back on and start pedaling, and before you know it, you're coasting."

Ellen stared at her blankly. "I don't quite get the analogy."

"Whatever." Linda shrugged. "You know what I mean."

Fortunately Ellen was saved by a knock on the door. At Ellen's invitation Jenny stepped in and Linda jumped up.

"Hi, Jenny. Gotta run to my class, we'll talk later," she said pointedly to Ellen.

"Have a seat, Jenny. You all ready for finals?"

Jenny slumped in the chair across from Ellen's desk, her gaze focused on the floor. When she looked up, Ellen noticed she could barely keep her composure.

"Jenny? What is it?"

Jenny's face crumpled and she buried her face in her hands. Ellen got up and closed the door, then knelt beside Jenny's chair. She smoothed her hair down her back and coaxed her into talking.

Between sobs, Jenny managed to divulge that her father's health, which had always been precarious, had worsened. She had a younger brother in high school, and her mother had asked her to come home to Connecticut to help out. Hopefully she would only have to stay through the summer, and once her father improved she could return to school in the fall to continue her research for her thesis.

"I'm so sorry to cancel out on you at the last minute." Jenny sniffed and wiped her eyes.

"Jenny, my research should be the least of your concerns. Of course you have to go home and be with your family now. Can I do anything?"

Jenny shook her head. "Thanks, Professor Webster, but I need to pack. I'm flying home tomorrow morning."

"Well, you have my cell number. Call me if you need anything, all right?"

Jenny managed a weak smile. "Thanks, I will."

After Jenny left, Ellen gathered the term papers and grabbed her purse. She still had to head over to Admissions to talk to her contact about Sandra's son. On her way back to her office she would swing by the history department office to see if she could find a last–minute replacement for Jenny. She didn't have much hope, with most students either already employed or headed home for the summer, but she could try.

Her friend in Admissions didn't know who had Jeremy Powell's file, but said he would look into it and let her know. He gave her a recommendation form to complete and she said she would touch base with him Monday. At the history department office, she asked if anybody knew a graduate student who wanted to do research for her during the summer term, but the response wasn't encouraging.

Ellen figured if it was meant to be, she'd find someone. Otherwise, well, it wouldn't be the first time she'd done research on her own. She did hate eating by herself in strange restaurants and having no one to talk to when a particularly interesting document came to light. Such important finds thrilled Ellen, and being able to share them with someone, particularly someone who understood, made such discoveries all the better.

When Ellen returned home after her mother's appointment, she started preparing dinner for herself and Kate. She looked forward to spending time with her, and that familiar flutter in her stomach reasserted itself whenever she thought of her. Tonight she planned to make chicken Marsala, garlic mashed potatoes, and asparagus. Filling, not too fattening, and yet a tad more elegant than the usual. A nice bottle of merlot and perhaps some candles on the table... Ellen shook herself out of her reverie.

This isn't a date, Ellen. Kate was no more interested in her than Ellen was in Joan's coterie of men. Still, she wanted the dinner to be nice. She hoped Kate could find something relaxing about her time in Ellen's condo. She couldn't imagine what it would be like to be cooped up day after day. It still bothered her that Kate had chosen to escape her problems in this particular way, and she hoped she could help get her out and into the world again.

Kate arrived at seven and brought a bottle of champagne and glasses. "I've been saving this for a special occasion," she said, popping the cork and pouring it into champagne flutes. "Congratulations on the end of classes, and here's to a fruitful, productive sabbatical." She touched her glass to the rim of Ellen's and took a sip.

"Thank you, Kate, how thoughtful. But you should be saving this for your next important career move." Ellen had intended to ease into the topic, but her words popped out at the first opportunity.

"Yes, well, the champagne won't keep that long. There's no use in letting it go bad." Kate took another sip and leaned against the kitchen counter, watching Ellen cook.

"Surely there are other things you can do. If not in television, then what about newspapers? You're extremely talented and smart, Kate. I bet lots of people would love for you to work for them."

Kate's irritation rose. What did Ellen know about her life and her ability? "Look, Ellen, I appreciate what you're saying, but television was my life. I focused my entire career on getting into broadcast journalism. Starting with college at Northwestern and the *Chicago Tribune*, then into research and reporting at the *Post*, and finally with Channel 5. A couple more years there and I would have been on national news. But that's over now. No one's interested in an anchor with a five-inch scar across her face. It just isn't happening."

Ellen finished chopping fresh sage and dropped it into the frying pan. "Okay," she said slowly. "So what are you going to do? Sit in your dark condo for the rest of your life? You have too much to offer, Kate."

"Actually"—Kate poured herself another glass of champagne— "I have quite a bit of money put away. At some point I'll travel. I've always wanted to go to the Far East. Who knows, maybe I can open a liquor store in Bangkok." She hooted at the thought.

Ellen sighed. Kate obviously wouldn't take the conversation seriously. And Ellen didn't have time before she left to solve Kate's problems for her.

During dinner, Ellen decided to shift the conversation to less controversial subjects. "You went to school in Illinois. Is that where you're from?"

Kate nodded. "I grew up in Chicago. You?"

"Virginia girl," Ellen replied. "Just across the river in Alexandria."

"So that's where your love of the Civil War comes from. You leave in three weeks and you're on the road by yourself for a while. I'll bet that's relaxing."

"Well, my research assistant was supposed to go, too, but she had to cancel at the last minute. I prefer the company. It gets lonely after a while."

"When I did research for the *Post*, I thoroughly enjoyed the solitude. Just me, my computer, and a vast library. I could've stayed like that forever, but of course I didn't see a lot of growth potential there."

Ellen stared at Kate, her fork frozen in midair. Kate took a bite of mashed potatoes and looked up at her.

"What?" Kate's hand flew to her scar.

"You loved doing research?" Ellen asked.

"Yeah, what about it?"

"How would you like to get outside, into some fresh air?" Ellen beamed. "Virginia isn't exactly the Far East, but it is lovely this time of year."

Chapter Ten

It took quite a bit of convincing, but Ellen finally managed to get Kate to agree to come along. She didn't know how good Kate would be with the research, but she didn't care. She wanted to get her out of the house—mission accomplished.

Ellen sang while cleaning her house that morning and continued to hum as she walked up the street to Lambda Rising. The small bookstore's rainbow flags drifted in the breeze out front. She waved hello to the staff behind the counter and began to peruse the lesbian section. Last night at dinner, trying to find an excuse not to join Ellen on her trip, Kate declared she knew nothing about the Civil War other than the North won.

"Hey, Ellen, can I help you find something?"

"Good afternoon, Heidi. I'm looking for something on the Civil War, but fiction, if you have it."

"We just got one in that might be what you're looking for." She led Ellen over to the new releases section and handed her a book.

"Have you read it?"

"Not yet. We just unpacked them this morning and put them on the shelf. But I'm taking a copy home."

Ellen scanned the blurb on the back cover. It sounded interesting, and it took place in Washington and Richmond. They would visit many of the locations included in the book. Hopefully the novel would interest Kate enough to divert her attention from her problems. Ellen picked up a copy and paid at the front counter.

❖

Kate sat at her office desk staring at the computer screen, her eyes glazed over at all the Web sites devoted to the Civil War. No way in hell could she ever absorb enough of this stuff to help Ellen. *What the hell was I thinking?* Ellen was this brilliant professor of history and Kate knew squat. She'd be totally useless—useless as a researcher and useless as a news anchor. She turned her monitor off in disgust and pushed away from the desk.

Wandering around, she headed for the bar where she poured herself a scotch. The first sip instantly calmed her and she thought about calling Ellen and telling her the deal was off. It was one thing to know your life was a failure and an entirely different thing for someone else to know it.

But she was relieved to be going with Ellen. Not having her to talk to, even only once or twice a week, was almost unbearable. She was still a little afraid to go outside, to be around strangers, people who might know who she was. They would point and say, "Hey, remember her? What's her name? She used to be a news anchor, but look at that face." Kate's stomach turned over.

Ellen hadn't finalized her plans yet, so Kate planned to pack enough for at least two weeks, hoping that would be enough. They wouldn't be far from home, though, so she could come back and regroup. The doorbell rang as she stood in her bedroom, and she went to answer it, knowing it was Ellen.

"Hey, I brought you a present." Ellen handed her a book.

"What's this?" Kate read the title.

"It's a pizza, what does it look like?"

"Very amusing."

"It's set during the Civil War in the Richmond and Washington area. Since nonfiction can be dry, a romantic fictional approach might interest you more."

"I hate to say it, but this is more my speed—history lite."

Ellen chortled. "That's okay. It'll be fun to have you along."

Kate felt odd. No one had ever said she was fun. No one would have dared. Clearly Ellen didn't know her that well…yet. "Thanks, I'll start reading it tonight."

"Enjoy." Ellen turned away.

"Hey." Kate called her back. "Uh, you feel like having dinner?"

"Oh, I'd love to, but I can't. I'm having dinner with my family and some of my father's associates. Believe me, if I didn't have to go I wouldn't. I'd much rather be with you."

Kate felt inordinately pleased. "Well, if you get home early, perhaps a nightcap?"

"Uh, well, my friend Sandra will be with me."

Kate felt the thud in the pit of her stomach. "Oh."

"Another time?"

"Yeah, sure. Well, have a good time."

She closed the door and leaned against it. So Ellen had a girlfriend. Why shouldn't she? She was stunning, intelligent, kind, and thoughtful. But Sandra didn't deserve someone as fantastic as Ellen.

Kate returned to the liquor cabinet. It was ridiculous, really. She didn't even know the woman, but somehow she knew she wasn't right for Ellen. And now Ellen was taking her home to meet her parents. Could it get any worse?

❖

Ellen stepped out of the shower and toweled off. She had bought a new dress to wear tonight and was hoping Sandra would find it alluring. Plus, she couldn't wait to prove to Joan that she could find an attractive, accomplished woman, better than any of the men her sister continued to try to set her up with. Her parents would like Sandra as well, especially her father, who had been a federal judge.

She put on the black, low-cut dress, accentuating her best features. A pair of diamond stud earrings and a spritz of Chanel and she was ready to go. The phone rang and, glancing at the caller ID, she saw it was Sandra.

"Hi," she said warmly.

"Hey, Ellen. Look, I hate to do this to you at the last minute, but something has come up at the office and I won't be able to make it after all."

Disappointment seeped into Ellen but she tried not to show it. "Oh, I'm sorry to hear that, Sandra. Do you think you can make at least part of the evening? Dessert?"

"I don't think so, but I'll try. Things are hectic right now. The senator is facing an important challenger this year, and they'll be debating next week in Albany."

Ellen waited for her to offer to get together at another time, but when she didn't, Ellen hurriedly reassured Sandra, if not herself. "I understand. Politics waits for no one, I suppose. I'll talk to you later, then?"

"Sure, sure. Have a good night." The line went dead.

She listened to the dial tone for a moment longer, then put down the handset. She needed to shake off her unease. Sandra had to work late, that's all. No big deal. Ellen was used to structure, academic calendars, regularly scheduled departmental meetings. She wasn't familiar with the hectic, ever-changing pace of Washington politics. She couldn't begrudge Sandra her work. She'd have to adapt.

Besides, everything was new and eventually things would settle down. She'd have to go without Sandra, and the thought of Joan pressing men on her made her shudder. Next time, she'd have a gorgeous woman on her arm. That would shut Joan up.

❖

"So Joan tells me that you're a history teacher?"

Ellen glanced at the middle-aged, balding man who had taken up residence on the sofa next to her. He had introduced himself by handing her his business card: *James Guilford III, Orthodontist.* If he hadn't given her his card, she could have easily identified his profession by his glaringly perfect set of teeth. Having spent the entire cocktail hour boring her with the details of his work, he had surprised her by asking her a question.

"Professor of history at Georgetown, actually," she said with a trace of acid in her voice.

"Being a teacher is a wonderful occupation, especially for women. Students learn more from women and appreciate the feminine touch."

That did it for her. "If you'll excuse me, I really should be helping out in the kitchen."

As she struggled to keep from running from the room, it dawned on her he probably thought her being in the kitchen was equally "feminine." She sighed and pushed open the swinging doors. The caterers were finishing dinner while her mother gave last-minute instructions.

"Oh, good, Ellen, come taste this. Is it too salty?"

Ellen dutifully sipped from the spoon her mother held out to her. "It's fine, Mother, don't worry. Everything is perfect, but the guests want to spend time with you. So come out of the kitchen and join us."

"All right, all right. Let's begin dinner in five minutes."

The caterer nodded his agreement.

"I thought you were bringing someone with you tonight," Barbara Webster said as they strolled into the dining room.

"I was, but something came up at the last minute." Ellen picked up an olive from the dish on the dining room table and popped it into her mouth.

"Someone special?"

Ellen could hear the hopeful tone in her mother's voice. "Too soon to tell, but it has possibilities."

She didn't want to get her mother's hopes up, let alone her own, but a part of her wished to have one special person to fill the void in her otherwise full, rich life.

"Well, I hope we get to meet her next time." Barbara squeezed her hand.

"Thanks, Mom. I hope so, too."

Ellen switched place cards at the table so she wouldn't have to sit next to the orthodontist, as Joan had evidently planned. After dinner, when they all retired to the living room for coffee and dessert, Ellen excused herself.

As she exited the bathroom off her old bedroom, she heard her cell phone ringing in her purse on the nightstand and was surprised to see Kate's name on the caller ID. "Kate, are you all right?"

"Yes, everything's fine. I was wondering, that is, if you don't mind, I was hoping on your way home you could stop at the CVS down the street."

"Sure, what do you need?"

"I've run out of bandages and need an assortment of different sizes."

"What do you need bandages for this late at night?" Ellen tensed at the possibilities. "Have you hurt yourself?"

"Oh, it's just a little cut, no big deal. Once it stops bleeding it'll be fine."

"What do you mean, 'once it stops bleeding'?" Ellen panicked. "How bad is it? What did you do?"

"Now calm down, Ellen, it's just a cut. Although I think I can still feel some glass in there, I—"

"Glass? In the wound? I'll be right there." Ellen picked up her purse.

"No, Ellen, I didn't mean for you to leave your party."

"It's almost over anyway. I'll be there as quick as I can." She dug around in her purse until she found her car keys.

Making excuses to her parents, she almost avoided Joan altogether but was cornered at the front door.

"Ellen? Where are you going? It's still early." Joan looked anxiously over Ellen's shoulder into the living room beyond.

"Something unavoidable has come up, but I made my excuses to Mom and Dad."

"But Jim Guilford was just saying how impressed he is with you. Do you want me to give him your number?"

Ellen folded her arms across her chest. "Over my dead body, Joan. I am not in the least bit impressed with Mr. Guilford."

"Now, Ellen, you've just met the man. Give him time."

"I already did, Joan, and his time's up." She pushed open the front door and sped to her car.

After stopping at a pharmacy in Alexandria, she raced along the George Washington Parkway and didn't stop until she pulled into the underground garage in her building. She pounded loudly on Kate's door and called out, afraid Kate might have fainted or was more seriously injured than she'd let on.

"Jesus Christ," Kate exclaimed, yanking the door open. "Is the building on fire?"

"I wasn't sure if you could hear me," Ellen said, scanning Kate for injuries.

"The guy in the building across the street can hear you, for crying out loud. Oh, and by the way, he said to tell you to keep it down."

Undaunted, Ellen pushed her way inside and made Kate sit on the couch. She saw the towel wrapped around Kate's hand and braced herself. Slowly unwrapping the damp cloth, she took Kate's hand and scrutinized it. "Where are you hurt?"

"Right there." Kate pointed to a spot on the tip of her index finger.

"Where?"

"Right there," Kate repeated, squeezing the finger until a tiny drop of blood oozed out.

"You mean to tell me that's your bloody gash?" Ellen nearly collapsed with relief.

"I never said it was a bloody gash."

"I drove like a bat out of hell thinking you were seriously injured and this is all you have? I left my parents' party early for this?"

"You're the one who decided to leave early," Kate said defensively. "All I asked you to do was stop and pick up some bandages on your way home."

"But you scared the hell out of me."

Kate peered at Ellen curiously. She was obviously upset, but Kate couldn't figure out why. It actually seemed Ellen cared about what happened to her. The thought began to fill a hole in her heart she didn't know existed.

"I'm sorry, Ellen. And I'm sorry you left the party early. I hope Sandra isn't too upset."

Ellen shook her head. "The party was dull and Sandra couldn't make it after all."

Kate caught a smirk forming on her lips but stopped it instantly. "Oh, I'm really sorry."

"Yeah, well, I'm just glad you're okay. Sorry if I overreacted." Ellen examined Kate's finger but couldn't find any glass.

They went into the kitchen where she washed and dried the finger and wrapped a bandage around it. When she finished, she lifted the finger to her lips to kiss it, as though Kate were a child and she wanted to make it feel better. When she glanced up, Kate's eyes focused intently on hers. She couldn't describe the swirling emotions she saw there, but a tremble that began in her knees crawled up her spine to the back of her neck.

"Thanks," Kate murmured.

"You're welcome," Ellen whispered, still holding on to the finger. The sound of her heart thudding in her ears and the feel of white-hot heat spreading through her body took her by surprise.

A second later they separated, an awkward silence filling the space between them.

"Well, it's late and I should let you get to bed." Ellen picked up her purse and headed for the door.

"Yeah, talk to you tomorrow." Kate was confused about what had just happened. No one had ever come to her rescue before. She was intrigued. Someone actually cared for her. The last time she could recall anyone caring for her had been her dog Jake. She was heartbroken for years after the collie had passed away. Oh, but there was her first girlfriend back in college. She thought she had been in love then, but when the woman dumped her a year later, Kate thought her heart would never mend. The memory of it made her think of Ellen in a different light, and it made her uneasy.

Ellen was being extremely kind, but Kate didn't want her to feel sorry for her or anything like that. If Ellen thought they could be buddies, she was dead wrong. And Ellen surely wouldn't think of her romantically—she was too attractive and accomplished to be interested in her. Even if she were, Kate was unable to return the feelings. Ellen was the type of woman who wanted forever. Kate had never wanted that before, and especially now it seemed impossible.

❖

Ellen pushed her cart down the personal-care aisle, selecting last-minute items for their trip tomorrow. She was looking forward to spending more time with Kate, especially since the cut-finger incident. Something had sparked between them. She had felt it and was sure Kate had as well. At least she hoped so, or was it just wishful thinking? The more she dwelled on it, the more she believed it was impossible. Kate was drop-dead gorgeous, while *she* was overweight and plain—nothing special. What could Kate possibly see in her?

She finished collecting what was on her list for both of them and headed toward the checkout. As she rounded the aisle toward a cashier, she saw Linda and Janice in line.

"Well, hello, you two."

"Ellen, how are you?" Linda hugged her. "We thought you'd left already."

"Tomorrow. I was going to call tonight to say good-bye, but you can always reach me on my cell, too."

"Yeah. We phoned a couple of weeks ago, Saturday night, I think, but you weren't home. We didn't leave a message, though, and then things got so busy." Janice began placing items from their cart on the conveyor belt.

"I was at my parents'," Ellen replied. "It was a dismal party, and Sandra had to work late."

Linda looked at her oddly. "Saturday night? Just before finals?"

"Yes." Ellen placed a separation bar on the belt and began to unload her cart.

Linda glanced at Janice, who shook her head quickly. But not quickly enough.

"What?" Ellen asked.

"Nothing." Janice's shrug seemed phony.

"Spill it," Ellen demanded. "What about Saturday night?"

Her friends were silent for several seconds, then Linda said, "We, uh…saw Sandra…that night."

"Oh?" Ellen supposed that must have been late, too late for her to drive all the way to Alexandria.

Linda didn't answer. When they put the last item on the belt and began a conversation with the checkout person, Ellen knew something was going on.

"Come on, you two, you're supposed to be my best friends."

Linda sighed heavily. "We saw her at Rosie's…around seven o'clock, I guess it was…"

She and Janice ventured nothing further, and from their awkwardness Ellen knew Sandra hadn't been alone. She stood very still, the familiar pain of rejection clutching at her heart and stomach. "I see."

While she finished checking out, Linda and Janice waited for her by the exit. They walked her to her car and helped load her groceries in the trunk.

"Listen, Ellen—" Linda began.

"No, it's fine. Look, we haven't dated that much. We never said our arrangement was exclusive. Both of us are free to see whomever we please."

"But she lied to you." Janice sounded angry.

"She was probably trying to avoid hurting my feelings. It's okay, really." Ellen closed the trunk and opened her car door. "Listen, I've got to run. I have a ton of stuff to do before I leave in the morning. Would you guys mind checking in on General Beau a few times? Kelly takes wonderful care of him and plays with him far more than I do. But he does like you both and variety is always nice."

"We'd be glad to," Janice said.

"Have a great trip." Linda hugged Ellen tightly. "Be careful, and call us when you discover something interesting. And let us know when you'll be back in town so we can get together for dinner."

"Will do." Ellen waved as they headed toward their car, but when she could no longer see them, she dropped her cheerful demeanor.

Buckling herself into her seat, she tried to catch her breath, tried to prevent the tears that welled up inside her. *It's no big deal. It's no big deal. She's just been really busy for the last three weeks.* She stared out the windshield, willing herself not to care. But it was no use. She put her hands on the steering wheel, placed her forehead on her hands, and let the tears drip silently onto her hands and the steering wheel.

The life and spirit ebbed out of her, leaving a defeated, empty feeling. Sometimes it was so exhausting to maintain a happy exterior.

Chapter Eleven

The morning of the nineteenth dawned gray and dreary, and rain drizzled sporadically like confetti remnants the day after a party. Ellen stowed the luggage in the trunk of her car and placed a small cooler on the floor behind the driver's seat. She had filled it with water, fruit, and healthy snacks. Not her normal travel fare, but she didn't want Kate to think she lived off Snickers bars, potato chips, and Cokes, even if she did and had the figure to prove it.

Normally Ellen looked forward to her research, and she should have felt especially exhilarated having Kate, the object of her fantasies, along for the ride. But the incident with Sandra had left her in an emotional tailspin, a nosedive she couldn't climb out of. If Sandra wasn't interested in her, what on earth made her think someone like Kate would ever be? Ellen understood that a reality check was precisely what she needed so she wouldn't make a fool of herself, but it dampened her spirits.

With the luggage all accounted for, she now had to get Kate into the car, a feat she didn't look forward to. Last night, when they discussed the details of the trip, Kate had tried to come up with every excuse she could. However, Ellen could sense that her heart wasn't in the protests, and the argument had faded away with the night. She slammed the trunk closed and went upstairs.

"You're sure about this," Kate said the moment she opened her door. She wore a Cubs baseball cap, the brim pulled low over her face.

"Yes, I'm sure." Ellen grasped Kate's arm and coaxed her out the door. "Let's go to my place so I can say one last good-bye to Beau, then we're off."

After kissing her cat several times and making sure the note she'd left for Kelly was in the usual place, she locked her door and they took the elevator to the garage. Ellen pressed the remote door-unlock on her key chain and Kate scurried to the passenger-side door of Ellen's car. Once inside, she slouched in her seat and slid on a pair of dark sunglasses.

Ellen hoped Kate would eventually relax and enjoy herself. "It'll be okay," she said as she started the engine. "Breathe in and out and you'll be fine."

"I'm not a child," Kate snapped, but she inhaled deeply.

Ellen rolled her eyes. It was going to be a long day. While she was glad for the company, she had to remind herself this wasn't vacation. This was work, even if Kate was wearing cologne that made her pulse quicken.

They took Interstate 66 out of Washington and headed southwest toward the Manassas battlefield. Ellen wanted to begin with a visual inspection of the battlefields between Washington and Richmond. The first major battle of the war—First Manassas or First Bull Run, depending on which side you fought—was the logical starting point. Getting a feel for the landscape was always important in understanding a battle, and besides, she loved the process.

Kate sat quietly as Ellen drove, puzzled by her lack of exuberance and chattiness. Ellen seemed unusually withdrawn, especially for the start of what should be an exciting day. Maybe she was just getting into the zone, like Kate used to prior to going on air. *It's really none of your business.*

By the time they passed Centreville, the mist began to dissipate and the sun finally peeked out from behind rapidly disappearing clouds. They turned into the drive off Sudley Road, pulled into the near-empty parking lot in front of the visitors' center, and went inside. In the back of the building, beyond the damp grassy fields, stood the widow Henry's home with its obelisk monument to the battle. Ellen scanned the bank of trees off to her right where Stonewall Jackson had earned his famous nom de guerre, imagining the row of cannon he brought to bear on Union troops.

She led Kate past the Henry house, and as they crested the hill, she could see in the distance Matthews Hill and the Stone House down below. An eerie fog, caused by a combination of warmth and receding mist, spread across the ground, giving the landscape an ethereal glow. Ellen had chills and tingled like she always did when she walked a battlefield. She could feel the anguish suffered there long ago.

"So." Kate glanced about. "Where was Lee situated and where was Grant?"

Ellen smothered a grin but kept her eyes fixed on the distant hill. "Lee was in Richmond and Grant out west," she murmured. "Confederate Generals Beauregard and Johnston fought Union General McDowell in the First Battle of Manassas. It was the first major battle of the Civil War."

"I thought Fort Sumter was the first."

"Technically it was, but with limited troop engagement and no fatalities, so it doesn't really qualify as a major battle. Actually, after the bombardment, the North saluted the lowering of the flag at the fort by firing cannon. A spark caught nearby ordnance on fire and exploded, killing two Union soldiers."

"So it got the ball rolling?"

"Militarily, yes," Ellen said. "There were other minor skirmishes, but First Manassas was an all-out battle between two armies."

"And the North won, right?" Kate asked.

Ellen laughed. Switching her attention from the surroundings back to Kate, she was caught off guard. Kate stood in profile, her scar on the opposite side, her hair blowing gently in the breeze. It was the first time Ellen had seen her in natural sunlight, and she was every bit as breathtaking as she appeared on television. Even outdoors she required no touchup to her flawless skin. Ellen wished she would remove the cap and sunglasses so she could see her fully.

"Actually, First Manassas was a disaster for the North," she said. "Thanks to badly uncoordinated troop movements and poor generalship, portents of what was to come. In fairness, the South wasn't much better. The tide turned in their favor only after more Confederate troops arrived late in the day. A brigade from the Shenandoah Valley even came by rail, the first time trains were used in such a way."

Kate observed a few visitors listening to Ellen's comments and was proud to be with someone so knowledgeable. It was like having a private tour guide. "How many were killed?" she asked. She found herself like one of the visitors, caught up in Ellen's vast knowledge and the enthusiasm evident in her descriptions. Standing on the battlefield while Ellen pointed to critical sights and heart-wrenching moments made the history that much more alive. Kate could almost hear and smell the battle, and she marveled that such things could happen in America. History in school had never been so real.

"About five thousand casualties, more than the death toll of the Revolution after eight years of fighting. The country had never seen anything like it, but in retrospect, it was minor compared to later battles."

Ellen pointed out troop placements and movements, oblivious to the gathering visitors. Every once in a while, someone would glance at Kate, then stare in recognition. She would turn and pretend to look at something of interest elsewhere, hiding her scar and squelching the urge to flee. After walking the fields together, with Ellen taking notes and saying hello to some of the rangers she knew, they returned to the car and headed out of the park.

"Where to now?" Kate asked.

"Fredericksburg. Have you ever been there?"

Kate shook her head. "I may have driven past it once."

"It's another important battlefield."

"But this time the North won?"

Delighted that Kate was making a game of this rivalry, Ellen said, "Nope. Different generals, too, although Lee was there. George McClellan was in command of the Union army and managed to stop Lee's advance, but President Lincoln said he had 'the slows,' so Ambrose Burnside replaced him. He tried to attack Richmond a couple of months later, and the Rebels defeated him at Fredericksburg."

"What happened to Ulysses Grant?"

"He was busy fighting out west in Tennessee at the time."

Kate was confused. "Exactly how many generals were in command of the Union army?"

"Well, depends upon how you look at it." Ellen merged into traffic. "The Union army had a few different commanders in different places before the president appointed Ulysses Grant general-in-chief. And that didn't happen until about a year before the end of the war. There were mistakes made. Most military historians think McClellan was inept in the field, for example, but concede his administrative strengths. I find all the personalities, from politicians to generals, an interesting subject for study. Some were brilliant, some simply in the right place at the right time. Oh, to be able to time travel and ask them all questions."

Watching Ellen speak, Kate couldn't help but be drawn in by her enthusiasm. When Ellen was discussing history, her face lit up with interest. She was passionate about her job, which Kate always respected in someone, no matter what their field. That was how she had been in television.

Recalling her unemployment and the reasons behind it, she folded her arms across her chest and slumped in her seat. She thought about the tourists who had gawked at her, fixated on her scar, and she gazed out the window at the passing countryside, not really seeing it.

Ellen noted Kate's silence and body language and considered asking her what was on her mind, but she had enough on her plate. She turned on the radio. Traffic jams on I-95 were a regular occurrence and she wasn't in the mood to get held up in a line of cars for hours. Despite her attempts to keep her mind on her research project, she was still plagued by Sandra's behavior. Though it was true that they'd never agreed to be monogamous, they hadn't said anything about *not* being monogamous, either. It hurt that Sandra had chosen someone else over her—especially since they'd already agreed to attend her parents' party. Something, or rather someone, had obviously been more appealing. She hadn't heard from Sandra in three weeks. Sandra had dumped her.

Kate swiveled in her seat and reached into the back. "So, do you have any beer in this cooler?"

"Hardly," Ellen said wryly. "Bottled water, fruit, and some trail mix in the zippered pouch." At Kate's frown, she added, "I thought we'd have lunch in Fredericksburg. The town is quite historic. It was the home of George Washington's mother. Depending on how things go, we could spend the night there."

Kate shrugged. "Fine with me."

"There are some excellent resources I'd like to study at the University of Mary Washington." Ellen paused. "Perhaps you could help me organize my work."

"Why not? It'll give me a chance to feel useful for a change."

Ellen kept her eyes on the road but Kate's bitter tone hurt her. Of course the future was still in the back of her mind; how could it not be? Ellen vowed to involve Kate more in her work so she could forget about her job, her accident, and her future, at least for a while. She was determined to find the extremely intelligent woman inside that sexy body. Of course, it would be nice to find the sexy body too, but that was asking a little too much.

When they reached Fredericksburg, Kate finally got the beer she wanted at the Olde Towne Wine and Cheese deli. Each time Ellen had been in the brightly painted yellow building it had been packed, and today was no exception. After a pleasant lunch, they ambled down Sophia and Caroline Streets before heading to the main battle sites. Ellen led Kate to a stone wall that at one time had a commanding view of the Rappahannock River and Stafford Heights beyond.

Pointing to the other side of the river, Ellen said, "Over there were two Union divisions, led by Edwin Sumner and Joe Hooker. They assaulted the ground we're standing on, called Marye's Heights, which was held by Confederate General James Longstreet."

"The Union attacked this?" Kate surveyed the steep slope. "I don't know much about military strategy, but if someone told me to climb this hill with an army shooting down at me, I'd tell them to go to hell."

Ellen grinned. "And you'd be right. You can't tell now, because of all the construction and trees, but back then this was virtually open space for hundreds of yards. It was yet another Union disaster, a horrible waste of men and a pointless assault. Union soldiers spent the night huddled behind the masses of dead men lying on the hillside, trying to keep warm and avoid getting shot. That was in December 1862."

"What a bunch of idiots," Kate muttered. "How could the Union have such incompetent morons leading these men?"

"Good question. I don't think people these days realize how incredible it was that the country made it through. This was one of the worst moments in our history. The odds were overwhelmingly against him, but Lincoln preserved the Union. He was a remarkable man, to say the least."

As they strolled back to the visitor center and museum, the wind picked up and the clouds began to roll in, whipping Ellen's hair back and forth against her face. She was so focused on taking notes at different points along the way that Kate could observe her without reservation.

The more time she spent with Ellen, the more impressed she was. Ellen treated her as an intellectual equal, sharing her knowledge as though they were partners in the endeavor. Kate could imagine what an incredible instructor she must be; she might have changed majors in college to take classes from someone with Ellen's classic face and voluptuous body.

She was chagrined to realize they'd lived next door to each other for years without her noticing how striking and charming Ellen was. How had that happened?

The first drops of rain drove them and a number of other tourists indoors, and Kate spent some time in the museum looking at artifacts while Ellen talked with a couple of the rangers. Everywhere they went, Ellen knew all the park employees, who seemed genuinely delighted to see her. From there they headed to Simpson Library at the University of Mary Washington, where Ellen took out her laptop.

"I'm going to see if I can find Fran Jenkins, one of the librarians here. She's an old friend and—"

"Yeah, yeah," Kate interrupted. "You know everyone."

Ellen's eyes danced. "Only the ones who are as into history as I am. Fran can get me access to original documents pertaining to the battle. They have some excellent diaries of locals who lived here at the time and recorded the events. You're welcome to come along."

"Thanks, but I've had a little too much history too fast. I wouldn't want to wear my brain out this soon."

"Suit yourself." Ellen had been worried that Kate would be bored. The Civil War wasn't everyone's cup of tea. If things didn't work out, she could always take her home and come back on her own. But even with Kate's lack of interest, she'd rather have her along than drive by herself.

She must have looked apprehensive, because Kate said, "Don't worry. I brought my book and am going to sit here and indulge myself. If you need me for anything, just come get me."

Ellen shook her head. "You'll be entering all my notes tonight. Part of your bedtime routine, if you can stand it."

Kate regarded her with a stare so direct Ellen didn't know where to look. "I'm open to any bedtime routine you want to suggest."

Surprised, Ellen didn't know what to say. Was it an innocuous flirtatious comment, or was she trying to read more into Kate's innuendo than was intended? Either way, her entire body trembled.

❖

Kate sat down at the small desk in her room and powered up the laptop. They'd checked into the Richard Johnston Inn, a quaint eighteenth-century hotel. After sharing a meal they ordered in, Kate claimed tiredness and excused herself. At first she'd expected to make slow progress inputting Ellen's notes, but she soon became enthralled by the firsthand accounts of men and women who lived through the battle of Fredericksburg. Soldiers with families in the town had watched helplessly as their homes were burned and looted. Women wrote of the anguish of canvassing the field the day after the battle and seeing the faces of the dead and dying. Before she knew it, Kate had stopped typing altogether and sat engrossed reading the notes instead. An hour later, ideas began pouring into her head about this aspect of Ellen's research.

Driven by an odd impulse, she set up a separate Word document and made some notes of her own after she finished her work for Ellen. When she looked at the bedside clock it was nearly midnight, and she shut the computer off and undressed for bed. She reached for the book Ellen had given her and picked up where she had left off. After another hour of reading, she finally turned off the bedside lamp, but thoughts and ideas continued to race through her mind until she forced herself to think of something else.

Ellen. She had done so much and was still doing an enormous amount for her. And Kate had shown her very little appreciation. She had taken for granted that Ellen would be there to shop for her and fulfill any need. Had she even thanked her? Not a simple thanks, but heartfelt gratitude for her selflessness. Kate was chagrined to admit that she hadn't. But that was about to change. She'd be the best damned research assistant Ellen had ever had, and hopefully that would help make up for her ingratitude.

She closed her eyes and allowed the images to appear of Ellen standing on Marye's Heights, the wind playing with her hair and blouse. The air had been slightly chilly and Ellen's blouse had clung to her full breasts, her nipples evident through the fabric. A slight twinge in Kate's groin surprised her since she hadn't felt aroused in a while. Then self-doubt insinuated itself into her thoughts. Ellen was exquisite. Kate was damaged goods, jobless, and directionless. What could they possibly have in common?

CHAPTER TWELVE

She was driving too fast and knew it, but she was late. The truck in front of her was exasperatingly slow, and each time she tried to pass, an oncoming car in the opposite lane forced her back into her own. Her stomach knotted at the lateness of the hour and, determined to make up time, she pushed the Porsche faster. Finally, her patience all but exhausted, she committed to passing the truck. As she swung around him, everything blurred. Suddenly she was in the backseat of another car, someone else at the wheel, and they were tumbling over and over into a ditch. She screamed. When she came to, the little girl from the SUV lay beside her in the ditch, her lifeless eyes staring blankly up at her.

Kate sat up in bed, her heart pounding. She couldn't breathe at first and forced herself to calm down until she heard rapid-fire knocking on the door adjoining her room.

"Kate, it's Ellen, are you all right?"

"Coming." Kate slid out of bed and slipped on a T-shirt, still in a fog.

"I heard you call out." Ellen peered at her closely when Kate opened the door.

"Sorry," Kate mumbled, pushing a hand through her hair. "What time is it?"

"Nearly eight."

Kate realized Ellen was staring at her barely covered legs,

exposed to mid-thigh by her T-shirt. A familiar tingling sensation spread from her stomach and radiated outward. Her nipples tightened in response. "Should I put something on or do you prefer me as is?"

"I thought you might want to grab breakfast before we checked out," Ellen stammered.

Kate was amused by Ellen's obvious discomfort. "Yeah, sure, let me hop in the shower. Go ahead and get a table and I'll meet you in twenty minutes."

Ellen waved as Kate entered the restaurant. Dressed in blue jeans and a form-fitting black tank top, she made heads turn as she approached. Ellen's temperature rose and a familiar yearning pulled at her. Even though she had been spending more time with Kate, her body's reaction each time she saw her still surprised her.

Kate sat down hurriedly. "Christ."

"What?"

"Can we go somewhere else?" Kate dropped her head so her hair hung down in her face.

"Well, yes, sure, but why?"

"Because everyone is staring."

Ellen scanned the room. All the diners appeared to be engrossed in their meals and conversations. "What do you mean, Kate? Nobody's staring."

Kate glanced up. "They were when I walked in, and when we're not looking they'll do it again."

Ellen gazed at her, then caught on. "Oh, Kate, they were staring at you because you're beautiful."

"Oh, please. No one thinks this thing is beautiful." She pushed aside her hair and turned her face, exposing her scar to Ellen's view.

A pang of regret seared Ellen's heart, but she refused to let Kate pity herself. "Kate, you are still a very desirable woman. Both inside *and* out. And never let anyone tell you otherwise."

Kate winced. If Ellen felt sorry for her and was trying to make her feel better, she was failing miserably. She wanted to run and hide, to get away from this room full of prying eyes. But when she thought she might bolt, a waitress appeared to take their order. Ellen hesitated, obviously watching for her reaction, and Kate sighed. "Coffee and toast."

After waiting a few moments for Kate to continue ordering, Ellen realized she had finished. She wanted eggs and sausages, but knew for appearance's sake she should order the fruit bowl. But fruit always left her hungry an hour later and she wound up making up for it by ordering something decadent for lunch. Her initial impulse won out. "That's all you're having?" she asked after the waitress left.

Kate shrugged. "I usually don't eat breakfast. My stomach doesn't wake up until noon." She leaned toward Ellen. "Hey, I was thinking last night about your research."

Surprised, Ellen was nevertheless pleased at Kate's interest.

"You're going about it all wrong."

Ellen stared at her. Grateful to the waitress for arriving and pouring coffee, she took the opportunity to collect herself. "Oh?"

"Yeah. Right now you're gathering data about the different military strategies employed in the early stages of the Civil War, am I right?"

"Well, that's just the initial—"

"Oh, could you make that rye toast, please?" Kate said to the waitress and put three packets of sugar in her coffee. "So, I was thinking. You're looking at both sides of the conflict, but everybody loves the underdog. We all know who won the war. You need to focus on the South. What drove their strategy? What compelled a man to join up when the average soldier didn't own slaves? What was his relationship with the elite ruling-class command?"

As Kate spoke, she gestured enthusiastically, like a Hollywood screenwriter pitching a script. Ellen dug into her breakfast, letting Kate get her thoughts off her chest. Clearly she had done her homework, even if on a very basic level.

When Kate finally stopped speaking, Ellen wiped her mouth with her napkin and placed it back on her lap. "But, Kate, you've fundamentally changed the project that my funding is based on and that my publisher is expecting to receive."

"But we'll give them something so much better." Kate grabbed Ellen's wrist as though trying to infuse Ellen with her enthusiasm. "You could blow them out of the water with a very intense, personal approach to the battles. What the participants thought, felt, believed, desired. It would be awesome."

Ellen forced a smile. She didn't have the heart to point out that what Kate was suggesting simply wasn't possible, on so many levels, not the least of which was she'd be expected to return every cent she'd already spent if she submitted a manuscript anything like the one Kate envisioned. Her publisher was expecting a book based upon her proposal. Anything else would be unthinkable.

However, she warmed to Kate's passion, thrilled to see her finally take an interest in something. Ellen's research might pull Kate out of the depression, moodiness, anger, and self-pity she'd been lost in for weeks. She couldn't remember Kate talking so animatedly before, and Kate's lingering grip on her wrist was causing a fluttering sensation in her chest.

Ellen relented halfheartedly. "Well…I'll think about it."

Kate beamed. "Excellent. This is going to be great."

When she removed her hand from Ellen's wrist and picked up her coffee cup, Ellen instantly felt the loss. With her other hand, she rubbed the tingling spot Kate had left behind. She warmed to Kate's enthusiasm and rationalized that once they were mired in the research, Kate would forget about her proposed change. The details and the sheer amount of data often bogged her down, so they would most certainly overwhelm Kate. She would let it go for now, but she had to be careful not to dampen Kate's interest.

❖

"What's next?" Kate asked when they had finished eating.

"On to Richmond." Ellen chuckled at her private joke.

"What's so funny?"

"Oh, nothing, really. 'On to Richmond' was a phrase the North espoused from the early stages of the war—Richmond, the capital of the Confederacy, being the ultimate goal."

Kate looked at her blankly. "And you think that's funny?"

Ellen shrugged sheepishly.

"Ellen, you need to get out more."

Kate rose from the table while Ellen paid the bill and they drove out of town at a leisurely pace. Ellen flipped open her cell phone and pressed a speed dial key. "Hi, Kelly, it's Ellen. Just checking in. How's Beau?" She listened for quite a while, smiling at Kelly's ebullient report.

Kate watched the countryside pass by, relaxing as the car headed south. Eventually Ellen said good-bye and hung up.

"Everything okay?"

Ellen nodded.

"Are you going to check in with Sandra, too?" Kate waggled her eyebrows. She meant it as a joke but was curious how things were going with Ellen's friend. And if she was honest with herself, she was a little jealous.

The remnants of a still-lingering smile slid off like an ice cube on a hot griddle. Kate was unprepared for the look of pain that replaced it. The two of them had seemed to be getting rather cozy. Obviously something had changed.

She had a powerful desire to strangle this Sandra woman for putting that look on Ellen's face. Her anger was so intense the words burst out before she could censor herself. "What did she do?"

Ellen was embarrassed and humiliated by her stupidity at having allowed Sandra to use her so patently. She didn't want Kate to know what an idiot she could be.

"Oh, nothing. It's just one of those things. Turns out we're not as compatible as I'd thought. We went our separate ways, that's all."

Kate could see the tension in Ellen's face belying her casual words. She also caught the shine in Ellen's eyes even as Ellen pretended to look at traffic in her side-view mirror. Never good at subtlety, Kate plunged ahead.

"Well, she's an idiot," she said with more heat than she had intended. "The moment I met her I thought she was an idiot. She doesn't deserve you and you're lucky to be rid of her. I can't figure out women sometimes. They find a good woman and don't even realize it, then move on. Somebody needs to beat the shit out of them. Give me the word and I'd be happy to do it for you."

Ellen struggled to regain her composure. She was almost tempted to give Kate the go-ahead. Yet at the same time, a thought nagged her. Why did Kate assume Sandra had dumped *her*? Was it an automatic response anyone would have, knowing what Ellen looked like and how compelling Sandra was? Did people think a frumpy-looking woman had nothing to offer and someone like Sandra would naturally want a better catch?

"What makes you think Sandra moved on?" Ellen's delivery was a little sharper than she intended, but she was ticked. "As a matter of fact, *I'm* the one who decided Sandra wasn't my type. She was looking for more than I was prepared to give. I'm not ready to settle down—just wanting to have a good time."

Ellen's admission startled Kate. For some reason, Ellen hadn't seemed like that kind of woman. Slightly disappointed, Kate sat quietly, absorbing this contradictory information and trying to reconcile it with what she had believed about Ellen. The entire time Ellen had taken care of her, she had exuded a powerful sense of safety and compassion. Kate could be herself with Ellen. In fact, Ellen seemed to be someone a person could settle down and make a home with. Kate definitely did not get the impression that Ellen was out for one-night stands. That had always been her territory.

"I want to stop at the Virginia Historical Society first. It's a wonderful resource and an old friend of mine is the director there. The museum is usually closed on Sunday mornings, but as a special favor he offered to let me come in this morning. Okay?"

Kate shrugged.

By the time they reached downtown Richmond a driving rain had begun, filling the gutters and flowing down the streets. Ellen found a parking space behind the museum and they dashed inside. Ellen introduced Kate to the director, Albert Berg, and Kate accompanied them throughout the building, viewing artifacts and documents. Each time the director tried to discuss Ellen's research,

Kate inquired about documents pertaining to her own area of interest for Ellen's work.

As they moved to another area of the building, Ellen sensed that Albert was increasingly hesitant and rather confused as to where she was heading with her research. Ellen had to admit even she was becoming confused and definitely frustrated at Kate's usurpation of her project. If she didn't take back the reins soon, Kate could sabotage the entire endeavor. But how could she do so without dampening Kate's spirit?

When Kate became engrossed in letters from soldiers writing home about their experiences in camp, Ellen suggested she stay and read them while she left with Albert to examine weapons in the museum's collection. She was intrigued when he showed her a recent acquisition—an actual window built by slaves and later removed from Libby Prison in Richmond during the Civil War. The prison had housed many Union prisoners over the war years but was no longer extant.

Relieved to finally be alone with Albert, Ellen returned the focus of her research to her original plan. She could sense his equilibrium return as well.

"Your research assistant seems to be on a different page than you," he observed.

Ellen was embarrassed at what must appear to be lack of control on her part. "She's actually a friend of mine who came along when my research assistant cancelled out at the last minute," she explained. "I'm happy to see her take such an interest in the research, even if it is somewhat incompatible with mine."

"She's the Kate Foster from Channel 5 news in DC, isn't she? The one in the terrible auto accident?"

"Yes," Ellen said. It had been a while since she'd thought of Kate that way.

"It's a shame about her face." Albert shook his head. "I can see now why she isn't still on television. She was a very attractive woman."

The heat rose to Ellen's face. "She *is* an attractive woman," she said defensively. "She's only taking time off to recuperate and do me this favor. She'll be back at work soon."

"Of course, I'm glad to hear it." He changed the subject quickly. "In here is the collection I'm sure you'll find very useful."

Several hours later Ellen emerged from the darkened room to search for Kate and found her seated at a table busily entering information into the laptop. Ellen placed her notes on the table and sat on a chair opposite her.

"Whatcha doin'?" Ellen peered at the notepad Kate was referring to as she typed.

"Just finished entering some great stories I found. You should read this stuff. This one guy who writes home to his sweetheart is very touching. You could include it as an example of the emotional strain these soldiers were under and how it impacted their lives and the lives of their families. That would be an entire chapter all by itself. Then follow it up with camp life and what they did for fun. God, I could spend all day here."

Ellen watched the excitement spread across Kate's face. She was simply breathtaking when she was so animated. Ellen was drawn to Kate's mouth, the full lips and the quirky turn at the corner when she smiled. And when she pursed her lips in thought, Ellen almost stared at them.

"I'm so glad you're enjoying yourself." Ellen handed over her notes. "When you get a chance, if you could enter these into the computer as well, then we can move on to the next round. I need to review them in the morning so I can see where I need to proceed or if I need to gather more data."

Kate glanced at Ellen's notes, then resumed typing. "Sure. I'm almost done with this."

"I thought we'd take a break and grab something to eat. Then I'd like to show you the White House of the Confederacy and the nearby museum. I think you'll enjoy it."

Kate shut down the laptop and stowed it in its case, then shoved Ellen's notes into a side pocket and flung the strap over her shoulder. "Great. I'm starving."

The rain continued to come down as they exited the building, but not as strongly as before. They ate a quick lunch, then visited the house where Jefferson Davis lived while in Richmond during his presidency. The building had been preserved much as it was during the Civil War, and they rambled through the home and the museum for nearly two hours. When they returned to the Virginia Historical Society, Kate resumed poring over the diaries while Albert led Ellen to the photograph collections.

As Ellen and Albert walked away, she glanced over her shoulder at Kate working away at her self-designated project. Ellen worried her bottom lip, thinking about how to talk to her about getting back on track. She needed to discuss it with her soon, because she was already losing Kate's attention and time to data she would never use. Time was very precious to her on this project. Tonight over a nice, quiet dinner might just do the trick.

❖

The restaurant, Julep's, offered Southern cuisine in the historic River District of Richmond. Ellen loved the pecan-encrusted chicken stuffed with Brie, and along with a chilled glass of wine, the ambience, and Kate, she could almost allow herself to think of the dinner as a romantic one.

Kate was stunning in black trousers and a stark white collarless shirt open at the throat. Unfortunately, she still let her hair hang down and forward, hiding the scarred part of her face. Ellen wanted to see her, all of her, and she wanted to brush the strands away and tuck them behind Kate's ear. In the restaurant's muted lighting, Kate was as strikingly handsome as she had ever been and Ellen yearned to touch her, to be connected to her on a more intimate level. She so wanted this to be a date, to flirt and tease, then go back to Kate's hotel room. She didn't realize she had sighed out loud.

"Something bothering you?" Kate murmured, her lips caressing the rim of her wineglass.

Ellen was mesmerized, watching the lips gently open to receive the red liquid. For a moment she didn't answer, overcome by the delicious sensations flooding her body. "Hmm? Oh, no, I just…it's that…" Ellen stumbled, trying to recover. "Well, actually, I wanted to discuss something with you."

Ellen was dressed fit to kill. Kate couldn't guess whether it was intentional or not, but it certainly had her attention. Ellen wore a sage green silk blouse that fell in supple folds down her arms and chest and formed a vee at the décolletage. Kate was constantly drawn to the curvaceous breasts exposed to view. Her heart rate kicked up a notch at the vision, and she tried to maintain a conversation but was failing miserably. She couldn't form coherent sentences because she could think only of running her tongue in the crevasse of Ellen's cleavage.

Looking up to discover Kate's perusal of her breasts, Ellen felt little pinpricks tingle up and down the most sensitive parts of her anatomy. Was it possible Kate could be interested in her, or was this just the standard lascivious stare her breasts received from men and women alike? They didn't see her looks, personality, or mind, just her tits. Coming from anyone else the attention would have made her angry. But for some reason, coming from Kate, it was a turn-on.

"I'm sorry, did you say something?" Kate asked as though from someplace far away.

Ellen thought hard, but couldn't recall what, if anything, she had been saying. What was happening? Was she imagining Kate's desire, or was she so engrossed in her fantasies that they had seeped into her waking reality? She needed to get a grip on her sanity to survive the rest of this trip. "I don't remember now, but it must not have been important."

After paying the bill, Ellen retrieved her raincoat and they stood under the awning watching as rain cascaded over the edges. They had a bit of a walk to the parking lot, and Ellen kept hoping the rain would let up enough for them to get there. But it didn't look as though it would happen anytime soon.

"Nothing to do but make a run for it." Kate grimaced.

"But your nice suit will be ruined." After thinking a moment, Ellen removed her coat, which was too warm anyway, and held it over her head. "Here, share it with me and at least you won't be completely soaked."

Kate wrapped an arm around Ellen's waist, gently pulling her close. The nearness of Ellen, along with her intoxicating fragrance, caused her heart to turn over. She tried not to bury her face in Ellen's thick blond waves and instead hunched under the coat, taking a corner of it to help hold it over them. "Let's go."

They ran as quickly as two people trying to stay huddled under a coat could, and Ellen squealed as each step splashed water up their calves. By the time they reached the car, both were as wet as if they held nothing. Kate stood over Ellen as she entered the driver's side and then ran to the passenger door, tossing the coat in the backseat.

They groaned and shook the water from their hair as Ellen started the car and turned on the defroster. The windows were completely fogged from the heat and humidity, and they sat waiting for them to clear. Out of breath and still giggling, Ellen glanced at Kate, who peered curiously at her, a strange mixture of emotions flickering across her face. Ellen's breath continued to burst forth in loud pants from the exertion of running. As she watched, Kate seemed to inch forward ever so slightly, one loud heartbeat at a time. Her lips came closer and closer like a heat-seeking missile until they found their target.

God.

Kate's lips were firm but pliable and, oh, so talented. Ellen melted into her, opening to receive Kate's questioning tongue. She relinquished all thoughts, all resistance to Kate's command, and within seconds was spinning out of control.

Way too soon Kate pulled back, her eyes heavy-lidded as her focus remained on Ellen's lips. "The windows are clear," Kate whispered.

Tearing her gaze from Kate's mouth, Ellen saw indeed that the windows were clear enough for her to drive.

"Let's go," Kate said.

Needing no further encouragement, Ellen backed out of the parking space and headed to the downtown Marriott.

❖

Registration took far too long. All the while, Ellen could feel Kate's presence at her back. She didn't need to see Kate in order to feel the waves of arousal emanating from her. For the first time, Ellen knew it wasn't just her imagination or her overactive fantasies. Kate had kissed her, and it was definitely not a kiss of friendship. Ellen's knees gave out, and she held on to the counter in front of her. The desk clerk handed Ellen her key and turned to Kate. "Ms. Foster, here's your key." Her glance strayed to Kate's scar despite her obvious attempts not to stare. "I was a big fan of yours, Ms. Foster. I was so sorry to hear about your accident."

With a brief nod, Kate took the card from her outstretched hand, mumbled her thanks, and headed for the bank of elevators. Ellen almost had to run to keep up.

They hadn't spoken during the drive from the restaurant to the hotel, but an exciting, anticipatory tension had filled the silence. Now Ellen felt something shift. A wall descended upon Kate's features and a blank, empty expression filled her eyes. Ellen thought it had to do with the front-desk clerk, but she couldn't be certain. All she knew was that her body was primed and she wasn't sure she could turn it off.

Inexplicably nervous, Kate was unsure of her next move and, stranger still, unsure if she should even be making a move. The desk clerk had brought home to her what she had almost forgotten—she wasn't the irresistible stud she had once been. She was a "was," someone who had once been somebody, but was no longer.

Did Ellen feel sorry for her? From the beginning Ellen had tried hard to help her. She was a genuine person. Maybe she simply wanted to boost Kate's ego by sleeping with her. Very warmhearted, but Kate wasn't looking for that kind of pity from anyone.

They found their rooms and paused at Kate's door.

"Ellen, back there in the car, I—" Kate broke off awkwardly, unable to find the right words to ease the tension between them. "Er...thank you for dinner."

"You're welcome." Ellen searched Kate's face for some sign as to where things were heading. Kate's inability to meet her eyes spoke volumes.

Ellen was so used to rejection she had her response down pat. Reject before being rejected. And yet she had felt so sure about Kate's feelings. But she thought she had sensed the same interest from Sandra.

"We need to get to the Historical Society early," she said. "I want to follow up on some documents pertaining to Lee's and Davis's exchanges during the battle of Fredericksburg. Spellbinding letters and full of excellent data. So, get some sleep and I'll see you in the morning."

"You, too." Kate hesitated, surprised by Ellen's readiness to sweep aside what had transpired between them in the car. Crushing a small stab of self-pity, she said sincerely, "I really enjoyed tonight."

"The pleasure was all mine." Ellen's voice sounded stiff. Her discomfort was obvious.

Feeling foolish for hovering in her open doorway, Kate stepped inside and said, "Good night, Ellen."

Ellen mumbled a reply and turned away so quickly Kate had no doubt that her well-meaning friend was relieved not to have to follow through on that kiss.

Regret pierced Ellen as she escaped into her room. Why had Kate retreated into herself? Was it because the clerk had stared at her? Did it have anything to do with the clerk at all? Ellen was convinced of what she'd seen in Kate's eyes back in the car. She'd felt it all the way to her toes. She had never seen a look like that directed at her before. She hadn't mistaken its meaning. *Desire.* In that moment, Kate had wanted her. Ellen *knew* it.

She wished she could recall that special moment and infuse it into the present. It was slipping away and she didn't know how to get it back. Not without Kate's help.

She sank down onto her bed and contemplated touching herself, but a momentary release seemed pointless. Only Kate could quench this thirst. Would she ever have that pleasure? Ellen wondered about Kate's motives. Her confidence must have taken quite a blow. Was she flirting with someone "safe," a woman she knew she could have if she wanted? Kate was stunning. What could she possibly see in Ellen? And what about Ellen's research? They would have to face each other every day and get through the work that needed to be done. Could they continue in a professional capacity, or was it time for Kate to consider returning home to get her life back on track? Just the thought made Ellen ache.

She turned on the bedside lamp and picked up the Lincoln book. Hopefully she could distract herself for a while and then fall back to sleep. It wasn't too much to ask, was it?

❖

Kate stared at the ceiling, unable to find a position comfortable enough to sleep. She had read for a while but gave up when she realized she couldn't concentrate. Her body tormented her, begging her to relieve it of the pulsing tension that threatened to consume her. She tried to remember the last time she had sex and was shocked to realize it had been four months. She seldom had to resort to masturbation. If she wanted someone, she merely looked at her. When her body demanded attention, she simply made a date and took care of it. But now things were different.

She slept in the nude except on the coldest winter nights. But it was hot in Richmond and she had covered herself with only the top sheet. The cotton fabric rubbed her most sensitive areas when she shifted, and each one screamed its needs. Finally succumbing to the temptation, she rationalized that then she could sleep.

When she slipped her hand under the sheet she was surprised to find a pool of moisture waiting. With two fingers she drew slow circles around her swollen clit, and instantly the tension in her belly heightened. Her other hand found her nipples taut and sensitive, and she pinched the right one gently. The pleasure that hummed throughout her body blossomed and she increased the speed of both hands. Within moments she felt the explosion rip through her and she moaned her satisfaction into the empty room. Slowing the circling of her right hand, she finally stopped and sighed. It would have to do…for now.

CHAPTER THIRTEEN

Ellen thought anyone watching her and Kate at breakfast would have seen nothing amiss. Even she was hard-pressed to notice anything out of place on the surface. But the tension inside her resembled a jack-in-the-box—the coil kept in place by a tightly hinged lid. One gentle turn of the crank would release all her lurking frustrations and closely guarded words, and she suspected Kate felt the same way.

They returned to the Historical Society and, once ensconced in the museum, were able to return to safer ground and discuss Ellen's research.

"Could I see my notes from yesterday?" Ellen asked.

"Sure." Kate hastily retrieved the papers from the side pocket of the laptop case and handed them to her.

Ellen stared at them blankly. "No, I mean all the data you entered into the laptop. I need to see the layout of all the data side by side in order to draw comparisons."

Kate's face reddened. "Oh."

When Kate said nothing more, Ellen realized she hadn't entered the data as she had requested. Granted, they had gone out to dinner and...well, kissed. But Kate had hours before that to get it all into the computer.

"I'm sorry, Ellen. But I had to finish entering the information I gathered from the soldiers' diaries." Her face lit up. "You're going to love what I've got here. The stories will move you to tears. And just look at these."

Kate clicked on a couple of folders and pulled up a slide show. "These are actual pictures of the soldiers whose diaries are housed here in the museum. They've been donated by the descendants of the men and other museums and sources around the country. It's amazing that this stuff survives. I'm telling you, Ellen, this is a human-interest story of the first degree. People are going to eat it up."

Ellen fought her rising temper. This wasn't at all what she needed for her book, and her building resentment at seeing her research lying in a pile of disorganized papers added to her frustration. Still, she forced it down, trying not to let her disappointment show. Kate had been making progress, and then the kiss had seemingly unraveled all she had accomplished. Ellen didn't want to hurt her feelings any more than they had been, but she also needed to get her research going in the right direction. Her direction.

"That's okay, Kate. I'm sure you'll get to them today. I'll review what I've got here, then head back into the maps and military communiqué area that Albert showed me yesterday. If you need me you can find me there."

Kate watched as Ellen left. She felt guilty at not getting Ellen's work done. But she'd make up for it today. She opened Ellen's database and began to input the data from her notes. After a while, she was nodding off; the details of Ellen's research were so boring. She just couldn't see where Ellen was heading. Kate's collection of stories and anecdotes, which she had organized in a logical fashion, was much more appealing.

She picked up a book about a Confederate soldier named David Freeman, who claimed to be the Confederates' youngest soldier. He had enlisted in the army at age eleven and served all four years of the war. She began to read his story and, before she knew it, several more hours had passed. She looked up at the clock on the wall in time to see Ellen coming from the desk where she had been talking to the director.

"Are you hungry yet?" Ellen asked.

"I am. I was thinking Greek. When we were driving in I saw a little place a few blocks away. Interested?"

"Perfect."

They walked the few blocks and ordered gyros, carrying them to an outside table in back of the building.

"So how goes the research today?" Kate asked.

"I discovered some interesting field maps of Fredericksburg drawn by Confederate General McLaws that correspond to ones I've seen in the National Archives. Albert is having copies made for me. Along with the correspondence between Lee and Davis, I'm getting a very good idea of how Lee planned to defend the town, when he developed the strategy, and what the Confederates' thinking was during that time."

"Interesting," Kate said, with more emphasis than she felt.

They sat at an umbrella-shaded table and ate their sandwiches and sipped iced tea. It was a picturesque day and the sun had dried all evidence of the previous day's rain. The air smelled of damp grass and lush vegetation, and Kate began to relax. She still felt a little unsettled, recalling her body's reaction to Ellen in the car yesterday. If things had been different, she could have pursued Ellen as she used to pursue other women, vigorously and with passion. But Ellen could have anyone she wanted, had said as much when she told Kate that she had dumped Sandra. Why would she settle for an unemployed, scarred, and washed-up former news anchor?

Although Ellen focused on a table of young lovers, she could feel Kate's eyes on her. She wanted to meet the intense gaze but was afraid to see the bland affection of friendship. She wanted more from Kate and wondered why Kate had kissed her if she didn't intend to take things further. It was confusing, but she didn't want to make their relationship more uncomfortable by bringing the kiss up again.

After returning one last time to the Historical Society, Ellen sat down at the computer while Kate browsed a collection of diaries in the adjoining room. A series of similarly bound leather volumes drew Kate's attention and she lifted one from the shelf.

Ellen was appalled that Kate had managed to input so little

of the data she had collected in the past two days. At this rate, she would never have it in time to make comparisons, and her lack of typing skills would only make the situation worse.

Glancing at the computer screen, she noticed a folder labeled "Kate" and double-clicked on it. She was surprised to see several documents that had been created within the past two days and now realized precisely what Kate was spending her time doing. After several more hours of one-fingered typing, Ellen finally gave up and shut down the computer. She zipped it up in its case, gathered her notes for the day, and searched for Kate.

Her temper high, Ellen knew it was time to talk with her. This was, after all, her book, not Kate's, and she couldn't afford to finance Kate's foray into a beginner's view of the Civil War. She found her intently reading a worn brown leather book, so engrossed in it she hadn't noticed Ellen enter the small room. Ellen was trying without much success to keep her anger in check, but seeing Kate waste her time reading diaries was too much. She cleared her throat loudly, and Kate looked up from the volume.

"Oh, hey," Kate said. "You're not going to believe this." She held up the book for Ellen to see. "This is a diary of a young girl in Virginia during the war, and it's got to be one of the best I've read so far. It's chock full of interesting historical bits that—"

"Kate." Ellen could stand it no longer.

Kate stopped speaking. "What?"

Ellen took a deep breath, not wanting what she was about to say to cause more problems than she was intending to solve. "Kate, we need to review exactly what my research entails and how we need to go about recording it. I asked you to come along when my RA cancelled out on me because I thought you had the intelligence and the skills to help me. Plus, I was hoping you would develop at least a passing interest in what I was doing. And you have, and I'm glad you have, but your interest is taking you off on a tangent unrelated to what I'm trying to accomplish."

She paused, wanting to take the sting out of her words. "I need you to refocus, Kate, and concentrate on inputting the data *I* collect. In your spare time you can do all the extracurricular reading you like. I think it's great. And I'd love to hear all about what you've discovered. But right now, we need to get back on track before all I'm trying to do is lost or unavailable to help me. Do you think you can do that, Kate?"

Kate sat in her chair, stunned. All along she had assumed what she had been doing was directly related to Ellen's research. She thought they had agreed to pursue the direction Kate was taking, which would be much more interesting than Ellen's original idea. Suddenly she felt the ground shift under her feet and couldn't think of a response. She stood up and placed the book back in its place on the shelf. Picking up her notepad and pen, she stared at Ellen, keeping her face expressionless. "Okay, got it. What now?"

Ellen frowned. Kate's emotionless delivery made it clear that her feelings were hurt. She couldn't do anything about that now, but with time she was sure she could smooth things over. She glanced at her watch. "Well, I think we should call it a day. The museum closes in half an hour. An extra day here will get us caught up and then I'd like to move on. Is that all right with you?"

Kate shrugged. "It's your call."

It wasn't exactly the cheerful response Ellen was looking for, but she took it nonetheless.

"Okay, how about dinner? I hear there's a great Italian restaurant not far from the hotel. You up for it?"

Kate walked out of the room and Ellen followed. "Thanks, but I'm beat. Plus, I need to enter all your data from yesterday and today, so I'll be catching up with that tonight in my room. I'll just order room service."

Kate picked up the laptop and headed to the parking lot. If Ellen expected nothing more than her services as a data-entry clerk, that's exactly what she would give her. Nothing more, nothing less. But she still intended to pursue her own research, for she was finding the diaries far more interesting than she had ever thought possible. Even better than most of the stories she had worked on in the newsroom.

Back in the hotel, Ellen started a bath and ordered room service, seeing no point in going to a nice restaurant alone. She missed discussing the day's activities with Kate over dinner, but she was glad they had cleared the air—that *she* had cleared it. She didn't quite know where Kate stood, except that she seemed pissed. Ellen would let her sleep on it tonight and then make nice over breakfast. She didn't like having Kate upset, but guessed it was Kate's way of processing what she had said. She would much rather have things the way things were, preferably just before the kiss.

❖

Kate had almost finished inputting the last of Ellen's data and looked at the clock on the laptop. It was after one and she had been at it for six hours. She downed the last of her scotch and stood and stretched. She couldn't rid herself of a slowly simmering tension or, rather, anger. She was restless and had taken frequent breaks. Now, pacing from the table to her window, she looked out at nothing. After a few minutes, she had forgotten why she got up and returned to the computer, angrily punching in the remaining data.

Ellen's reprimand had startled her. The professor had fire under her seemingly gentle exterior, and Kate had received an appetizer of it. Well, two could play that game. If Ellen wanted to keep things on a professional—read platonic—level, Kate would oblige. But there would certainly be no more kissing, no matter how much Kate wanted it.

She turned out the light, crawled into bed, and couldn't relax for a long time, her mind still occupied with the conversation at the museum. But as she fell asleep, all anger dissipated, replaced by thoughts of kissing…and more.

CHAPTER FOURTEEN

The next day they communicated only when necessary, a situation Kate didn't enjoy but was proud enough to maintain. When she announced that she had entered everything Ellen had given her, Ellen praised her lavishly, entirely out of proportion to the task. And though Kate brushed the compliment away as nothing, secretly she was pleased.

By the end of the day she was exhausted from the strain of being on her best behavior and didn't know how much longer she could be nice—it wasn't in her nature. And she so wanted to remain angry at Ellen, who she felt had treated her like an incompetent or a child. But each time Ellen stopped by the table where she was working and brushed against her, Kate's mind turned to mush. The anger evaporated and she leaned closer, breathing deeply of Ellen's tantalizing fragrance.

By midafternoon Ellen had achieved what she had set out to accomplish and decided now was a good time to take a break, even though the museum would be open for another two hours. Kate had worked especially hard, and Ellen decided to make an overture to her. She found Kate working on the laptop, concentrating on Ellen's notes.

"How's it going?" she asked, trying to be as friendly as possible.

"Almost finished." Kate kept her eyes on the screen. "If you've got more notes, just put them on top."

"No more notes. I'm done here. There are a couple of hours left, so if you want to do some research of your own, that's fine with me."

Kate glanced up. "It's not really *my* research."

"But you've taken such an interest in it," Ellen insisted. She didn't want to see Kate neglect her work. It had mattered to her. "What you've described so far sounds intriguing."

Kate frowned. Ellen had already decided she couldn't use the material, so why bother? She was expending a lot of effort on something that was going nowhere. She did find it interesting, but what difference did that make? She had written better stories as a cub reporter.

She shook her head. "There isn't time for it. Besides, it's not going to become a book."

"But that's the point." Ellen's voice rose a notch. "It could be a book. You could write your own book." Suddenly she saw a possibility for Kate's future. "You're a journalist by profession, a writer. You could take any story you've ever come across and write a book about it. Stories about people, about their emotions, those are the kinds of things you're good at."

Kate was taken aback. Writing a book seemed sedate compared with the fast-paced, noisy newsroom she had been accustomed to. While she enjoyed what she had uncovered in the past few days, the actual work had begun to bore her and she felt restless. She needed contact with people and the energy and unpredictability that entailed, not writing in an enclosed room.

"I don't know," Kate said slowly. "Doing this short-term is one thing, but a steady diet of it doesn't appeal to me."

Ellen didn't want her to give up so easily. "Well, think about it. Don't close the door on the possibility too soon." She could see it so clearly now. Kate was smart and intuitively knew what would make a good story. Writing suited her perfectly. And she wouldn't have to leave her condo and be exposed to prying eyes, her one great fear. At least she would have ample time to readjust to society without having to deal with it on a daily basis.

As they drove back to the hotel Ellen thought about where to go next. She needed to cover quite a few other sites, but intended to visit some such as Chancellorsville and Spotsylvania on the way back to DC. She wanted to travel to the Shenandoah Valley on another occasion and leave the out-of-state research for last.

Glancing toward Kate, she asked, "Have you been to Williamsburg?"

"Isn't that a Revolutionary-era town?"

"Well, yes, although there was a minor Civil War battle there, too. I thought we'd detour by there since it's so close and it's on the way to Norfolk, our next stop. Williamsburg is one of my favorite places, and I'm also interested in the Revolution. It's an enjoyable sightseeing place, and on our way back from the coast, we could meander along the James River and see some of the plantations."

After leaving the downtown area and merging onto the highway, Ellen drove west, arriving in Williamsburg an hour later. As they immersed themselves in the living history of the Colonial district, Ellen thought again about Kate becoming a writer. The prospect excited her.

The temporary break from work took a little of the edge off their strained relationship, or so it seemed to Ellen. They wandered from shop to shop, exploring the replicas of eighteenth-century products for sale, as well as the shops dedicated to preserving the kinds of trades that had existed. By the time they made it to the capitol building it was getting late, so they stopped in at Christiana Campbell's for dinner.

Ellen ordered a glass of wine and perused the menu. She was thoroughly enjoying herself, and she loved being with Kate. The sights and sounds of Williamsburg heightened her senses more than she could remember, probably because of her growing feelings for Kate. While Kate had been somewhat subdued, Ellen sensed that she was getting over her earlier hurt feelings. She regretted being responsible for them, but now she could smooth things over.

"So what are you having?" Ellen asked her.

"The chicken sounds good. What's spoon bread?"

"Oh, you must try it, it's heavenly."

Kate glanced at her. The way Ellen looked at that moment in the candlelight, her face expressive and alive, took her breath away. Try as she might, she couldn't stay angry and was once again drawn in by Ellen's beauty. She couldn't really blame her for wanting to write her book the way she wanted to, even if it was rather dull. She had no right to impose her opinion on Ellen's book and certainly shouldn't try to change it. Kate recalled her final day in the newsroom, when she had been angry over someone editing her copy without her permission. She had been ready to rip them a new one. She sighed, recalling her last day at the station. She missed the work and the excitement and knew she'd been good at it—was still good at it. It was where she belonged.

The dinner and the wine helped heal the slight rift in their relationship, and as they left the restaurant, Ellen didn't want the pleasant evening to end. They meandered down the Duke of Gloucester Street to the car, the shops they passed locked and dark. Ellen inhaled deeply of the smells she always associated with Williamsburg: the lush gardens, the dirt street, the old wooden buildings. At times like these she wished she had been born in another era.

Kate felt Ellen relax and wanted nothing more than to put her arm around her and walk side by side. In fact, she had to make an effort not to. She consoled herself by breathing in Ellen's scent, floral and feminine, and a warm rush of arousal spread through her.

"We can drive on to Norfolk tonight, get in late, and find a hotel." Ellen didn't sound enthusiastic.

"Can't we just spend the night here?" Kate asked. Ellen seemed so happy at the moment; Kate didn't want to dispel her mood so quickly.

"Williamsburg doesn't fit into my budget. The Inn itself is prohibitive, although it wouldn't be my first preference anyway."

"And what would be your first preference?" Kate probed.

"Mmm, one of these." Ellen gestured to a couple of quaint Colonial guest houses nearby. Each had a small plaque indicating its name and an even smaller one stating that it was a guest house. "They're separate accommodations, but still part of the Inn."

Kate noticed a small private garden behind each house and perceived the charm that drew Ellen. "Why don't we just find out if one's available? My treat."

"Oh, no, I couldn't."

"Why not? You've been working hard for days. You deserve a break, at least for one night. Tomorrow we can drive on to Norfolk and get back to work."

Kate watched as Ellen paused and the wheels turned in her head. "Come on," she said.

The twinkle in Kate's eyes made the offer doubly hard to resist. Ellen thought about the last time she'd spent the night in Williamsburg, which had been a favorite escape for her and Chris, her partner years ago. Chris had been a grad student in the same program and was as passionate about history as Ellen, the only thing they had in common. She had come to associate Williamsburg with Chris and therefore hadn't spent as much time here as she would like. It was a pity, since she loved the place and it was so close to DC.

But spending the night again, this time with Kate, took on an entirely new meaning. Not that anything would happen, but she had always considered the place a romantic getaway. She was enjoying herself with Kate, and the pull of attraction was drawing them closer. "Well, I suppose we could just inquire…"

Kate didn't give her a chance to change her mind. She grabbed Ellen's hand, turned up a side street, and headed for the Inn and the front desk.

"The upstairs of the Orlando Jones Office is available. It has two twin beds."

"What about downstairs?" Ellen asked.

"I'm afraid that is booked," the desk clerk replied, looking up from her computer expectantly.

Ellen frowned. "Are any of the other Colonial houses available?"

After searching again, the desk clerk shook her head. "Sorry, I do have a few vacancies in the taverns, but no other houses."

Kate glanced at Ellen. "What's wrong with the place that's available?"

"It's one room," Ellen emphasized.

Kate looked quizzically at her. "So?"

Ellen's ears felt warm. She didn't want Kate to think she was a prude, but she didn't want her to think she was easy. Just the idea of sleeping in the same room with Kate made her body twitch. She wouldn't be able to sleep knowing Kate, wearing only a T-shirt, was in the bed next to her.

It finally dawned on Kate what Ellen was implying. They would be sharing a room. Though the notion wasn't completely unpleasant, perhaps Ellen had second thoughts about being that close. The kiss they shared had been a momentary, spontaneous aberration. Obviously, Ellen wanted to move on and not give Kate any ideas. What did Ellen think she was going to do, ravish her?

"There are two beds," the desk clerk said helpfully.

Ellen glanced at the woman and blushed.

"We'll take it," Kate said emphatically. She pulled out her credit card and slapped it down on the counter.

They parked behind the house and climbed the steps to their room. Although it was relatively small compared to others Ellen had stayed in, the dormer windows and the period furnishings gave the room a quaint charm and she stood admiring it. Once again she felt transported back in time and closed her eyes to relish the sensation.

As Kate unpacked, she surreptitiously observed Ellen, wondering at the strong feeling she appeared to have about the hotel, the town, and history in general. Something about her intensity made Ellen more alluring, as though merely being in the historical milieu made her a totally different person.

"Um, if you need to get into the bathroom first, that's fine," Ellen offered.

"No, I'm good, go ahead." Kate grabbed the hem of her shirt and drew it up and over her head, then tossed it onto the bed she had chosen to sleep in.

She was obviously unconcerned with her effect on Ellen, who looked everywhere but directly at her. Helpless, she dared to peek at Kate's trim figure, and as she admired it, she noticed several scars she hadn't seen before. One ran from Kate's left shoulder down her arm and the other along the left side of her body. During their time traveling together, Ellen had completely forgotten the accident. All that mattered was her work and being with Kate. Seeing the scars rekindled the forgotten memory, and it pained Ellen to imagine what the accident had cost Kate.

Glancing up, she was startled to realize Kate had caught her staring and noticed Kate's angry expression mixed with hurt. Kate turned her back on Ellen and continued to undress, and once more Ellen looked away from her. She was embarrassed to have been caught staring and wanted to correct Kate's predictable impression that she had done so because of her scars. She opened her mouth to explain, but words simply failed her. No matter what she said, Kate probably wouldn't believe her.

Ellen gathered her overnight bag and pajamas and headed for the bathroom. After she finished and returned to the main room, Kate was sitting on her bed, placing a book and a travel clock on the nightstand. Even wearing an old T-shirt and a pair of boxers, she was absolutely stunning. Ellen hoped that the loose pajamas she wore covered as many of her shortcomings as possible.

Ellen sat on the bed next to Kate's. "Kate," she began.

Kate looked up from her book to see Ellen dressed in pale blue silk pajamas. She had removed what little makeup she wore, and her freshly washed face made her look even younger. The silk pajamas clung to her curves, inviting touch. Kate could only imagine how smooth Ellen's skin was underneath.

"I…" Ellen didn't know what to say. She wanted to apologize for staring, she wanted to apologize for hurting her feelings, and she wanted to say she was sorry for everything that had happened to her. But how could she express something like that and not sound pitying?

"What?"

"I want you to know how glad I am you decided to come with

me. I really enjoy having you along and appreciate all you're doing for me."

Kate was surprised. Somehow she felt that this wasn't really what Ellen had wanted to say, but it was nice to hear nevertheless.

"Thanks," she replied, nonplussed. "But I should be the one to thank you. You've done a lot for me, when I needed it most. I owe you a lot." *I could kiss her right now. I've done it a million times before with other women. I can do it again.*

Ellen blushed. "I think you've more than made up for it by the torture you're enduring at my hands."

Being deliciously tortured by Ellen's hands flashed through Kate's mind. She even dared to glance at them resting in Ellen's lap. "I've enjoyed the research, really I have. Some of what I've read has been absorbing. I can see why it captivates you so."

"And I hope you find it enticing enough to continue your research," Ellen replied. "You have the makings of a very good book on your hands. I hope you don't abandon it because of me."

Kate realized that Ellen was trying to make amends for their earlier disagreement and waved it off. "Don't worry about it, Ellen. You were right. I was trying to shape your research in another direction, and that wasn't fair to you. I came along to help, not make your work more difficult."

A large weight lifted from Ellen's shoulders, and the small knot in her stomach finally untied. She sighed and felt like giggling as relief surged through her. "Well, now that we're back on track, I'd love to see what you have so far. It would be interesting bedtime reading, but it could also help me with my work. That is, if you don't mind."

Kate shrugged. "Fine. It's not as academic as what you're doing—purely a subjective project."

Ellen chuckled. "Oh, Kate, very little research is objective. All scholars, including historians, bring their own bias to their work."

Kate loved to see Ellen laugh. Not only her mouth but her entire face became animated, which made her even more attractive, if that was possible. She peered at the expanse of skin exposed at her throat and noticed how the shadows drifted down her cleavage in the muted light of their room. A surge of arousal, both physical and emotional, rushed through her, and its unexpectedness surprised her.

In the past she would have immediately acted. Ellen was extremely alluring, and it would be so easy to lean across the space separating the two beds and kiss her. She sensed the attraction was mutual. Neither of them had faked the kiss in the car. Maybe, just maybe, Ellen was attracted to her too, despite her scars?

The panoply of emotions racing across Kate's face fascinated Ellen. She didn't know what to make of it, and she didn't really care. For a moment, she felt reconnected to Kate, without any of the previous misunderstandings and hurt feelings, as she had in the car seconds before they kissed. Warmth permeated her body and all the right places began to tingle. It was a sign. She trembled involuntarily. *God, I wish she would lean over and kiss me again.*

Feeling awkward, Kate smiled sheepishly and got up to brush her teeth. By the time she returned to bed, Ellen was already under the covers, her glasses perched on the bridge of her nose and a sheaf of papers in hand. The moment had passed.

Chapter Fifteen

Kate wasn't looking forward to returning to the city or, rather, her life. She enjoyed being on the road, living in an entirely different world. In fact, her old life had begun to fade and the one she was living now had become her reality. Being lost in the past had consumed her time and attention, and mercifully she had been able to avoid thinking about the future. But eventually she would have to face what awaited her return, and Kate finally felt as though her old strength was returning. The future still scared her, but it didn't seem as insurmountable as it had when she left.

She also had never spent so much alone time with another woman. She had come to know an attractive woman without sleeping with her, and actually enjoyed it. As her respect for the person who was Ellen increased, so did her desire for her. No one was more surprised at this self-discovery than Kate, and her introspection increased at the revelation.

"A penny for your thoughts," Ellen said.

"Trust me, they're not worth that much. I guess I'm not looking forward to a dirty condo and laundry." Kate contemplated her problems. She was unemployed with no prospects, and she had the scars that drew others' attention even when not in a city where people knew her. Money didn't concern her yet, but what should she do with her life? She had a lot to offer still, a sharp mind and talent that was very marketable. She couldn't return to the way things were, but she had no clue where to go from here.

"Well, you better get the chores over with as quickly as possible. We've got a lot of work ahead of us. And I want to take a look at what you've done so far on your project. I can't wait to read it."

Kate smiled wryly. "It's not much, really, certainly not enough for a book. It would make for light reading in *Reader's Digest*."

"What are you talking about?" Ellen demanded. "It's going to be great. You just need to gather more information and decide how you want it all to come together. I can help you, it'll be fun."

Kate appreciated what Ellen was trying to do, but she wasn't about to fool herself. Her passion remained fixed in television news—that would never change. She diverted Ellen's attention back to the battlefield where Ellen spent the next few hours mapping out barely visible trenches and talking with the rangers.

By early afternoon they were on the road again and headed into the city. Every passing mile Kate's depression settled more heavily on her, and she wondered how much scotch she had in the house.

When they arrived at their building, Kelly, Ellen's cat sitter, ran outside to greet her. "Hi, Ellen," she said as she helped grab a bag from the backseat of the car.

"Hi, Kelly, how's the General?" Ellen lifted her large suitcase out of the trunk.

"He's fine. We played with his feather toy this morning and now he's sleeping."

Delaying the moment when she had to enter her empty condo, Kate carried the bags to Ellen's and lingered, watching as Ellen played with her cat. After a few minutes, Ellen got up and went into the kitchen, pushing the playback button on her answering machine.

"Hi, Ellen, it's Sandra." The honeyed voice was distinct. "I was missing you and—"

Ellen pressed the Stop button immediately and glanced at Kate.

Kate didn't think her life could get any worse. A high-powered, attractive DC attorney was chasing the one woman she was interested in, and she was jealous. Previously she had used the women she was "dating" to satisfy her physical needs. None of them had much depth of character. Of course, she had to admit, she hadn't selected them for their character.

But now that Kate had finally found someone she cared about, her entire career was gone. Some catch she turned out to be.

"Well, I better get home and do some laundry." She rose from the couch and shuffled to the door. "I still have some data to enter into the computer and a lot of reading to catch up on."

"Hey, why don't you come over for dinner when you're done? We could order Chinese, watch a movie, you know, take a break and relax."

Kate was tempted, but didn't want to prolong the inevitable. Ellen needed to move on with her life, and Kate was an energy vampire. She could feel herself sucking the strength and energy from Ellen and knew eventually Ellen would have to withdraw. "I don't know, I'm a little tired."

Ellen watched as Kate withdrew both physically and emotionally. She didn't want her to go, especially not like this, but she couldn't force her to stay. "I'll call you later," she insisted. "You'll be starving by then and I know you don't have even half of what I have in the fridge, and I don't have anything."

Kate left and Ellen stood staring at the door. Sometimes Kate could be so frustrating. She was angry that Sandra had called and that Kate had overheard. She knew it wasn't the only reason Kate was feeling down, but she felt certain it had pushed her over the edge. She dialed Sandra's number.

"Ellen, it's so good to hear from you. I heard you went out of town."

"Yes, I started my sabbatical, Sandra, remember?"

"Oh, right."

Ellen could tell Sandra didn't remember at all.

"Well, I'm glad you're back," Sandra continued. "I was hoping we could get together, you know, dinner, and well, whatever."

Ellen could hear the grin across the line. The sexual innuendo wasn't lost on her. It just didn't mean anything anymore. Still, it surprised her. "I don't know, Sandra. I got the impression you weren't really interested in anything...steady."

There was a brief pause over the line.

"Now where did you get that idea?" Sandra sounded defensive. "I've had an extremely busy schedule, but that's not unusual. I thought we had a good time that night, didn't you?"

Ellen wasn't so sure. She remembered feeling awkward—aroused, but awkward. More than anything else she had been self-conscious, about her body and what Sandra thought of it. She also didn't feel a lot emotionally, but she had chalked that up to not knowing Sandra well enough. She immediately recalled Kate's kiss in the car and how turned on she had been, how she had lost sense of time and place. It was more powerful than anything she had ever experienced, with any woman.

However, Kate didn't seem to be interested in her. The kiss notwithstanding, now that Kate seemed to be coming out of her shell, she would want to get back to her own life soon. Ellen needed to focus on her needs and not Kate's. What time they had together on the road had been wonderful, and she would miss it terribly. But she couldn't hope to have Kate all to herself for long. At least Sandra wanted to be with her, for whatever reason, had in fact already slept with her. Ellen had finished helping with her son's application. If that was all Sandra wanted, why was she calling now, asking to see her again?

"What did you have in mind?"

❖

Kate looked around her condo and didn't recognize it. Nothing seemed familiar, and while she had never considered it her home, now it was completely alien, filled with furniture and things, but nothing of sentimental value. She could have walked into a hotel room and felt equally at home.

She dropped her bags on the floor just inside the door and left them. Entering the kitchen, she found the half-full bottle of scotch and was relieved she wouldn't have to go to the liquor store. Pouring three fingers, she barely made it to her large chair and collapsed. She picked up the remote and turned on the television. She hadn't watched it since she left and thought she might catch up on the latest news. Instead, she clicked to a movie channel and settled in with Katharine Hepburn and Glenlivet.

❖

The ringing phone woke Kate and she stumbled into the kitchen to grab it before it could annoy her again. She hadn't answered the phone in a while, either. "Yeah?"

"Are you ready for Chinese yet?" Ellen asked.

"You know, you're right, I am hungry after all. But I didn't get any laundry done."

"Well, bring it over. Doing laundry by yourself should be illegal anyway."

Kate couldn't help it. Just the sound of Ellen's voice made her feel good.

A few minutes later she tossed a load into Ellen's machine and turned it on before taking a sip of the wine Ellen had poured. Ellen set the boxes of Chinese food on the table.

"Nothing fancy tonight"—Ellen gestured at the cartons—"but there's something so satisfying about Chinese. And not having much to clean up after days of eating out has its rewards, too."

"Not to mention the leftovers," Kate added. "You've ordered enough for the Confederate army."

"Well, I didn't know what you'd like."

Kate glanced at Ellen's curvaceous hips and full breasts and knew exactly what she liked. She took another gulp of wine, and the slight buzz that had begun with the scotch returned. She felt warm inside, not entirely due to the alcohol. Being with Ellen left her blissfully content.

After dinner they settled in front of the television. A Hitchcock movie was playing and normally Ellen would be excited about seeing an old black-and-white. She was relaxed, full from dinner, and comfortable in jeans and a chenille sweater. But as she sat on the couch next to Kate, all she could think about was how right it seemed.

The couple of hours Kate had left to go home had been unsettling. They had been in each other's company for days—talking, sharing, eating, and, yes, at times arguing. But their brief separation had brought back all Ellen's loneliness, and for a moment she thought she might cry. She didn't want to return to her old ways. Perhaps that was why she had said yes to Sandra. But Sandra didn't make her feel the things Kate did.

"I love Cary Grant and Ingrid Bergman together, don't you?" Ellen sighed.

"Yeah, but he's an asshole in this movie," Kate replied. "How could he treat her that way and make her go back to that guy? He's clearly poisoning her."

"But Cary loves her, you'll see."

"He has a heck of a way of showing it."

"Oh, Kate, you're such a realist. Can't you see how romantic they are together?"

"Romantic? I wouldn't make the woman I love go back to that guy and his criminal friends. That's not romantic."

Ellen glanced at her. "Okay, so what do you think is romantic?"

Kate hesitated. "Romance is when the woman you love consumes you. She is your everything—all that matters, all that ever was and ever will be. You will gladly endure anything, any hardship, to avoid inflicting a second of pain on her. And you will love her until the day you die, never taking a moment of being with her for granted. After that, you will thank your lucky stars that someone as magnificent as she ever thought of loving someone as insignificant as you in return."

Ellen couldn't move. The entire time Kate spoke, she had looked into Ellen's eyes. Her heart beat erratically, and her face felt too hot to touch. She tried to catch her breath, but the more she tried, the harder it became to get air. "Oh, Kate," she whispered. Tears burned her eyes for all the possibilities she never dared imagine.

The alcohol had loosened Kate's self-restraint and she knew it, but she didn't care. Being with Ellen made her feel whole, and she couldn't take one more minute of wondering what it would be like to touch her. The kiss in the car was seared in her mind, and her body had awakened to the memory of it. She was on fire and had to have Ellen, here and now, if only this once. Would Ellen be able to see past her scars? More important, could she?

Kate had always found kissing someone side by side awkward, so she dared to roll over and settle gently on Ellen's lap, facing her, her bent legs bearing her weight on the couch. She towered over Ellen and leaned in, bracing her hands against the back of the couch. "I would like very much to kiss you…again," Kate murmured.

Ellen looked up into the hazy passion in Kate's eyes. *So this is what it feels like.* The inability to catch your breath, your heart pounding wildly in your chest, the feeling that wherever that person touched you, she left a trail of fire behind. And even though the fire burned intensely, it felt so good you never wanted it to go away. Ellen wanted to reply but her mouth was completely dry. She licked her lips to moisten them.

The tongue was all it took. Considering it an affirmation, Kate captured Ellen's lips with her own. *God.* This kiss was better than she remembered, and she hadn't forgotten anything about that first one. She pulled back slightly, a mere fraction of an inch from the supple mouth. Opening her eyes, she sought Ellen's, needing to know it was all right, that she didn't want her to stop.

It took Ellen a moment to realize Kate had stopped kissing her. She was lost in the sensation of warm, tender lips that aroused her like nothing before. She was already wet, amazed the kiss was all it took. She opened her eyes, afraid to think this was as far as it might go…again. The need in Kate's eyes enveloped her and she ran her fingers through the dark tresses at the nape of Kate's neck. "Please," she whispered, pulling Kate back down to her mouth.

The tentative embrace changed quickly in intensity. Their lips sought each other until that wasn't enough. Ellen opened her mouth and invited Kate's searching tongue inside, letting it fill her questioningly. When Kate sucked Ellen's tongue back into her mouth, Ellen moaned, encouraging her further.

Kate tried not to rush things, but her body simply would not obey. Her hands wandered of their own accord, finding Ellen's face first, then sliding down her neck, shoulders, then back to her neck. After hesitating briefly, she smoothed them down the front of Ellen's sweater, until they swept over the stiff nipples that pressed into the palms of her hands. Ellen arched up into her hands and she cupped both breasts, gently stroking the stiff peaks with her thumbs. Her passion overcame her insecurities, and she was transported back into the old Kate, the Kate whom women begged to touch.

Ellen pulled away from Kate's mouth, gasping for air, her body out of control. Her hips were lifting off the couch, needing to find contact with Kate, whose center painfully eluded her. Her hands moved from Kate's waist to her back, rubbing firmly, pressing her to move even closer.

Kate pushed her down onto the couch. When Ellen was on her back, Kate stretched out on top of her. The full-body contact was exquisite, and a rush of wetness pooled between Ellen's legs as their two centers connected. Almost immediately, they moved rhythmically as one, the overwhelming instinct to connect as natural as breathing. Without warning, Kate pushed Ellen's sweater up, but before she could go further, Ellen stopped her.

"Wait," Ellen panted.

Kate froze.

"I…God, I…" Ellen didn't know what she wanted to say. She worried Kate wouldn't find her body pleasing, and she didn't think she could stand it if she didn't.

"Are you okay?" Kate whispered.

Ellen nodded, her body screaming to be released from the delicious torture Kate was inflicting.

Kate kissed Ellen's stomach, her tongue tracing a line slightly above the waist of her jeans, leaving a trail of wetness behind. Ellen's body stiffened ever so slightly and Kate paused in her path. "Do you want me to stop?" Kate searched Ellen's eyes.

"No…it's just that I…I want you…" *Fuck it.* "I don't want you to be disappointed, that's all."

Kate's mouth dropped. "Are you insane? My God, you're exquisite. It's all I can do not to force myself on you. What on earth would I be disappointed in?"

Ellen struggled not to let tears spill out and ruin the moment. *She thinks I'm exquisite. Me.* She ran her hands across Kate's cheeks and into her hair, pulling her down into a searing kiss. Instantly the ache in her groin developed into a pounding throb. Gently pushing Kate away, she struggled to sit up. "I need to get more comfortable than on the couch. Come on."

She took Kate by the hand and led her into the bedroom. At the foot of the bed, she helped Kate lie down. In the pale light that filtered in through the blinds, she saw Kate reach toward the bedside lamp. "No, leave it off."

Kate drew her hand away from the lamp and pulled Ellen alongside her on the bed. The pace slowed measurably as Kate returned to kissing and nibbling along Ellen's lips and neck. Ellen sensed Kate's hesitation and knew if she wasn't going to blow this, she needed to make changes, and fast. She wanted Kate, wanted to make love with her, had in fact fantasized for quite some time about doing just what they were doing now. That Kate had confirmed her physical response to Ellen only made it more real. Ellen took a deep breath. Reaching down, she took hold of her sweater and drew it up and off her head.

Kate stopped what she was doing and stared. Her hands were obviously shaking as she took Ellen's breasts in her hands and worshipped them with her mouth.

"Oh, yes," Ellen said encouragingly. Her body ached to be touched and her mind was lost in the pleasure of Kate's tongue and lips on her nipples. She pressed Kate's head firmly into them, wanting her to devour them; she could easily come with that sensation alone. She tugged on Kate's shirt, letting her know she needed contact with her skin as well, and Kate quickly obliged. Within seconds she had stripped off her jeans and then helped slide Ellen's off her.

Finally skin to skin with no barrier in between, Kate took her, with her mouth, fingers, body, and mind. When Ellen felt her slip down between her thighs, she opened to her, inviting all she could give. And when Kate's lips and tongue enclosed her, drawing her deeply into her mouth, Ellen knew she could no longer hold back. "Please, go inside," she begged.

Kate moaned just to hear Ellen and willingly inserted first one and then two fingers into her hot, wet center. With her fingers stroking inside and her lips and tongue sucking the head of Ellen's clit, she felt Ellen's body rock faster, taking her in as far as she could go. Sliding in to a familiar spot, she felt Ellen jerk once and then let her entire body loosen as she called out Kate's name. Kate didn't stop, soothing her with her tongue until Ellen ceased to buck. The aftershocks continued and Kate held her until it was over.

After a few minutes to let Ellen relax, Kate withdrew her fingers and crawled up to settle beside her. Ellen fell into her arms and began to cry.

"Shh, it's okay." Kate brushed her lips across Ellen's damp forehead.

Ellen laughed. "It's more than okay. It felt so damn good I can't stop myself from crying. How embarrassing."

"No, it's not. I'm flattered. You were absolutely wonderful. Thank you."

Ellen's eyes were barely open. "Thank *you*. That was a first."

"Crying after sex?"

"No." Ellen yawned. "Having an orgasm like that."

"Now, I *know* you've had sex before," Kate teased.

"Mmm, sex, yes. An orgasm, no."

Stunned, Kate couldn't move, unable to respond. But no response was necessary. Ellen was sound asleep.

CHAPTER SIXTEEN

Kate smoothed her hand across the arch of Ellen's hip, finding the dip inward to her waist. She could not recall ever having felt anything so curvaceous, so womanly. She thought of the women she had been with in the past, women who were thin and flat, almost one-dimensional. Ellen looked like a woman in a Rubens painting: flared hips, full breasts, round ass, and highly desirable. She wondered at Ellen's initial modesty, her unwillingness to be seen as she was. Kate thought about her own body, which she had studiously avoided having Ellen touch.

She ran a hand across her face, down her left shoulder, arm, and side. The raised strips of skin, the result of her scars, were smooth and sensitive. None of them mattered much to her, except the one on her face. It now defined her and what she would become. She tried not to dwell on it too much, but now, being home again, she stared at her future, which was a gaping black void. She remembered a special report the television station's science team did on black holes. At the time she couldn't grasp the concept of nothingness in space. Now she had a good idea.

But it was time to start figuring out what she was going to do. She was tired of her self-imposed confinement, tired of watching television, and tired of having no direction. She had always needed action, needed something meaningful to make her feel like she was making a difference. Being with Ellen, someone who had such passion and interest in her field, made Kate realize that she needed to feel that again, too.

She returned her gaze to Ellen sleeping on her side next to her. Her hair spilled across the pillow, her face wore a peaceful expression. Ellen looked so much younger, almost childlike in her sleep.

At the foot of the bed General Beauregard stretched and looked her way. He definitely appeared annoyed. Stalking toward the headboard, he banged his head into Ellen, causing her to stir. She reached up and petted him, scratching gently behind his ears. "Good morning, Beau," she whispered groggily.

"I think he's hungry," Kate said.

"He's *always* hungry." Ellen rolled over to face Kate. "Good morning." She leaned close for a kiss. The warmth of their lips and the slow dance of their tongues put Kate's body on alert. "Mmm, that's a nice way to wake up in the morning."

Kate grinned. "Yes, very nice." She pulled Ellen into her, their bodies pressing firmly against each other. Kate felt the ache between her thighs rekindle and she moaned into Ellen's mouth.

"Let me touch you," Ellen whispered.

She reached out to Kate, but before hand could meet skin, Kate intercepted her. "It's not very pretty."

Ellen gazed steadily into her eyes. "Do you think that really matters to me?"

Kate paused, then kissed Ellen's palm. She guided Ellen's hand to the scar that ran from her left shoulder, down her arm, and then where it skipped to her rib cage. The entire time she watched Ellen for any sign of hesitation or revulsion, but all she found was compassion.

"Let me really look at you." Ellen tried to convey as much tenderness in her eyes and her touch as she could. She knew exactly what it was like to not want someone to touch or see her body. She gently pulled the sheet from Kate's body. The scars were about half an inch wide and still red, but not as angry as those Ellen had first seen on Kate's face. With time they too would fade. But all Ellen could see were the small breasts, the flat stomach, and the triangle of dark hair that glistened with moisture. A pull in her groin signaled her desire.

"You're beautiful, Kate…as I imagined you'd be." Ellen was in awe and instinctually drew the sheet up to cover herself. Kate's body made her ashamed of her own. Kate was in great shape whereas she was fat and flabby.

"No." Kate prevented Ellen from hiding behind the sheet. "We both need to see each other the way we really are."

Ellen's eyes burned from unshed tears. She gently pushed Kate back on the bed and ran her hand up her stomach to cup her breast. With a flick of her thumb she brought Kate's nipple to attention, then replaced her thumb with her mouth. She sucked gently, the nipple hardening between her lips, and when Kate groaned, her body reacted. Running her hand to the vee between Kate's thighs, she couldn't restrain herself from dipping in to feel what she had fantasized about for several years. Kate was hot and wet, and Ellen slid her fingers directly to Kate's opening and inside.

Kate gasped and was so ready that Ellen felt her instantly clamp down on her fingers. Sensing Kate's need, Ellen pushed as far as she could, stroking inside Kate with her fingertips. Then slowly she withdrew completely, only to plunge back. Picking up speed, she thrust faster, all the while sucking Kate's nipple. Kate arched up off the bed when the orgasm slammed into her, and Ellen felt each successive ripple wash over her.

Ellen was stunned by Kate's responsiveness. It was over all too quickly, and she had so wanted to make it last, to never end. She thought she might cry again, but she didn't want to scare Kate away. Even her fantasies had never come close to this reality.

She climbed on top of Kate, kissing her way from her breast to her throat, nipping and soothing with her tongue as she went. When she reached Kate's mouth, she pressed her lips to Kate's, pushing them open with her tongue, and lazily sucked Kate's.

The phone rang. Ellen stopped sucking and sighed, glad it hadn't rung while Kate was trying to come. She let her answering machine pick up. She had called her mother last night, and knew she would call back before she went for her morning walk.

"Hi, Ellen, it's Sandra."

Ellen froze. Thoughts of running to the machine and ripping

the cord out of the wall ran through her mind. But it was too late. She would only confirm the suspicion in Kate's mind that she had something to hide. *Shit. Please don't say anything bad.*

"I'm looking forward to tonight, and, uh, why don't you wear that sexy outfit you wore when we went to the symphony? You looked hot." A breathy sigh came over the phone and Ellen cringed inwardly. "I just wanted to let you know that I couldn't get reservations at Al Tirimasu's until late tonight, so I switched to the Regent Thai instead. Hope that's okay. See you around seven."

The machine clicked off and Ellen wanted to die.

Thoughts of Ellen playing the field raced through Kate's mind. *And why shouldn't Ellen see whomever she wants? She's highly desirable*, and so was Sandra, although Kate still held a low opinion of her. *She must be great in bed.* How could Ellen ever think Kate would be someone long-term? She had absolutely nothing to offer, and besides, Ellen had clearly stated her interest in playing the field.

"Sandra had called while we were gone," Ellen quickly explained. "I didn't think this was going to happen between us, otherwise—"

"It's okay. You don't have to explain anything to me."

Kate was wondering how to extricate herself from Ellen's bed without seeming overly eager to get away. She didn't want to go, didn't want to leave Ellen's warmth and tenderness, but clearly Ellen had plans. She used to be smooth at a quick fuck and an equally quick escape. But now the emptiness in the depths of her stomach made her want to run without her usual witty excuse.

Ellen felt the tension descend over both of them and desperately wanted to make Kate understand. But what was there to understand? She had made a date with Sandra. And she'd even decided if Sandra wanted to take her to bed again, she'd probably go. But now everything had changed with Kate. What that meant, she wasn't sure. Did they have a future? Did it matter? Simply being with her made Ellen happy, but it wasn't enough.

"You know what? I'm starved." Kate got up to go to the

bathroom. "How about I take a quick shower, and if you've got some coffee, that would be great."

Ellen watched as Kate walked away. "I could scramble some eggs and make toast?"

"Perfect," Kate called from the bathroom. She studied herself in the mirror. There it was again. The scar. Oddly, it was becoming less of a shock to her, had in fact become somewhat familiar and more a part of her. Still, she loathed herself at the moment and wanted nothing more than to slink back to her condo. She shook her head disgustedly. *What an ego you've got, Foster, thinking Ellen wanted more than a casual fuck.* She turned on the shower and stepped in, letting the hot water wash the tears away.

Ellen got the coffee going and set a pan on the stove. Reaching into the refrigerator, she first fed Beau, who demanded attention, then retrieved the eggs and milk. She cracked several in a bowl and beat them with a whisk. The activity felt good, and she sloshed a little over the sides until she calmed down. Sandra's timing couldn't have been worse. Ellen needed to let Kate know things were different now, at least she hoped so. She'd tell Sandra tonight that she didn't want to see her again. With Kate in her life, she had everything she needed.

Kate walked into the kitchen, her hair wet and hands shoved into the back pockets of her jeans. Ellen could tell she was about to bolt, and she needed to defuse the situation.

"I was thinking we'd go over to the National Archives and do some research today. Their holdings are enormous, and we'll have to skim through a lot that's superfluous before we find what we need."

Kate sat down at the table. "I need to do some running around today, get some groceries, respond to mail, you know. How about you give me a call tomorrow?" She glanced at the door. She wanted to escape, to never again recall the tousled look of Ellen's hair in the morning, the way her robe separated loosely, revealing the sloping curve of a breast.

Ellen stared at her. "*You're* going to go out? By yourself?"

Kate shrugged. "Guess I have to start sometime, and now's as good as any."

They ate in silence, Ellen trying to absorb Kate's newfound sense of freedom. She was rapidly pulling away from her, and Ellen didn't know how to stop her. While she had wanted it for her all along, she felt a bit hurt that Kate no longer needed her.

Kate finished eating, the eggs tasting like sand in her mouth, and made excuses that she had to leave. She wanted to go home, close the door, and never come out. How could she have been so blind to who Ellen was? She'd certainly been fooled. *That's because you* are *a fool, you idiot.*

Ellen walked Kate to the door. "Kate." She hesitated. "About last night…"

"It was amazing," Kate replied, her throat tight with emotion. "Thank you, for everything you've done for me."

"But I want to explain about Sandra. Please, don't—"

"No, it's okay, really, Ellen." Kate backed away as though Ellen's touch might burn her.

Kate opened the door and ran into a woman about to knock. She mumbled her apologies as the woman stared open-mouthed at her, her gaze fixed on Kate's scar. Anger flared inside Kate and she opened her mouth to say something rude, but caught herself. After all, the woman was probably another of Ellen's girlfriends. She strode down the hallway, feeling the eyes of both women on her back as she entered her condo and locked herself inside.

Ellen closed the door behind her sister. "What are you doing here, Joan?" *What is it with everyone's timing this morning?*

"My God, was that Kate Foster, leaving your place at"— she glanced at her watch—"eight thirty in the morning?"

"What of it?" The heat rose to Ellen's cheeks.

Joan looked disapprovingly at her and Ellen flushed in anger.

"You cannot tell me that you and she…that you were… How could you?" Joan spluttered. "And that horrible scar." Her face contorted with disgust.

Ellen's anger was now barely controlled fury. "You will not say a word about Kate." She emphasized each word as she spoke. "She is a kind, caring woman who has been through hell, and if you say one more insulting thing about her or us, I swear I'll—"

Joan raised her hands. "Fine, fine. Do what you want. If you don't care about the gossip, why should I? I'd have thought you would at least have better taste, that's all."

Ellen collapsed onto her chair at the kitchen table and sighed. She felt defeated, not because of her sister, but because nothing mattered anyway. Kate had practically run away. Ellen probably wouldn't be able to revive the relationship. Everything had looked so promising last night. How did it all go wrong so quickly?

"What are you doing here?" she asked tiredly.

"Mom said you were back in town. I wanted to talk to you and was coming into the city anyway. Dad's sick."

Ellen frowned. "And? Sick as in he has the flu?"

"Do you think I'd come here in person if that's all it was?"

A cold fist gripped Ellen's heart. "What's wrong?" She was almost afraid to ask.

"Well, we don't know yet." Joan sniffed. "He's been having stomach pains for a while and is going in for tests tomorrow."

"Tomorrow! Why the hell didn't anyone tell me?" Ellen wanted to scream.

"I was all for calling you, but Dad didn't want to worry you when he didn't even know what it was. Besides, you were out of town. By the time you got back, the tests would have been over. But you need to spend more time with them, Ellen. They're getting so old. I'm always the one helping them. I knew something wasn't right with Dad, but he kept brushing me off. If you were there more often you'd have noticed it, too. Dad listens to you. If you had said something sooner he might not have let it go so long."

Ellen was all too familiar with Joan's guilt ploy, but this time it succeeded. She tried to justify her infrequent visits by saying she had a demanding job while Joan was solely occupied with her family and the club. Joan had more time and also lived closer. But the justification sounded hollow even to her ears. She was only an hour away, and her job wasn't so demanding that she couldn't visit once a week.

"I'll shower and then go see them." Ellen jumped up from the table and headed for her bedroom. "You can let yourself out."

❖

Kate finally sat down at her answering machine and listened to a dozen or so messages, all from her agent. His insistence that she call him became more vehement with each call until finally his anger dominated. Surprised, since Dean knew better, she grabbed a beer and reluctantly picked up the phone.

"Where the hell have you been?" he shouted into her ear.

"Whoa. Hang on just a minute, Dean. What's going on?"

"I have called and called you. At least have the decency to call me back."

"Okay, I'm calling you back now. I was out of town, sorry. What's got you so bent out of shape?"

"Only the biggest goddamn offer you're going to get. No kidding, Kate, this is a tremendous opportunity."

Kate rolled her eyes. "I'm not interested in a single-watt in Kansas."

"You're not in Kansas anymore, Dorothy. It's CNN."

Kate's hand with the beer bottle in it froze halfway to her mouth. "What?"

"Yeah, what nothing," Dean scoffed. "Do I have your attention now?"

Kate was confused. "CNN wants me on the air?"

"No, not exactly," Dean admitted. "But they're looking for a managing editor—no small potatoes."

"In Atlanta?" Kate was shocked.

"Not Atlanta—London."

Kate slowly put the bottle down on the coffee table and sat back on the couch. She was stunned, unable to wrap her mind around this surprising news.

"Admittedly it's not an on-air gig," Dean explained. "It's behind the scenes. The guy there now is moving on to an executive position in Atlanta, and they need someone to fill his shoes. He kept a pretty tight ship and they don't want to lose that."

"Why me?" Kate was still in shock.

"They've had their eye on you awhile, it seems. You've got years of experience in print journalism, and I'm sure the Pulitzer played a huge part. They know you can write and they're definitely interested."

Kate didn't know what to say. It wasn't exactly the job she'd always wanted, but it was an incredible opportunity. The challenge alone intrigued her, but she had another reason for being interested. Despite her scar, no one would know who she had been. She could rebuild her reputation from scratch.

"Kate? You still there?"

"Yeah, uh, when do they want to meet with me?"

"I've been able to hold them off for a week, but I need to give them something soon."

"Give me until tomorrow and I'll call you."

"Make it the first thing in the morning," Dean insisted.

"Don't worry, I will."

She hung up and stared at the wall that divided her condo from Ellen's. London was far enough away to be an escape, yet in every other way it was a large political city like DC. In many respects she had been cocooned in Washington, seeing the news from an American perspective. In London that would shift, giving her a broader world view of events. The offer most definitely had appeal. For the first time in a very long time she was excited about the future.

She took another beer from the refrigerator and twisted the top off, then took a long, thoughtful pull. Ellen, who had been trying to get her to focus on her career, would be pleased with this turn of events. Well, the time had come and it hadn't even been of her own doing. The opportunity had fallen into her lap, to use a cliché. London.

It would be far away from Ellen as well. Her stomach churned painfully, but she had to admit that it was for the best. She was, she realized, falling for a woman who thought of her as another fling. Staying in DC and living next door to Ellen to watch her women come and go wasn't something she could endure for long. She had always resented when the women she dated became too clingy, yet here she was hanging on to Ellen, who was more interested in having a lot of women in her life.

Kate dragged back to the couch and picked up the book she had finished reading, the book Ellen had given her. She fingered the pages, remembering the battle scene and reflecting that she had walked the very soil those soldiers had fought and died on a hundred and forty-odd years earlier. It hadn't seemed possible that such violence had occurred in this country. History, a subject that had never before particularly interested her, had come alive under Ellen's tutelage.

And more than that, Kate had come alive under Ellen's touch. For the first time, she had experienced more than just a physical response to a woman, and the cruel irony that Ellen didn't reciprocate wasn't lost on her. The Fates were paying her back for all the years she had used and discarded women.

Ellen had a date tonight with Sandra, but this time Kate wouldn't be at the peephole to watch for their return. She couldn't bear the thought. She would call Dean tomorrow and tell him to set up an interview with CNN. She wished she could tell Ellen about it—wanted to be able to confide in her—but this time she would wait until she had made a firm decision. She didn't want to get Ellen's hopes up. And she certainly didn't want to watch Ellen's positive reaction to the news. That was something she hoped to never see.

CHAPTER SEVENTEEN

Igo in tomorrow for tests and should know the results within twelve hours. There's nothing to do but wait."

Exasperated by her father's calmness and lack of details, Ellen still didn't want to make it a big deal. His symptoms were probably nothing to worry about, just the signs of old age. At least that's what she tried to convince herself.

"But don't they have any idea, some sort of guess as to what it might be?" she asked.

"They've said it could be any number of things," her mother replied. "But of course they don't want to alarm us by saying it's anything major. Except for the discomfort, everything else is fine, so there's not much to do at this point."

Her mother's face was pale and strained. She kept glancing over to the man she had been married to for nearly fifty years, touching his arm. Ellen couldn't bear to watch the gesture, which seemed as if her mother was trying to keep the connection with her father alive, and got up to take her coffee cup to the kitchen.

"I thought I'd hang out here today," Ellen mentioned casually. "Maybe we could go catch a movie or something later. What do you say?"

"Honey, we'd love to," Barbara replied, "but we have plans. There's a fund-raiser this afternoon for the shelter, then a dinner."

"Should you still be going?" Ellen glanced at her father.

"I'm not dead yet," Ira replied haughtily. He got up from his chair and danced a little jig, making her and her mother laugh.

"Okay, okay." Ellen held up her hands.

"Now go on home and do what you need to do," he insisted. "How's the research going, anyway?"

"Fine," Ellen said. "I'm in the beginning stages, but it's coming along." Of all the members of her family, her father had been the most supportive of her academic pursuits. His love of history and the law had instilled in her the same passion. As a little girl, he had taken her on jaunts all over Virginia, and they had walked the land together as he told her about the battles that had occurred there.

"Well, then, you'd better get back to it." He folded his arms across his chest, clearly waiting for her to move.

"All right, but I'll call you later." Ellen grabbed her purse and took out her keys.

Her mother walked her to the door, her arm wrapped around Ellen's shoulder. At the door they kissed each other on the cheek, and Ellen hurried to her car.

As she started to pull out of the driveway, she picked up her cell phone and dialed Sandra's number. "Hi, Sandra, it's Ellen."

"Hey, you got my message earlier?"

"Yes, but that's not why I'm calling." Ellen took a deep breath. "I'm afraid I'm going to have to cancel this evening."

"Oh?" Sandra paused. "Well, I'm disappointed, of course, but not a problem. How about tomorrow night, then? You'll be in town for a while, won't you?"

"Yes, but that's not the point, Sandra. I don't want to cancel dinner only for tonight, but for all nights."

There was silence on the other end.

"So you're saying you don't want to see me anymore?"

"Yes, Sandra. I'm sorry, I really am, but I don't think it's going to work out between us, so it's best to end it now."

"But I thought we were having a good time," Sandra argued.

"That's just it," Ellen replied. "I want more than a good time, and I think I've found it."

There was another pause, so lengthy Ellen thought she'd lost the connection.

"I see. So it's someone else, is that it?"

"Yes."

Ellen had nothing more to say. She felt that way about Kate, but the greater question was if Kate did as well. But even if Kate didn't, Ellen couldn't settle for less.

"I guess that's it, then."

"I guess so."

"Good-bye, Ellen."

"Good-bye, Sandra."

Ellen flipped the lid closed. She sighed, releasing the tension in her stomach. That was easier than she thought it would be. She had to do it, especially now. Her father's health brought everything into perspective for her.

Life was too short not to try for what she wanted. If she didn't make a full-out effort to be with Kate now, she never would. Never again would she be so close to having the woman she'd always desired, and she couldn't let anything, or anyone, get in her way. All she had to do now was drive home and find out how Kate felt.

When Ellen stepped off the elevator to her floor, a maintenance man stood on a ladder replacing light bulbs in the hallway fixture. She stepped around him, walked directly to Kate's door, and knocked.

"If you're looking for the lady who lives there, she left about ten minutes ago."

Ellen frowned. So Kate actually had gone out on her own. Well, that was good, wasn't it? It showed courage and was the first step in getting on with her life.

"Thanks," she replied. Once home, she thought about doing some work, but her mind wouldn't stay still. Finding General Beau belly up in a patch of sunlight by the sliding glass doors, she sat and petted him for a few minutes. He stretched and rolled, letting her scratch every part of his body. She was about to quit when she heard a sound in the hallway and went to investigate. Peering through the peephole, she saw Kate enter her condo. Her heart rate picked up as she took a deep breath and walked next door.

When Kate opened her door, Ellen felt a rush of arousal. "Hey, I saw you come home and wondered if you had a minute to talk."

"Yeah, sure, come on in."

Kate gestured to the living room and Ellen sat on the couch, noticing that Kate preferred to sit in the chair opposite. She felt awkward, not knowing how to begin or what she wanted to say. All she could do was drink in how sexy Kate was in a pair of torn jeans and a white tank top. They accentuated her athletic figure, and Ellen recalled how delicious that firm, flat stomach felt against the palm of her hand.

"So you went out for a while?" she asked. "Good for you, Kate. I'm proud of you."

Kate blushed. "Yeah, but not for long. I barely made it to the liquor store and back."

She had felt anxious when she left her place and stepped out onto the street. The traffic and noise were all too familiar, but it was good to be in her city and back to normal. She was taking control again, in a small way.

The owner of the liquor store recognized her and, after a brief glance at her face, continued ringing up her purchases. He actually said it was good to see her back and she had cleared her throat nervously, not knowing how to respond. She waved good-bye and returned home. The experience had been both exhilarating and scary, and she had done it.

"But it's a start, and that's what's important. After today, it'll get easier," Ellen said. After a slight lull in the conversation, Ellen figured now was the time to tell Kate why she wanted to see her. "Kate, I—"

"To tell you the truth, I went out because I had to." Kate sat forward on the edge of her seat. "I talked to my agent this morning. I've been asked to consider a position with CNN."

When Ellen heard the words the muscles in her face went numb. She was surprised and happy and devastated all at once. Atlanta was only a two-hour flight, but it was still far away. A heavy weight descended on her, and she wasn't sure she could breathe. "That's great news, Kate," she replied without emotion. "I hear Atlanta is a nice place."

"It's not in Atlanta," Kate said. She couldn't read Ellen's expression. Was she happy or not? Did Ellen care if she stayed or left? She wanted to touch Ellen, to relate with her like they had last night. Their union had been incredible, and she thought it had meant something to each of them. But she wasn't so sure now. Ellen had distanced herself, and she didn't know how to reconnect.

Through a dense fog, Ellen realized Kate had said she wasn't moving to Atlanta. A spark of hope ignited somewhere in her inner darkness.

"You mean you'll be here in DC?" she asked, the blood beginning to flow through her body again.

"No. In London."

Ellen couldn't control her jaw. "London?" The word came out as a squeak. "You're moving to London?"

"Well, I don't have the job yet. I'm going to talk to them."

"But they asked to see you, right?" Ellen asked. "That's a pretty good sign."

Kate shrugged. "We'll see."

Ellen gazed at Kate, trying to gauge how she felt. She longed to tell Kate what she really wanted. She didn't want her to go to London. She wanted her to stay. She wanted to take Kate to bed and show her how much she loved her so she would never be tempted to leave. But did she have that right? Kate needed the job, needed to feel important and useful again. Could Ellen ask that of her? Was it fair?

Kate wasn't sure what Ellen's silence meant, but the lack of conversation and the awkwardness spoke volumes. Maybe Ellen had nothing to say and was simply being polite by sitting there. She probably had other things to do. She had that date tonight with Sandra; perhaps that was where she was really focused. The sex last night had been fantastic, and Kate had craved nothing more than to pull Ellen into her arms at the door and take her to bed. But she knew she wasn't the only woman waiting for Ellen.

"So, when will you know?" Ellen asked, her voice catching in her throat. God, she couldn't break down in front of Kate. Not now.

"I have to tell them tomorrow if I'm interested. Then it's up to them as to when we'll meet."

Ellen nodded as though she were in a dream. Everything seemed to move so much slower. She cleared her throat and breathed deeply. She had to be supportive. Kate was making tremendous strides in getting her life back on track. "Well, of course you must go talk to them, at the very least. It sounds like a wonderful opportunity, Kate."

"Yeah, it is," Kate agreed. There it was. Ellen wanted her to go, thought it was a good move. That was all she needed to hear or, rather, what she didn't want to hear.

"Well, I've got some things to take care of before I tell Dean to call them. I haven't updated my resume in years."

Ellen stood to leave. "Yes, you'd better get to it, then, and I should leave you alone. I've got a lot of work to do, too."

"I guess you'll need help, now that you've lost two assistants. Perhaps we can call a temp agency and they can find someone for you."

Ellen grimaced. A temp agency could never replace Kate, in more ways than one. "Don't worry about it." She shook her head. "I'll work something out." Every muscle screamed for her to stay. What could she say, what could she do to not have Kate leave her?

Kate watched Ellen's back as she headed for the door. If only she could touch her, make her understand how she felt. If she could make Ellen love her, want only her. She had never been in a monogamous relationship, hadn't wanted to. It surprised her that she would want one now, with Ellen, but she knew it felt right. Ellen felt so good in her arms. She was so female, so sexy and desirable. Ellen was all those things and something she couldn't quite name. She was simply Ellen. And Kate was attracted to everything about her. She wanted to know her, wanted to spend time with her. But as she moved past Ellen to open the door, Kate knew she had to take this job offer.

Ellen stopped and gazed up at Kate. She couldn't read the look in her eyes, those deep, dark eyes that swirled with emotion. But she would never forgive herself if she didn't touch her one last time. She cupped Kate's chin, stroking the downy cheek with her thumb. Then with one last brave attempt, she stood on her tiptoes and kissed the cheek, lingering for as long as she dared before she pulled away.

"See you later, Kate." Her eyes burned as she stepped into the hallway.

Kate watched as Ellen entered her condo. A large lump in her throat hurt as she swallowed and leaned heavily against her door. She would call Dean in the morning and tell him to go ahead with the CNN interview. She had no reason to stay in DC. She needed to get away, as far away from this city and Ellen as she could. London was the perfect solution.

Feeling suddenly reckless, she decided to visit an old favorite hangout down the street. The bar in the Childe Harold was close by, and the bartender knew what she liked to drink and didn't talk to her. Everything she liked in a bartender. If people wanted to stare at her, let them. She didn't give a damn anymore.

❖

The Childe Harold was a two-story restaurant on Connecticut Avenue with the main dining room upstairs, the bar and some booths downstairs, and a few tables out front. Kate sat in the bar and, as expected, a shot of Chivas appeared magically before her. She downed it in one swift gulp and had no sooner put the glass down than the bartender refilled it. She held up two fingers this time and he nodded.

After a couple of sips, she sat and watched the basketball game without really caring who was playing, let alone winning.

"I don't believe my eyes."

The familiarity of the voice caused Kate to swivel abruptly in her chair. "Sergei?"

A tall, well-built man in his mid-forties with a neatly trimmed beard approached her with arms open wide. He enveloped Kate in a crushing bear hug, then released her to hold her at arm's length. Unabashedly, he examined the scar on her face—not in shock, but with great interest. "It makes you look even more roguish than you did before," he pronounced loudly.

Kate couldn't help but grin. Sergei had made her feel at ease ever since they met in Moscow when Kate was on assignment for Reuters. Sergei worked as a reporter for a Russian television station. He was interested in her photographer at the time and had taken them to his house, introducing her to Russian vodka. She wound up smashed and slept on the couch while the two men got to know one another more intimately.

"What the hell are you doing in DC?" she asked as he pulled out the stool next to her.

"I am looking to marry a handsome, young American and then get citizenship. What are you doing?"

"We haven't gotten gay marriage approved yet, Sergei. But we're working on it."

"Ah," he scoffed. "It will happen sooner or later. You Americans always get what you want eventually. In the meantime, I suppose I shall have to drown my sorrows in all the good-looking men in Dupont Circle. You know many of them, yes? You can introduce me?"

"I know some, yes. But seriously, what are you doing here?"

"Ketel One Vodka," he told the bartender, then sat down. "We finally got approval to open a station here in Washington, and you are looking at the one and only reporter. I have a cameraman who is cute, but not a man—I think maybe your type. And a producer who is a drunk and got his job because his brother is connected in Moscow. Not exactly perfect, but at least I am here. I love everything American." He took a large swallow of vodka. "Ahh, that is good. Let's go upstairs later and have a big steak next. Now, what are you doing, Kate? I heard about your accident and the job, the bastards."

"Yeah, well, I've got a possibility with CNN in London. I found out about it today."

He leaned back and looked at her, obviously impressed. "So you are celebrating alone?" He shook his head. "It is good that I came along to help out. Bartender, another round here." He tossed back his vodka and peered at Kate. "But you do not look so happy."

Kate averted her eyes, staring into her glass of amber liquid. "It's a good opportunity and all that, but…"

"But what?" he finally asked.

Kate struggled with her answer. "I'm not sure I want to leave DC...right now."

"Why? Is there another opportunity?"

Kate shook her head. "More like another person."

She watched as Sergei scrutinized her face and then understanding replaced his confusion.

"Could it be that the rogue Kate Foster is in love?" His brown eyes sparkled and the creases at the corners deepened.

Kate sipped her scotch and didn't reply. She was miserable and in no mood to discuss her situation.

"And what is her name?"

"Ellen Webster."

"And she must be sexy and smart to have caught the attention of the great Kate." He grinned.

"Let's not go there, okay, Sergei?" Kate sipped her drink.

"Okay. Let's go get that steak."

As he stood up his cell phone rang, and he pulled it out of the inside pocket of his suit jacket. "Da?"

He listened for a minute, then slammed the phone shut. Kate waited until the Russian curses had subsided before asking him what the problem was.

"Mikhail, that idiot, that...I can't think of the words in English that translate well. He's our producer and he doesn't know shit. I'm sorry, Kate, but I must go to the studio. Let's get together again soon, okay? You owe me a steak."

"Sure, no problem," she said as he kissed her cheek, downed the few drops in his glass, and left.

Kate smiled, realizing Sergei had stuck her with the bill, again. She left money on the bar and stepped out onto the street. Glancing up at the threatening sky, she heard thunder in the distance. She headed home, and as she entered the lobby of her building she was surprised to run into Ellen exiting the elevator, two bags of trash in her hands. She was clearly not dressed for her dinner out.

"Hey, I thought you'd be out with Sandra." Kate took a bag from Ellen.

"Thanks," Ellen murmured, embarrassed at being caught in her sweats. Cleaning house was a way of working through her sadness, but this time it hadn't helped. "Dinner was cancelled."

Kate held the door for her as they headed out the back of their building and tossed the trash bags into the Dumpster. "Oh," she replied.

"In fact, I cancelled Sandra altogether."

Kate's step faltered. "Excuse me?"

"I realized Sandra wasn't someone I was interested in long-term. There was no point in taking it any further."

They reentered the building and rode the elevator together in silence. Ellen could smell the alcohol on Kate and wondered if she had been drinking alone or with someone. When the elevator stopped on their floor, she thought she saw Kate grab the wall for support. She had obviously had a little too much to drink, so Ellen instinctively reached for her arm to steady her as she stepped out of the elevator.

Kate glanced down at Ellen's hand on her arm. It burned where Ellen touched it, and Kate felt the sensation travel up her shoulder and spread throughout her body. She knew the alcohol hadn't caused the feeling, because it hadn't been there a moment ago. It was Ellen, all Ellen. She had that effect on her, and Kate leaned closer, aching for more. What was it Ellen had said out by the Dumpster? She wasn't interested in a long-term relationship? Kate shook her head to clear her thinking. No, she said she wasn't interested in Sandra long-term. Did that mean she eventually wanted *someone* long-term?

"Well, here we are," Ellen said as they approached Kate's door. She risked rubbing Kate's arm with her thumb, luxuriating in the delectable skin. But what she really wanted was to slide her hand around Kate's neck and pull her into a searing kiss. Instead, she simply let go.

"Ellen?" Kate called to Ellen's retreating back.

Ellen swung around. Something in Kate's eyes spoke more to Ellen than anything Kate could have said. It was pure want, and Ellen felt it rush through her body like a tidal wave, the undertow dragging her forward. She felt herself moving into Kate without conscious effort, as though the floor, instead of her own two feet, moved her. Suddenly they were in each other's arms, and from that moment on she had no thought. It was all primal and raw, and even if she had wanted to stop, she couldn't have. Somehow they were in Kate's condo, and before she knew it, they were in bed, undressed, and Kate was inside her. She was all skin and wet and hot, and she didn't know where her body ended and Kate's began. It was unlike anything she had ever experienced and she never wanted it to end. She felt the cataclysm in her body radiate outward and somehow, from some distant vantage point, knew that Kate too was coming against her, and they were one.

Ellen awoke in the dark, disoriented and for a moment unsure where she was. But the feel of Kate pressed into her back, her arm flung over Ellen's hip, reassured her and she sighed contentedly. What they had wasn't just sex. She knew they had moved on to something much deeper. Now what the hell would she do? Kate was on her way to London and probably wouldn't be back. Could she tell her not to go? Could she ask Kate to give it all away for a chance with her? If the situation was reversed, would Ellen give up her job for London? And just what was Kate thinking, what did she want? Her head hurt from trying to find solutions so quickly.

"Are you awake?"

Ellen rolled over. "Yes."

Kate's hand slid up to Ellen's waist and nestled in the deep curve.

"So you dumped Sandra, huh?"

Ellen struggled to keep the grin off her face. "Yes, *I* dumped *her*."

"She didn't deserve you."

Kate's hand danced lazily across Ellen's belly, slowly finding its way downward. Ellen closed her eyes and luxuriated in the sensations that coursed through her. Unbelievably, she was ready again and opened to Kate without reservation.

Something shifted inside Kate. The emptiness, the black hole that had always existed within her evaporated, and the missing piece that belonged there filled it. She took a deep breath and felt... happy.

CHAPTER EIGHTEEN

The interview in Atlanta had gone well, and the staff there wanted Kate to meet and talk with the people in London immediately so she could see the operation firsthand. She was nervous and excited but had a lingering sense of sadness. She knew it had to do with Ellen, because she couldn't stop thinking about her.

She had returned home the previous night after being in Atlanta nearly a week, and hadn't seen Ellen. She was anxious about leaving that evening for London and worried that she wouldn't see Ellen before then. Ellen's newspaper had resumed home delivery and had been picked up, so she knew Ellen was still home and not on the road. Perhaps she was avoiding her, which was just as well. Kate was never comfortable with good-byes, and even though she'd be returning in a couple of days, this time apart could very well be the precursor to a permanent relocation.

Downing the last of her scotch, she took one last look around, making sure she had turned all the lights and appliances off. If she did wind up moving, the condo would be the last thing she would miss about DC. It had never felt like home—more like a place to dump her stuff and sleep. She would miss Ellen, though. Something about Ellen's space made her feel at home, but more important, something about Ellen made her feel at home.

She grabbed the handle of her Tumi luggage and wheeled it out into the hallway, tossing her other bag over her shoulder. After closing her door and locking it, she walked to Ellen's and stopped, then knocked rapidly and waited for a response. When she didn't get one, she pressed her ear closer, trying to hear any movement inside. Finally, she gave up and reached into her bag for a notepad and pen. She scribbled a quick note and slipped it under Ellen's door, then pressed the elevator button. She was disappointed that she'd not seen Ellen before she left, but she'd be back soon and maybe they could have dinner one night. Maybe, if the mood was right—a little wine, some jazz—Ellen might take her to bed one last time.

❖

Ellen trudged home from the dry cleaners, nearly two miles from home. Her car was in the shop having its fifty-thousand-mile checkup, and since she hadn't taken it in until late in the day, it wouldn't be ready until tomorrow. She supposed she could have called a cab, but it was such a pleasant evening, and she was determined to exercise more to accompany her diet. This time she was serious about losing weight.

She was about halfway home when her cell phone rang, and she glanced at the caller ID to see her sister's cell number. "Hi, Joan," she said, switching the dry cleaning to her other arm.

"Oh, Ellen," Joan sobbed into the phone.

"What on earth is wrong?" Ellen was instantly on alert. She hadn't heard her sister cry like that since they were kids.

"It's Dad. Ellen, you have to come now." She broke into tears again.

Ellen's heart momentarily stopped beating and she leaned against a streetlight for support. "What happened, Joan? What's going on? Talk to me, dammit."

She could hear her sister blowing her nose into a handkerchief and sniffling before she returned to the phone.

"He collapsed a little while ago. The ambulance is taking him to Inova Hospital, and I'm driving Mom there now. You've got to hurry!"

The pain in Ellen's chest was almost too much, but she needed to calm Joan. "Okay, I'll get there as soon as I can. But you need to pull yourself together, if not for your sake, at least for Mom's. Who's in the car with you?"

"Me, Mom, and the kids. Robert is in Chicago." She blew her nose again.

"Shit," Ellen murmured, trying to figure out what to do.

"What's wrong?"

"Oh, nothing. My car's in the shop, that's all. But don't worry. I'll call a friend and either borrow her car or have her drive me. I'll get there as quick as I can."

She hung up and autodialed Linda and Janice's home number, but their voicemail picked up immediately. When she dialed Linda's cell, Linda picked up on the second ring.

"Hey, girl, what's happening?"

"Sorry, Linda, but I don't have time to chat. My dad has just been taken to the hospital and my car is in the shop."

"My God, Ellen. What can I do to help?"

"Can you drive me to Alexandria, or let me borrow your car?"

Linda groaned. "Oh, honey, I wish I could, but Janice and I managed to get away for a long weekend. We're in Rehoboth Beach right now."

"Damn!"

"I'm so sorry."

"No, it's okay," Ellen reassured her. "I'll find another way."

"Call me when you know something. I'll leave the phone on all night."

The lump in Ellen's throat barely let her speak. "Thanks, I will."

She kept walking, trying to think of what to do next. The hospital was miles from the nearest Metro stop. Getting a cab seemed to be her only hope, but she knew the drive wouldn't be cheap and she didn't have enough cash on her. She turned the corner to her street and was surprised to run into Kate coming out of the building.

"Kate."

"Ellen. I stopped by to let you know I was going out of town, but obviously you weren't there."

Just seeing Kate standing in front of her, after days of not having even spoken to her, opened the floodgates for Ellen. The stress of her father's illness and now the emotions associated with Kate all blended into a maelstrom of feeling, and the tears poured out despite her best efforts to hold them in.

Shocked by Ellen's reaction, Kate dropped her bags and threw her arms around her, holding her close. "Hey, I'm sorry. I didn't know you'd be so upset about my going to London for a few days."

Ellen's sobs increased and Kate held her tight. *Wow. Maybe I underestimated her feelings for me.*

Finally Ellen managed to get a breath. "No, it's not that," she sniffed. "I'm a wreck, that's all. My father has been taken to the hospital and my car is in the shop, so I don't have a way to get to Alexandria. Can I borrow your cab and some cash? I'll pay you back."

Kate's ego deflated a bit, but her concern for Ellen's father outweighed the pinprick. She gestured toward the man who had approached them, yet maintained a respectful distance.

"I'll give you anything you need, but I didn't call for a cab. My friend Sergei here has rented a car and was going to take me. Besides you, he's the only one I trust behind the wheel in DC. Sergei, can you can drive Ellen to Alexandria instead?"

Sergei bowed, his eyes lighting up at the mention of her name. "I would drive her into the jaws of hell if that is where she wished to go."

"Well, between here and Alexandria you may just have to do that," Kate replied.

"But what about your flight to London?" Ellen dabbed at her eyes with the sleeve of her suit from the dry-cleaning bag.

Kate hesitated only a moment. "Screw it, I'll grab another flight. This is more important."

The grateful look Ellen gave her almost made her melt. She took Ellen's hand and, without thinking, kissed it. The contact reconnected her with Ellen in a way she hadn't felt in days, and she refused to let go.

"Ladies?" Sergei had opened the back door of the car and stood waiting.

Kate tossed her luggage into the trunk and climbed in next to Ellen, allowing Sergei to play chauffeur. The entire ride to Alexandria she continued to hold Ellen's hand, reassuring her through touch, but also needing to reassure herself.

Sergei ran red lights and passed cars on two-way streets. More than once Ellen closed her eyes as the door handles of their car nearly scraped the door handles of the cars he passed.

"Uh, Sergei, how did you ever get a driver's license in this country?" she couldn't help but ask.

"What driver's license?" He glanced over the front seat at her with a genuine look of puzzlement.

They sped across the Fourteenth Street Bridge, Ellen giving directions once they were on the other side of the Potomac. Fortunately the hospital was just off Interstate 395, and when Sergei dropped them at the emergency room entrance, they ran inside and asked at the desk where Ellen's father was.

"He's in surgery now," the nurse told them after scanning her list. She directed them to the family waiting room, and they walked up just as a surgeon was leaving.

Still holding Ellen's hand, Kate hesitated outside the room. "Perhaps I should wait out here."

Ellen shook her head. "No, come with me, please."

Kate nodded and pushed open the door to the waiting room. Ellen was so relieved to find her mother laughing and Joan smiling that she was momentarily light-headed from the sudden swing of emotions. Joan's children were sitting on orange plastic chairs, playing tug-of-war with a magazine they both wanted to read.

"What is it?" she managed to ask.

"Diverticulitis." Her mother sniffed through her tears. "He's going to be fine."

"Thank God," Ellen said weakly, holding onto her mother for support. "When can he go home?"

"Not for a while," Joan replied. "They have to keep him to

guard against infection, but he should be able to go home in a week at the most."

Ellen shook her head. "Oh, he's not going to like that one bit."

"He'll have to," her mother said firmly. "I'll make sure of it."

Joan took Ellen by the arm and led her to a corner of the room. "What's *she* doing here?" Joan whispered angrily.

Ellen glanced over her shoulder. "*She* is missing a flight to London because of me. *She* and her friend drove me here, and if it hadn't been for them I'd probably still be in the city."

"I can't believe you'd bring that woman in here, at a time like this. At least take Mom's feelings into consideration."

"I intend on introducing her to Mom," Ellen snapped, her temper wearing thin now that the crisis was over. "Just exactly what is your problem with Kate?"

"Well, for starters she's scaring my children."

Ellen laughed. "Hell, Joan. Your children are probably scaring *her*."

She withdrew her arm from Joan's and ignored her momentary twinge of guilt for snapping at her sister.

"You doing all right, Mom?" Ellen hugged her mother tightly.

"Oh, I am now." Barbara Webster dabbed at her eyes with relief.

"Um, I'd like you to meet my friend Kate, Mom." Ellen extended her hand, and when Kate grasped it, she pulled her close. "She and her friend Sergei drove me over here."

"Thank you so much, Kate. I don't know what I'd have done without my family near me."

"It was no problem," Kate murmured. "I'm just glad Mr. Webster is going to be okay."

Kate had tried to remain as unobtrusive as possible, standing near the door in case she needed to make a getaway. Hospitals made her exceedingly uncomfortable, and seeing Ellen and her sister in the corner clearly arguing about her hadn't helped. She was pleasantly surprised to discover that the woman she'd run into leaving Ellen's place that morning wasn't another lover. Realizing now that everything was okay and that Ellen didn't really need her, she excused herself and looked for Sergei.

He was sitting near the vending machines, drinking a Coke and reading or, rather, looking at the pictures in *GQ*, and glanced up when she approached. "How is he?"

"He'll be fine. I've got to call my agent and let him know I'll miss my flight."

As expected, when she reached Dean, he wasn't happy. "You what? Kate, they're expecting you in the morning."

"I know, but my friend's father was more important. Reschedule the meeting and I'll be there."

"Maybe I can still get you on a flight out of Dulles tonight. Let me check and I'll call you back."

Kate bought a cup of coffee from the machine and sat next to Sergei.

"So that is Ellen," Sergei said without looking up from his magazine.

"Mmm."

He glanced up and stared at her until she met his gaze. "What does that mean, 'Mmm'?"

"It means, yes, that's Ellen."

He continued to scrutinize her until finally Kate squirmed in her chair. "What?"

"She is very womanly, unlike those girls I have seen you with before."

"Yes, Ellen's not like anyone I've met before," Kate admitted.

"And still you are going to London to pursue this job?"

Kate shrugged. "I don't have much choice. She's not in love with me."

Sergei's face lit up in surprise. "She told you that?"

"Not in so many words, but she wants to play the field, and she did tell me that."

"Bah." He waved her comments away. "You cannot believe everything a lover tells you. I saw the way she looked at you in the car. She clung to you the entire time."

"That was because of your driving, Sergei," Kate deadpanned.

"I got her here, didn't I? Seriously, Kate, she looked at you as only a woman in love can look. We Russians know all about love. There is more than the eye meets here—that is a new expression I learned—and I think you should talk to her. Tell her how you feel."

Kate's cell phone rang.

"I can't get you out until tomorrow, it's the best I could do," Dean said. "I've already talked to Tracy at CNN and they're not happy. They're on a tight deadline, and rearranging everyone's schedule to accommodate you isn't something they needed right now."

"Did you explain what happened?" Kate asked, slightly irritated.

"Yes. I did. But that's not their problem, Kate. They need someone in London ASAP, and your friend's personal issues aren't their primary concern."

"Okay, okay, I know. But I couldn't leave her like that. Tell them I'll fit in with whatever their schedules are."

"Just be on that plane tomorrow. United flight 922 leaves at nine twenty-six in the morning."

❖

It was late by the time they left the hospital. Ellen was able to visit briefly with her father, and then her mother told both her and Joan to go home. They argued for a while as to who should stay, but Barbara absolutely refused to leave, and there wasn't enough space in the room to accommodate more than one visitor. Eventually Ellen gave in and kissed them both good night.

She walked slowly down the hallway to the public waiting room, where she found Kate and Sergei watching the ten o'clock news. Seeing Kate with a look of genuine concern on her face warmed and aroused Ellen. Exhausted, she wanted to simply go home, crawl into bed with Kate, and be held. Without thinking or caring, she reached out to her, needing to connect with her, however briefly. The stress of the day was an excuse to do so, but only an excuse.

Kate welcomed Ellen into her arms, almost sighing aloud at the contact. It felt so right to have her there, and she wanted nothing more than to protect Ellen from the day's sadness. When she opened her eyes, she glanced over Ellen's shoulder at Sergei, who stood looking at her, a knowing smile on his face. She glared at him.

Reluctantly releasing her hold on Kate, Ellen turned and hugged Sergei. "I don't know how to thank you."

Sergei dismissed his involvement as minor.

"What about your trip to London?" she asked Kate.

"I have another flight out tomorrow."

Slightly disappointed, Ellen nodded. "I'm glad it worked out."

Sergei smiled. "I'm sure you must be exhausted. Let me drive you both home."

"Thank you, I am a bit tired," Ellen admitted.

They returned the way they had come, over the Fourteenth Street Bridge, but this time Sergei drove slowly. Ellen leaned slightly against Kate, and as the car swayed at curves and turns, she eventually laid her head on Kate's shoulder. She closed her eyes at the comfortable position, and Kate put her arm around her.

Sergei dropped them in front of their building and unloaded Kate's luggage for her. "Good night," he called as he opened the driver's side door.

"Good night, and thank you again." Ellen waved.

As they stopped in front of Ellen's front door, she felt awkward, wanting to invite Kate in, yet knowing she had a flight to catch in the morning. The thought of Kate moving to London made her ache all over, but there was nothing she could do, was there? "Well, I guess you should get some sleep. That flight to London is a long one."

"Yeah," Kate agreed. "I'm not looking forward to it."

"You're not?" Ellen asked hopefully.

"No, I hate flying, particularly into Heathrow."

"Oh." Ellen was disappointed, hoping for another reason.

Kate noticed the look of disappointment and wondered at its meaning. Even tired, Ellen was striking, her hair in slight disarray and her eyes puffy from crying. Kate had never seen anyone look more attractive. She leaned close, inhaling Ellen's fragrance, the smell of her shampoo, and recalled the taste of her skin. Aroused, she had to struggle to keep herself from touching Ellen. The poor woman had been through too much and certainly didn't need her hitting on her this late.

Ellen saw and felt the nearness of Kate. If she were to shift just inches her breasts would press into Kate's, and the thought made her tingle. She longed to be touched, longed to feel her skin against Kate's. She wanted to run her hands up and down Kate's body and feel it react to her touch. She knew every square inch of Kate, and she wanted to get to know each one all over again. She needed to feel alive again.

The air in the hallway was so thick with tension Kate could almost touch it. Neither had said a word and the silence was deafening. Almost without realizing she was moving, she stroked Ellen's flawless cheek, which was hot under her fingertips. She traced Ellen's jaw down to her throat, finding the base and resting her fingers in the notch of her collarbone. She wanted…so much, more than she ever thought possible in a relationship. Could she really give this up for a job? It would be much easier to crawl inside Ellen and shut out the rest of the world and never venture out of the safety of her arms. But what would happen after that? She couldn't stay there forever, and eventually Ellen would become bored. And she would become bored as well. If she was going to contribute in a meaningful way, she had to go to London—had to know if this job was what she was meant to do. But, God, it was killing her.

Ellen's heart beat erratically, and her knees trembled. Resting against her door so that it would help hold her up, she tried to regulate her breathing. Kate's touch electrified her and she had no control over her body's response.

"I'll miss you," she managed to get out. Her eyes filled with tears and she blinked them back. They wouldn't do any good now. Kate had made up her mind about London. Ellen's emotions were scattered in every direction, and she tried to gather them and put them back in their place. The day had been incredibly stressful, and she chalked up her lack of control to the scare over her father's health. The sudden relief that the event was minor had left her weak and drained. She didn't know what would have happened if Kate and Sergei hadn't been there. She was so grateful to have Kate step in and take charge. Kate's strength had buoyed her. Having Kate in her life completed her.

Kate was unable to speak. She would be gone only a few days, and then she would be back. This wasn't good-bye, not yet. But why did it feel that way? Was it just her, or did Ellen feel it too? If this was good-bye, she wanted to make the most of it. She pulled Ellen into her and found her lips moist and waiting.

Ellen almost fainted with relief that Kate had finally kissed her. It was so good, so right. Kate seemed tentative at first, questioning, but within seconds the kiss heated up. Ellen wanted to kiss her as though this was the last kiss she'd ever give, which it just might be. Tears rained down her face, and she clung to Kate, not wanting to let go.

Out of breath, they finally parted, their foreheads pressed together. Once Kate was able to breathe normally, she released her hold on Ellen and they leaned apart. Ellen brushed her tears away and rubbed a smudge of lipstick from Kate's cheek.

"I should let you get some sleep. You've had quite a day," Kate murmured.

"And you have a flight in the morning."

"I'll call you from London. You know, just to tell you how it's going."

Ellen brightened noticeably. "I'd love that, Kate."

Kate nodded, her eyes never leaving Ellen's face. If Ellen's day hadn't been like this, she wouldn't have been able to stop. She would have swept Ellen into her arms and carried her to bed. But she didn't.

CHAPTER NINETEEN

The cab dropped Kate off in front of Turner House on Great Marlborough Street, CNN's London headquarters. After checking in at the reception desk, she waited briefly for a young woman who led her up to the executive offices. Kate noticed the receptionist there looking at her, knew she was staring at the scar, and all her insecurities regarding her appearance resurfaced. She loosened the hair tucked behind her left ear and let it fall forward onto her face.

The door to the office directly behind the reception desk opened, and an elegantly tailored and coiffed woman emerged. Everything about her was perfectly manicured, and she walked as though treading a fashion-show runway.

"Ms. Foster, I'm Tracy Shelbourne, but please call me Tracy."

Tracy, an executive in the human resources department, was the first person she would meet with that day. "How was your flight?" she asked, leading Kate into her office and to a camel-leather couch.

"Just fine, thank you. Though your prime minister ought to condemn Heathrow as a national disaster."

Tracy laughed. "You wouldn't be the first to say so, Ms. Foster."

"Please, call me Kate."

"All right, Kate. I'd like to run down today's itinerary. Who you will meet with, their areas of expertise, the editorial staff that would report to you, and so forth."

During the next eight hours Kate met everyone from the top down. She was grilled by executives, some of whom surreptitiously gazed at her scar when they thought she wasn't looking. Their curiosity annoyed and embarrassed her, but she guessed it was natural. The scar was rather obvious. But hell, she wasn't interviewing for an anchor spot, so what did it matter? Some of the staff were engaging and explained their work, while others questioned her decision to leave print journalism for on-air work. They didn't ask why she was considering behind-the-scenes work. That was obvious.

She revisited the crazy pace of writers, and from the sound booth she observed the afternoon news program, one of the projects she would be working on. While she watched, she took notes on some issues that stood out to her immediately, and along with the thoughts and ideas she had prepared in advance, she knew she could converse reasonably well about the subject when it came up.

By the end of the day, jet lag had begun to take its toll, but she was expected to join Tracy, another executive, and the retiring managing editor for dinner later that evening. They gave her two hours to rest before they picked her up, but when she entered her hotel room, she collapsed onto the bed, sighing at the feel of the down pillows beneath her head. She didn't dare close her eyes because she knew she would be asleep in two minutes.

She thought of Ellen—where she was and what she was doing. Ellen had said it was all right to call her, though, and she reached for the phone. Hesitating, she replaced it in its cradle.

Then she retrieved a tiny bottle of Beefeater from the mini-bar and poured it into a cup of ice. Sipping the gin for courage, she picked up the phone again and made the call. After five rings, she was about to hang up.

"Hello?" Ellen panted.

"Hi, Ellen, it's Kate. Did I catch you at a bad time? You sound out of breath."

"No, it's fine. I was on my way out but thought it might be you, and I didn't want to miss your call."

Just hearing Ellen's voice made her feel better. "How's your father?"

"Much better. That's where I was going."

"Oh. I'll let you go. I can call back later."

"No, now is good. Mom and Joan are there, so he's not alone. I'll relieve Joan and hang out with them for a while. How's it going?" Ellen asked.

"Okay, I guess." Kate wished she could see Ellen's face. "It's too soon to tell. I've met with a bunch of people, so many that I forget. I've got a respite before dinner, but I'd rather be in jeans and a T-shirt at your place eating pasta and watching a movie. That, plus I'm ready to fall asleep any minute, so the prospect of putting on another suit and forcing a happy look on my face isn't appealing."

Ellen sat down on the sofa in the living room and curled her feet under her, feeling as though she was in high school again and getting a call from her latest crush. The butterflies in her stomach said it all, and she warmed to the sound of Kate's voice. "I'm sure they love you."

"Sure they do," Kate agreed. "What's not to love?"

Nothing. Ellen loved everything about Kate. The way her face lit up when she found a relevant piece of research, how her body tensed in the throes of passion, even when she was angry. "So, how much longer do you think you'll be there?"

"I have another full day tomorrow and fly back the day after that."

"Do you need me to pick you up from the airport?" Ellen asked hopefully.

"Oh, no, thanks. Sergei offered to do that." Now Kate wished she hadn't agreed to Sergei's offer, but she didn't want to impose on Ellen while she had a family emergency.

"Well, how about I make you dinner the night you get back?"

"Ellen, you don't have to do that." Though Kate said no, she thought otherwise. She couldn't imagine anything she'd rather do than be with Ellen.

"Please, I'd like to." Plus Ellen wanted to see Kate. She didn't know how many more nights she'd have in Kate's company, and she wanted to make it as many as possible.

"Well, okay, thanks."

Ellen tingled. She loved the way Kate's voice dropped a couple of octaves on the last sentence. The deep alto thrummed through her even across phone lines and the Atlantic Ocean.

During the silence that followed, not awkward, not uncomfortable, Kate thought of how Ellen's quiet breathing at the other end reminded her of the way Ellen had slept that morning after making love. She was painfully vulnerable in the patch of morning sunlight that filtered across the bed, her hair spread across the pillow. Kate sighed at the memory.

"Are you okay?" Ellen asked.

"Yeah, just a little tired," Kate replied. "I should let you go so you can visit your father."

Ellen didn't want to hang up but knew Kate had her own appointment. "I suppose," she agreed. "And you need to get ready for your dinner. I hope it goes well."

"Thanks," Kate whispered. *Does she really?*

❖

"We run a tight ship here, Kate," an executive producer explained. "Everything hums along like clockwork, and we like to keep it that way."

"I can appreciate that." Kate nodded, sipping her wine.

"We want the next managing editor to step into Stan's position and pick up where he leaves off. It will be a completely smooth transition, no hiccups whatsoever."

Managing Editor Stanley Giddings had been involved with the evening news segment for the past six years and with CNN for nearly twenty. He had worked his way steadily up the ladder and now was being rewarded with a promotion to Atlanta. Everything about CNN was first class, and Kate saw very clearly the challenges that the position presented.

Kate had seen the established practices and the organizational hierarchy from the bottom up. On the surface, it would seem that she would be another cog in a wheel of this smoothly oiled machine. No more incompetent reporters or equipment malfunctions, or at least with far less frequency than at Channel 5. But she saw some opportunities where she could contribute, as well as learn a thing or two. The job had tremendous potential.

They had discussed the job until Kate's head swam with details. She knew she could handle it. The salary was well above what she had been making, and the chance to make her mark in a huge organization such as CNN was certainly an added bonus. If she measured up to their standards and played by the rules, she would probably advance rapidly.

As they chatted amiably over coffee and dessert, she knew the executives were trying to get a sense of her as a person. She could tell they were wondering if she would be a good addition to the team, and she leisurely answered their questions. They had done their homework, knowing much of what she had accomplished in her career, details they hadn't just taken off a resume. If they had really gone to this much trouble, they would know about the accident and possibly about her personal life. It didn't seem to be an issue.

Tracy Shelbourne drove Kate back to the hotel and stopped out front, letting the engine idle. "I'll see you tomorrow, Kate. We can go over any questions you may have as well as any additional ones from senior management. Shall I pick you up about eight thirty?"

"Thank you, Tracy, and thank you for dinner. I'll see you in the morning."

Once in her room, Kate again fell onto the bed, exhausted. It had been a grueling day because of all the questions, but also because she had to be "on" all the time—a state she always disliked. She had never been a people person. She had always been about the work, discovering what needed to be done and then doing it.

She kicked off her shoes and undressed, turning the shower on as hot as she could stand it, then stepped in. Within seconds she relaxed, so much so she could almost fall asleep standing up. Deciding she'd rather be more comfortable, she shut the water off and quickly dried herself. She tossed the damp towel on the floor and dragged herself to bed, crawling in naked and moaning aloud with pleasure as she let the cool sheets soothe her tired body.

She thought about calling Ellen but didn't want to appear needy. Besides, Ellen might be having dinner with her family. Ellen's sister had already made her feelings about Kate clear, so she didn't want to exacerbate the situation. She sighed, thinking about that day and the kiss that had ended it. Just the memory of it made her ache, but she immediately repressed all thoughts about her physical response to Ellen.

Kate flipped over and punched her pillow into submission. She was exhausted, but her mind wouldn't calm down. If they offered her the job, she was moving to London and that would be that. Hopefully Ellen would think of her fondly, if she thought of her at all. But how could she forget Ellen? Even during her interviews, Kate had dwelt on her—her hair blowing in the wind on the heights at Fredericksburg, the curve of her hip as Kate ran her hand over the smooth skin.

Frustrated by her mind's tantalizing wandering, Kate picked up the remote. She turned on CNN and tried to focus on what else was happening in the world. Her personal world was simply too confusing and chaotic. She needed to see other people in the world experiencing disorder, too; then she could feel at peace. She hoped the distraction would work. About an hour later, it did. She slept, and dreamed, but this time the dream was not about the horrifying details of the car accident and the little girl's lifeless eyes. Kate dreamed of waking up in the hospital, alive. And sitting at her bedside was Ellen.

❖

Ellen carried a tray from the cafeteria into the hospital room where her mother sat at her father's bedside. Joan had gone home to take care of the kids, and her father had fallen asleep. So she and her mother shared spaghetti, the only item on the menu that held any appeal. While they ate, Ellen slowly related her feelings about Kate and her fear that now she had met someone she truly cared for, she was about to slip out of her grasp.

"Have you told her how you feel?" Barbara asked.

"I was going to, and then this job in London came up. I couldn't drop my feelings in her lap just as she was on the verge of finding her way back to the real world. It's a great opportunity for her. I'm sure she didn't think anything like it would come along for quite some time, if at all."

"But if she doesn't know how you feel about her, how can she make a truly informed decision?" Barbara glanced at her sleeping husband.

"Her choices would be me or the job. That's not a fair decision to have to make, and I couldn't ask it of her."

"So you're just going to let her go?"

Ellen winced, not liking the sound of the words, even though that was precisely what she had been thinking. The decision sounded grandly self-sacrificing in her mind, but saying it out loud was painful. Could she simply let Kate go? Did she have any claim on her? Did she really know that Kate loved her? She'd never said so. But during those nights in bed together, Ellen had felt they shared more than just great sex.

"I don't know. I don't want her to leave, but I don't think I can, or should, do anything to stop her."

Barbara stared at her. "Honey, you have to tell Kate how you feel. It's not fair otherwise. How can she choose if she doesn't know you love her? Isn't it possible she might choose you?"

Ellen's throat tightened and her eyes burned. She wanted desperately to believe what her mother was saying. But what if she told Kate how she felt and Kate still preferred London? Ellen didn't think she could recover from that kind of pain. The possibility was too much for her, and she pushed her dinner plate away, having lost her appetite.

"Well, if one good thing comes of it, I just may lose that weight I've been complaining about." Ellen's tears spilled over and she dabbed at the corners of her eyes with her napkin.

"Oh, honey," her mother whispered.

Her mother's fierce hug made the tears come faster. Ellen allowed herself to be rocked, much as her mother had done when she was a child. She felt safe, as she had back then, but Ellen was no longer a child. She was an adult, with an adult's breaking heart. And she wasn't sure it would ever mend this time.

CHAPTER TWENTY

Ellen stood in her kitchen preparing dinner for Kate when she heard a knock at the door. Glancing over to the microwave clock, she saw it was a good half hour before she expected anyone. She wiped her hands on the dish towel and opened the door to find Kate.

"Hey, you're early, but come on in." It wasn't until Kate stepped inside and stopped that Ellen noticed something wasn't right. "Kate?"

"I just got off the phone with my agent," Kate murmured.

"And?" Ellen suddenly found it difficult to breathe.

"CNN has offered me the job."

Stunned, Ellen couldn't think of a response. It was bound to happen, yet she couldn't conceive of the reality. She wanted to congratulate Kate, but the words wouldn't come. Her chest constricted and she gulped for air. If only she was alone right now, she would fall to the floor in a boneless pile and sob endlessly.

Kate felt miserable, wishing the job wasn't in London. It seemed like a death sentence instead of a great opportunity, because she couldn't ask Ellen to come with her. Ellen had her profession, her career right here in DC. And they hadn't known each other that long. Could she really ask her to run away with her? It was ridiculous to even contemplate.

"Congratulations, Kate." Ellen finally found her voice but was still unable to move. Suddenly she felt incredibly tired and could barely lift her arms to place them on the table.

"Thanks," Kate whispered.

Finally shaking her head and composing herself, Ellen returned to the kitchen to finish making dinner. At least in the kitchen she wouldn't have to pretend she was happy. She placed the dishes next to the sink. Squeezing her eyes shut, she leaned against the counter and struggled to regain control. This simply could not be happening. Somehow she'd been able to retain a speck of hope through it all. Maybe Kate wouldn't want the job, maybe the fit wouldn't be right, maybe they'd find somebody better suited to fill the position. But now the hope was gone. Reality had found her and moved in to stay. *God, it hurts.*

"When do they want you to start?" she called out.

"As soon as possible." Kate entered the kitchen and stood next to her at the sink.

Ellen could barely speak. "I'll miss our meals together."

Kate nodded. "So will I." She hesitated. "Ellen, I can't tell you how grateful I am to you for all you've done for me. I—"

"No." Ellen shook her head. She couldn't hear the words Kate spoke, not about that anyway. Her mind, her heart, her body screamed for words she wouldn't speak. She didn't want gratitude now. She wanted, needed, so much more. She was horrified to find tears form in her eyes. She was so close to keeping her emotions under control, had almost made it until after Kate left.

Kate saw the tears and wondered at them. Were they just tears at losing a friend, or was there more to them? If there was, surely Ellen would have said something. Was it too late now? Would it do any good? Could they see each other perhaps a few times a year, have great sex, then return to their separate lives? No. Kate wanted more than that. Living that way would only drive her crazy with desire. And it would eventually destroy her soul. She couldn't live that way. Better to end it now, while the pain was almost bearable.

Ellen's tears fell in streams and she brushed them away. She tried to pretend she was being silly, but losing Kate hurt too much to hide. Kate pulled her into her arms and she dissolved, crying freely, and buried her face in Kate's neck. She clutched at Kate's shirt, clinging to her, not wanting to let her go.

"Oh, Ellen," Kate whispered, kissing her forehead and rubbing her hands soothingly down Ellen's back. "I'll miss you so much." Her voice was raw, and she knew they were the last words she would speak or she would crumble, too.

Ellen pulled away from Kate and dried her face with her hands. Peering up at Kate, she tried to dismiss the tears, but she'd never been good at hiding her emotions. She pulled Kate to her and found her waiting lips. She kissed her hard, forcing her mouth open and finding the warmth inside. She moaned as the heat flooded through her down to her toes, wanting the fire to burn away her pain. The ache in the pit of her stomach warred with the one in her heart, and she pressed her hips into Kate to ease it.

Any thoughts of being tired disappeared when Ellen pressed into Kate. She slipped her hands from Ellen's back over her shoulders and down to her breasts. She palmed them roughly, feeling the nipples harden under her touch. For a moment the power of her need overwhelmed her and she worried she might hurt Ellen. Unbuttoning her blouse, she pushed Ellen's bra up and groaned at the feel of her hot flesh in her hands. Kate kissed her neck, let her tongue travel down Ellen's throat to her exposed nipples where she bit them roughly, sucking them into her mouth.

Ellen nearly collapsed at the sensation. The wetness between her legs spread, and she knew the slightest friction from Kate's leg between hers would set her off. She pulled Kate's shirt out of her pants and found the heated skin of her back, then dipped below Kate's waistband to the slight curve of her buttocks, soft and smooth to the touch. Blindly she found the button and zipper in the front and fumbled to unzip it.

"Bed," Kate demanded. "Now."

Not breaking their hold on one another, they stumbled and kissed, fondled and stroked their way to the bedroom. Once they had kicked off their shoes, they fell onto the bed, still entwined in each other's arms. Kate climbed on top, grinding her pelvis into Ellen's thigh, ready to come in an instant. But she needed Ellen naked, needed to feel hot flesh on hot flesh, nothing separating them.

They undressed each other, nearly tearing the clothes off their bodies. When they were finally naked, the feel of Ellen's skin on hers nearly made her come, and she wanted to bury herself in Ellen's lush body. She found Ellen's nipples again, desperately sucking and licking them so she would never forget how they tasted. Sliding down Ellen's stomach, she traced a wet line with her tongue to the pale triangle between her legs. She pushed Ellen's legs apart and sucked in her breath at the pool of moisture waiting there.

"God," Ellen gasped. "Please, please, Kate, whatever you do, don't stop."

Ellen was on fire and could barely form a coherent sentence. Her entire being was merely the flesh and nerves that Kate played at will. Nothing else existed.

Kate buried her tongue deep between Ellen's slick folds, probing and tasting Ellen's desire. Finding her clit hard and swollen, Kate pulled it in between her lips, flicking it rapidly back and forth with her tongue.

"Oh, yes, God, yes. Don't stop, please don't stop!"

The sound of Ellen's voice barely penetrated Kate's blind desire to take her. Spurred on by Ellen's words, she sucked harder and moved her fingers to find the hot opening, slipping in and filling her.

"Jesus, Kate, oh, Jesus, that's so good...so good."

Ellen's voice faded, as though she were calling from a great distance. Her muscles clamped down on Kate's fingers, drawing her in even deeper. She spread and flexed them, wanting to touch and soothe every inch inside of Ellen. Kate was driven, though, driven by a fire that filled her belly, and this time she simply wanted to fuck Ellen. She wanted to fuck her until she screamed and came and drenched her with her come. Pushing in, she rapidly withdrew almost entirely out of Ellen, then forcefully plunged in as far as she could go.

"Yes!"

Ellen reached down and grasped Kate's hand, roughly forcing her fingers inside. It felt so damn good to have her there, to feel her fingers fucking her. She'd never let herself go with anyone this way, never abandoned herself without concern as to how she looked. All she wanted now was to come, for Kate to make her come. She wanted Kate to own her.

Kate pumped her with all she had, thrusting in and out as fast as she could. She felt Ellen's body stiffen and knew she was at the edge. Leaning down, she put her lips back on Ellen's stiff clit. As before, she stroked it with her tongue, all the while filling and fucking her with her hand.

The incredible sensation was building and twisting, climbing higher and taking Ellen's breath away. It filled her belly and traveled up her body to her breasts and neck. With one last thrust it exploded, taking her along for the ride. "Kate," she called, sobbing into the air as she came convulsively. The tremors ripped through her along with her sobs, and she couldn't tell where one began and the other ended.

The force of Ellen's orgasm stunned Kate, and her tears finally fell. She stilled her hand, leaving it inside Ellen, and rested her head against Ellen's thigh. Despite her desire not to, she wept bitterly, for all that might have been. The accident hadn't changed only her appearance, but had redirected her life in a way she might never have chosen otherwise.

Finally withdrawing her fingers, Kate slid up to Ellen's side and enfolded her in her arms. She held and comforted her, knowing this was good-bye. When Ellen could finally move, she trailed her fingers from Kate's throat, down her belly to just above her hairline. Kate caught her hand. "It's okay. I want to just hold you."

Ellen shook her head. "No. I don't want to just hold you. I need you. I need to feel you come. I need to take you and make you feel that. If not for your sake, then for mine."

She withdrew her hand from Kate's grasp and continued her journey downward between Kate's legs. Her lover's thighs were coated with her wetness, and Ellen followed the trail of moisture to Kate's waiting folds.

Kate opened her legs wider. "Don't wait, I need you now," she pleaded.

With no further encouragement, Ellen slid inside, finding no resistance. She held her breath at the wonder of Kate and pushed another finger inside, filling her. This night she wanted to make it last, but Kate was having none of it.

"Faster, I'm so close."

After only a few thrusts, Kate jerked and came, her eyes half open. Ellen thought she had no tears left to give, but they fell lazily down her chin. She placed a gentle kiss on the tip of Kate's clit, drawing it into her mouth. Kate's body jumped at the added sensation, and she shuddered again before the first orgasm completely receded. When Kate was still, Ellen closed her eyes and wept.

❖

General Beauregard meowed and bumped his head into Ellen's head, waking her instantly.

"Ouch, Beau," she whispered.

He really did hurt. She petted him and he fell down next to her, wanting to be held, too. Ellen glanced at the clock on her bedside table. Three o'clock. Kate's arm rested over Ellen's hip and she nestled into Ellen's back. Being spooned by Kate felt so good, and she rolled over to face her. Startled to find Kate awake and looking back at her, Ellen touched her cheek soothingly. She tried to think of something to say, but couldn't. What could possibly be said about their lovemaking?

"Have you been awake long?"

"A little while," Kate replied. "My internal clock is screwed up."

Ellen stared at her, trying to memorize the way Kate looked at that moment—sexy, sleepy, and totally irresistible. God, she was so in love with her. What the hell was she going to do?

"That was amazing," Kate murmured.

"Mmm, yes, yes, it was," Ellen agreed.

Kate ran her fingers through Ellen's hair, scratching and massaging her scalp. Ellen yawned, wanting to stay awake, but Kate's touch was putting her back to sleep. Her body, completely sated, called to her for rest. Although she fought her fatigue, her eyelids drooped and she relaxed into the massage. How could she be so utterly content and so utterly unhappy at the same time? Her mind wouldn't work. Besides, it was senseless to ponder the impossible.

Chapter Twenty-one

When Ellen awoke she was alone in bed. She listened carefully for any sound from the bathroom or the rest of the house. Hearing nothing, she got up and threw a robe on, calling Kate's name. She could smell coffee in the kitchen, and when she went in, a note was lying on the counter next to the coffeemaker.

Ellen,

Had a few errands to run. See you later.

Kate

Bewildered by the abruptness with which Kate had left, Ellen poured a cup of coffee and sat down at the table. She couldn't think of anything she might have said or done to cause Kate to leave without saying good-bye. Last night had been so miraculous, her body still hummed. She had been certain Kate had enjoyed it, too, but now she wasn't sure.

Sighing, she left her coffee untouched and returned to the bedroom. Since it looked as though the day would be a long one, she might as well get back to her research. She had fallen far behind, unable to focus. But things were about to change. With Kate moving to London, all she would have was time.

❖

Kate jogged past the Lincoln Memorial as she rounded her lap on the Mall. She turned and headed back down Independence Avenue, feeling the burn in her legs and lungs. Running had always helped her work things out, but this time it failed her. She had avoided seeing Ellen this morning because she didn't want to talk about what was happening between them.

She had to pack and put things in storage, and quickly find a place in London. Fortunately the personnel department would help her in that regard, and she had left it completely up to them. She didn't care where she lived or what it looked like. Again, it would be someplace merely to sleep, nothing more.

It was time to pull away from Ellen emotionally. Kate had become far too attached, and last night had been a mistake. But she couldn't help herself. Ellen was so captivating, and Kate's body refused to listen to what her mind knew she shouldn't be doing. For the first time in her life, she might be falling in love. She wasn't completely sure, though, not knowing what that was like. But if it meant an overwhelming need to be near that person, a passion so intense it made her want to cry, and a pain so great at the thought of leaving it almost made her heart stop beating, then Kate had all the symptoms.

God, why now?

Turning left on Seventeenth Street, she slowed to a walk, her heart pounding and the sweat pouring down her back. The morning had already begun to heat up, and she hugged the tree line and the shade it provided. Crossing Constitution, she detoured onto the Ellipse, enjoying the park and the views it provided of the nation's capital. The White House was obscured by the dense foliage, but knowing it was there gave her a thrill.

Living and working here had been personally satisfying and professionally challenging. The Washington political scene was where the action was, what she had always been most interested in covering. New York and its financial news bored her, and California held no interest whatsoever. Past overseas jobs had temporarily held her interest, but she had never contemplated living abroad permanently.

Her hand rose involuntarily up to her face, her fingers tracing the lengthy scar line. It no longer revolted her, had in fact become a part of her and who she would become. It signaled a change from the old Kate to the new, and though in some respects she wished it wasn't there, in other ways she knew she might never have found Ellen without it. Kate had a job now, which was a good thing, but it took her away from the city she loved and the woman she loved. She supposed it was just as well, though, since if she couldn't have the woman she loved, the city would no longer hold the same appeal.

❖

Ellen's mother Barbara claimed her husband had alienated all the nurses on the floor and she was the only one left to tolerate his obstinacy, so he was able to go home early. With promises to take him in for checkups, she wheeled him to the curb and Ellen drove them back to their house. Joan was there preparing lunch while the children played in the backyard.

"Hallelujah, it's good to be home," Ira exclaimed. "And real food for a change. How about some wine to celebrate?"

"You will do no such thing," Barbara admonished him. "Don't get your hopes up. We're not having anything rich or exotic, just soup and sandwiches. Then you're getting into bed."

"Oh, no. I can't take being in bed anymore."

Barbara eyed him skeptically. "If I let you lie on the couch with the remote and a blanket over you, will you promise to be good?"

"Cross my heart," he replied, making the mark across his chest.

Once they had ensconced him on the sofa, she and her daughters prepared lunch. Barbara couldn't help but notice Ellen's lackluster movements and stopped what she was doing to watch. When she realized Ellen was pouring milk for the children in bowls and soup in their glasses, she finally intervened.

"What's the matter, Ellen?"

Joan stopped cutting the sandwiches in half and looked up.

"What do you mean?" Ellen asked.

Barbara looked down at the bowls and glasses until Ellen did likewise. Flustered, Ellen poured the soup back into the pan on the stove and took out new glasses for the milk.

"I guess I'm distracted," she admitted.

"Distracted about what?"

When Ellen didn't answer, Joan spoke up. "It probably has something do with that *woman*. I still can't believe you would see someone like that, Ellen. I mean, *really*. If you're going to insist on seeing women, at least you could find someone who isn't so...so..." Unable to find the word, Joan shivered as if she was disgusted.

"That's enough, Joan," Barbara said sternly.

"She's Kate Foster, Mom," Joan continued. "You met her at the hospital. Now she's unemployed because of that accident and her face is horrible. You shouldn't be getting mixed up with someone with her reputation, Ellen, that's all."

Ellen whirled on her sister, her fury finally unleashed. "She's a courageous woman, Joan, someone you should emulate. And she's not unemployed. She's just accepted a position with CNN in London." Her voice caught and her hand shook at the thought, and she leaned against the counter.

"Oh, Ellen," her mother said, reaching out to her.

Ellen hadn't meant to talk about Kate, not now, not with her father just home from the hospital, but thoughts about her were consuming Ellen. Kate had altered her life forever, and now she was about to lose her. It was all too much and she welcomed her mother's embrace.

"Honey, did you talk with her like I told you to?"

Ellen shook her head and brushed her tears away. "I couldn't, Mom. I just couldn't."

"Why not?"

"Because I'm in love with her, and I have to let her go and be who she needs to be."

"Love?" Joan exclaimed. "You're in *love* with a woman? Oh, Ellen, please."

The snap inside was almost audible to Ellen. Her relationship with her sister had always been tenuous, and now she didn't care that they were related by blood.

"What is it, Joan? What is it about my personal life and my preference for women that you don't like? Not that it's any of your business, but who the hell do you think you are that you think you can dictate to me who I may love and what I must feel? Don't you have anything else to occupy your life so you have to butt in on mine?"

"I have a lot going on in my life, Ellen. A husband and children, a home, family, and friends. That's what life is supposed to be, that's what's normal."

"Normal?" Ellen shouted.

"Girls, now stop it," Barbara said.

"No, Mom. Joan and I have been dancing around this for years. I'm sick to death of it and we're going to have it out once and for all, because I refuse to put up with her crap any longer. Tell me, Joan, what's normal? Having a couple of absolute brats and a husband who's never around?"

"How dare you speak about my children like that," Joan shrieked. "They're perfectly normal children and Robert is a perfect husband. His work takes him away from home a lot, and he can't always be around for family functions. He would be here if he could, and he—"

Suddenly gasping for air, Joan stopped speaking. She wailed and burst into tears, sobbing between gritted teeth. Then she covered her mouth with her hand and ran from the kitchen, leaving them staring in disbelief. Ellen glanced at her mother, unsure what had happened. They left the kitchen and searched for Joan, eventually finding her in the guest bedroom, huddled in a ball on the bed.

Barbara sat down next to her and put her hand on Joan's shoulder. "Oh, sweetheart, what's the matter?"

Joan continued to sob, her fist pressed into her mouth and her eyes shut tight. Ellen and her mother waited for the tears to subside, then waited until Joan could find her voice.

"Was it something I said?" Ellen said, trying to introduce a bit of levity.

Joan sat up abruptly. "It's always about you, isn't it, Ellen?"

Ellen was shocked by the venom in Joan's voice, but she didn't want to argue with her. Whatever was going on with Joan had nothing to do with her.

"You have the great job, *Professor*. Everyone admires your mind and your career. You travel and write books. You get to experiment sexually with women and God knows what else."

"Joan," Barbara snapped.

"Come on, Mother. I did everything you and Daddy wanted me to do. I married a handsome, successful physician and had two children. Hell, we even have a damn dog. I have the American dream, I have it all. Everything looks so great from the outside. But nobody knows what it's been like on the inside. No one knows, or cares for that matter, that Robert has been having an affair for at least a year now with another physician at the hospital."

Ellen felt as though Joan had hit her in the solar plexus. She grabbed hold of the edge of the dresser to steady herself. "My God," she whispered.

Joan sputtered. "God had nothing to do with it. Why do you think I spend all my time at the club—because I enjoy wasting time with the girls? I go to work out, every day, hours a day to stay thin and try to be attractive for a man who doesn't even care about me. Robert just decided he wasn't in love with me anymore, if he ever had been. His family had expected him to live the American dream, too. We were both so young and naïve, I know, but I loved him. I still do.

"But now, I'm invisible. Oh, sure, I still go to the club, still play tennis with my so-called friends. But my life is empty. My children are only concerned about when they'll be getting the latest technological toy and where they'll be spending their next vacation. I'm a servant, cooking and cleaning. I don't have any meaning or purpose or direction."

"You can change all that if you want to," Ellen said. "I'll help you."

"What? Go back to school? Become a rocket scientist? If your offer weren't so clichéd, so predictable, it would be laughable. It's too late. There's nothing left, I suppose, but signing the divorce papers. I presume that's what Robert wants."

"Who cares what Robert wants?" Ellen argued. "Take him for every nickel he's got and you won't have to worry again about money. Punish him. Take him to the cleaners, for God's sake."

"We'll get you a lawyer from your father's office," Barbara said. "Don't worry about a thing. And you get to keep the house, no question about it. Let Robert move in with his girlfriend."

"It's not a girlfriend, Mother, it's a boyfriend."

Neither Ellen nor her mother moved. The only sound came from Joan blowing her nose into a tissue. Then she pulled out another tissue and dabbed at the corners of her eyes. With one last sniff, she glanced up at her mother and Ellen.

"Surprise."

"Shit," Ellen whispered.

"Double shit," Barbara agreed.

"Yeah, it was a real eye-opener, that's for sure," Joan added

"No wonder you resented my lifestyle," Ellen murmured.

"Now don't go turning my problem into something about you," Joan warned.

"No, sorry, I'm not, really, Joan. But I can see how Robert having an affair with a man made you less understanding about my being attracted to women. Don't you see? It's not about who you love. It's about finding someone you can love at all. It's a very rare, very special discovery. Obviously Robert had these feelings long before he knew you. It didn't happen overnight. You weren't meant for each other, okay, so now what are you going to do about it?"

"The same thing you're doing about this Kate person," Joan tossed back.

Ellen blinked, confused. "What?"

"Nothing. I'm going to let him go. What else can I do?"

The full impact of Joan's words hit Ellen like a roundhouse

punch. For Joan, letting go of Robert was letting go of someone who no longer loved her, perhaps never did. And despite Joan's attempts to remain fit and attractive, he obviously didn't care how she looked. Ellen loved Kate. For the first time in her life she was deeply, hopelessly, passionately in love. And Kate didn't mind Ellen's weight, had said so and reinforced it with her actions.

She wasn't sure if Kate was in love with her, but that was it, wasn't it? She didn't know. Her mother was right. She needed to let Kate know how she felt, and then she needed to find out exactly how Kate felt. After that, well, she'd cross that bridge when she got to it. And even if it meant the London Bridge, well, she'd cross that, too.

"Thanks, Joan."

"For what?"

"You just helped me more than you'll ever know. Look, I'm sorry about Robert, but you know what? He's an asshole. You deserve better, and I know a guy in our department at GU who would love to take you to dinner sometime. Just say the word. But right now, I've got to run."

She left the guest room and found her purse where she had left it on a table in the entryway. Digging around for her keys, she nearly ran to the front door.

"What about lunch?" her mother called after her.

"Another time. Tell Daddy I love him and I'm glad he's home. I'll drop by tomorrow."

"But where are you going, Ellen?"

Ellen stopped, her hand on the doorknob. "I'm going to tell Kate I love her."

"And if she loves you, too?"

"If she loves me, too, then that's a lot, that's everything. If she does, then I'll be happy, happier than I've ever been."

"And what about London?"

Ellen paused, not sure how to solve that dilemma. "Somehow it'll work out. I don't know how, but it's got to. Maybe not right away, but someday. And that's all I can hope for. A someday."

CHAPTER TWENTY-TWO

Ellen stood outside Kate's door, her heart pounding rapidly as though she'd just run a marathon. On the drive over she had thought about what she was going to say and how she would say it. She had edited herself and revised and memorized the long speech and felt pretty good about it. Now that she was here, though, her nerve left her, and she hesitated. If she really wanted Kate, now was the time. Physically gathering herself, she knocked.

"Ellen?" Kate asked after opening the door.

"I love you," Ellen blurted, and felt the blood rush to her face.

For several heartbeats Kate stared, then opened her arms. Ellen fell into them and felt so many emotions—but primarily relief that she had made the right choice.

"I love you, and I want you to come with me to London." Kate was shocked by the realization and for saying it out loud. Thinking it was one thing, but asking Ellen to give up her life here astonished her. She couldn't possibly see how Ellen could quit her job and her family for the unknown in London. How could an American history professor find a career in Europe? And what about her family?

"Oh, Kate, if I could, I'd go with you tomorrow."

Kate's throat closed and for a moment she felt numb. Of course Ellen couldn't alter her life on a whim and for someone who was off in another country pursuing her own career. What was she thinking?

Ellen felt Kate stiffen in her arms and begin to pull away.

"What I mean is, I can't go with you right away. For one thing, my father isn't well, and while he'll make a full recovery, I need to be with my family now. On top of that, I still have my job at Georgetown and a commitment to my publisher." Ellen's mind raced with all the complications Kate's departure and her own responsibilities presented. She couldn't see her way clear without resigning her position, and she had lived her entire life within hours of her parents. Could she give up a career at a university she loved and a family who had always been there? What would she do in London? She supposed she could teach, but how would she find a position? And how well did she really know Kate? It had been only months since they'd gotten to know one another and fall in love. Was that enough to build a lifetime on?

"I'm sorry. I know I'm asking a lot of you." Kate drew her close once again. "But I love you and don't want to lose you. I haven't thought it all out and we'd have obstacles, but I want you with me, always. I've spent hours today thinking about you, and for the first time I want to spend the rest of my life with someone."

Ellen glanced up into Kate's eyes and saw the raw sincerity of her emotions laid bare. It was almost painful to look at her and she willed the hurt away. No one had ever given her so much, had wanted her so much, and her heart was full with a need so great she didn't know what to do with it.

"I suppose I could finish my research here and write the book in London," she thought out loud. "I have a colleague in the American Studies department at King's College who might be able to give me some advice on teaching positions in London…"

She could see the hope in Kate's eyes. She didn't want Kate to think it would be easy or even possible for her to find something quickly or in an area even remotely comparable to Georgetown, but for now, seeing Kate's pleasure was all that mattered. Ellen kissed her. She only meant to convey her love and a promise, but kissing Kate had never been that simple. Her hands wandered down Kate's back to her hips, and with the slightest pressure, Kate responded by thrusting into her. She wasn't sure if she or Kate had moaned, but it didn't matter; she was already lost in her own body's reaction.

They fumbled their way to the bedroom and quickly undressed.

The feel of skin upon skin made Ellen ache and she felt the wetness between them. She had never abandoned herself to someone so completely. The voice in her head that always accompanied a romantic encounter with someone, cautioning her about how she looked, was completely silent. This was Kate, whom she trusted with her body as well as her heart, and she let herself go. Lying on top of Kate, she arched up and pushed into her center. The contact was exquisite and she rocked forward, needing to feel more, wishing she could be inside Kate when she came. When Kate's hands reached for her breasts and stroked her nipples, she shuddered. She climaxed with an intensity so complete, she collapsed into Kate's arms, drawing it out for as long as possible.

Kate held Ellen, stroking her back and kissing her temple, trying to calm her racing heart. She was surprised to feel her eyes fill with tears, and she blinked them away. She couldn't imagine not having Ellen with her, not having this passion in her life again. Was it possible that Ellen would change her life for her? Would she be happy in London with just Kate and a career that might not fulfill her? Should Kate turn the job down and try to find something in Washington? Maybe Channel 2 would be interested in her.

"I love you," Ellen murmured.

A smile spread across Kate's face. "I love you, too." She thought about her flight tomorrow and at this moment didn't relish the thought. But she also knew that she couldn't delay the trip again. She needed to follow the entire thing through to the end—whatever that might be.

Kate stifled a yawn and her eyes drooped heavily. Ellen's deep breathing told Kate she was asleep and she held her tightly. She was so completely happy at that moment that she sighed contentedly. As she drifted off, a thought came to her that brought her back awake with a start. It was the best idea she'd had in a long time.

❖

Kate sat at the window seat sipping a glass of orange juice and leafing through the British Airways magazine. She'd brought a book to read, but knew she would never open it. The image of Ellen in bed that morning forced its way into her memory and she smiled inwardly. God, had it just been that morning that she had awakened next to her? It seemed like ages ago, yet the feel, smell, and taste of her lingered on her skin.

"Ma'am." Kate motioned to the flight attendant. "Another orange juice, please."

"I'd like to order some champagne and turn that into a mimosa. What do you think?"

Kate pulled Ellen in and kissed her, at first tentatively, then so hard she was certain her lips would be bruised. She stared into Ellen's eyes, afraid that if she blinked Ellen would disappear. "I think it's a great idea. Whatever you want."

Ellen was still in shock that in the middle of the night, Kate had somehow managed to book an extra seat on the flight, pack her bags, arrange for Kelly to take care of Beau, and still get them to the airport on time. She knew Kate was a determined woman, but she didn't realize how much. She thought she was going to like this character trait very much.

"Whatever I want? I like the sound of that." She took Kate's hand and stroked it.

"I hope you don't mind that I did this without asking you. I know you still have a lot of work to do on your book, but I thought a couple of weeks in London would give you a chance to see if you even like the city. And secretly, I was hoping you might stop in and see your colleague at King's College. It wouldn't hurt to find out about the possibilities of teaching there. I only hope your family isn't pissed at me."

"I love that you did this. It means everything to me. Mom was fine with it, and she knows how important this is to me. My father is doing very well, but I can be back on a flight and home if I have to. I need to do this, need to be with you so I can make a decision. We won't know what our lives can be unless we start somewhere."

"If you're not happy in London, we can think of something else," Kate insisted. "I can look for a job in Washington. Something will turn up eventually. I could—"

"Shh." Ellen pressed her fingers to Kate's lips. "One step at a time. Let's just wait and see."

Ellen leaned back in her seat and closed her eyes. Still holding Kate's hand, she felt their unbreakable connection. She had visited London many times and loved the city, but she couldn't help but think about her home, her career, her family and friends. *Could I give it all up for this woman?*

Kate lifted Ellen's hand to her lips, kissed it, then rested her cheek against it.

Yes, I could.

About the Author

KI Thompson began her writing career when her first short story, "The Blue Line," appeared in the Lambda Literary Award–winning anthology *Erotic Interludes 2: Stolen Moments* from Bold Strokes Books. She has published numerous short stories, as well as a novel, *House of Clouds*, a romantic saga set during the Civil War. Her forthcoming book, *Cooper's Deale*, will be released in September 2008. Kim resides in the Washington, DC area with her partner and two very spoiled but much-loved cats. Her interests include American history, Southwest Native American art and culture, and the culinary arts. She can be reached at www.kithompson. com.

Books Available From Bold Strokes Books

Deal with the Devil by Ali Vali. New Orleans crime boss Cain Casey brings her fury down on the men who threatened her family, and blood and bullets fly. (978-1-60282-012-8)

Naked Heart by Jennifer Fulton. When a sexy ex-CIA agent sets out to seduce and entrap a powerful CEO, there's more to this plan than meets the eye...or the flogger. (978-1-60282-011-1)

Heart of the Matter by KI Thompson. TV newscaster Kate Foster is Professor Ellen Webster's dream girl, but Kate doesn't know Ellen exists...until an accident changes everything. (978-1-60282-010-4)

Heartland by Julie Cannon. When political strategist Rachel Stanton and dude ranch owner Shivley McCoy collide on an empty country road, fate intervenes. (978-1-60282-009-8)

Shadow of the Knife by Jane Fletcher. Militia Rookie Ellen Mittal has no idea just how complex and dangerous her life is about to become. A Celaeno series adventure romance. (978-1-60282-008-1)

To Protect and Serve by VK Powell. Lieutenant Alex Troy is caught in the paradox of her life—to hold steadfast to her professional oath or to protect the woman she loves. (978-1-60282-007-4)

Deeper by Ronica Black. Former homicide detective Erin McKenzie and her fiancée Elizabeth Adams couldn't be happier—until the not-so-distant past comes knocking at the door. (978-1-60282-006-7)

The Lonely Hearts Club by Radclyffe. Take three friends, add two ex-lovers and several new ones, and the result is a recipe for explosive rivalries and incendiary romance. (978-1-60282-005-0)

Venus Besieged by Andrews & Austin. Teague Richfield heads for Sedona and the sensual arms of psychic astrologer Callie Rivers for a much-needed romantic reunion. (978-1-60282-004-3)

Branded Ann by Merry Shannon. Pirate Branded Ann raids a merchant vessel to obtain a treasure map and gets more than she bargained for with the widow Violet. (978-1-60282-003-6)

American Goth by JD Glass. Trapped by an unsuspected inheritance and guided only by the guardian who holds the secret to her future, Samantha Cray fights to fulfill her destiny. (978-1-60282-002-9)

Learning Curve by Rachel Spangler. Ashton Clarke is perfectly content with her life until she meets the intriguing Professor Carrie Fletcher, who isn't looking for a relationship with anyone. (978-1-60282-001-2)

Place of Exile by Rose Beecham. Sheriff's detective Jude Devine struggles with ghosts of her past and an ex-lover who still haunts her dreams. (978-1-933110-98-1)

Fully Involved by Erin Dutton. A love that has smoldered for years ignites when two women and one little boy come together in the aftermath of tragedy. (978-1-933110-99-8)

Heart 2 Heart by Julie Cannon. Suffering from a devastating personal loss, Kyle Bain meets Lane Connor, and the chance for happiness suddenly seems possible. (978-1-60282-000-5)

Queens of Tristaine by Cate Culpepper. When a deadly plague stalks the Amazons of Tristaine, two warrior lovers must return to the place of their nightmares to find a cure. (978-1-933110-97-4)

The Crown of Valencia by Catherine Friend. Ex-lovers can really mess up your life…even, as Kate discovers, if they've traveled back to the eleventh century! (978-1-933110-96-7)

Mine by Georgia Beers. What happens when you've already given your heart and love finds you again? Courtney McAllister is about to find out. (978-1-933110-95-0)

House of Clouds by KI Thompson. A sweeping saga of an impassioned romance between a Northern spy and a Southern sympathizer, set amidst the upheaval of a nation under siege. (978-1-933110-94-3)

Winds of Fortune by Radclyffe. Provincetown local Deo Camara agrees to rehab Dr. Bonita Burgoyne's historic home, but she never said anything about mending her heart. (978-1-933110-93-6)

Focus of Desire by Kim Baldwin. Isabel Sterling is surprised when she wins a photography contest, but no more than photographer Natasha Kashnikova. Their promo tour becomes a ticket to romance. (978-1-933110-92-9)

Blind Leap by Diane and Jacob Anderson-Minshall. A Golden Gate Bridge suicide becomes suspect when a filmmaker's camera shows a different story. Yoshi Yakamota and the Blind Eye Detective Agency uncover evidence that could be worth killing for. (978-1-933110-91-2)

Wall of Silence, 2nd ed. by Gabrielle Goldsby. Life takes a dangerous turn when jaded police detective Foster Everett meets Riley Medeiros, a woman who isn't afraid to discover the truth no matter the cost. (978-1-933110-90-5)

Mistress of the Runes by Andrews & Austin. Passion ignites between two women with ties to ancient secrets, contemporary mysteries, and a shared quest for the meaning of life. (978-1-933110-89-9)

Vulture's Kiss by Justine Saracen. Archeologist Valerie Foret, heir to a terrifying task, returns in a powerful desert adventure set in Egypt and Jerusalem. (978-1-933110-87-5)

Sheridan's Fate by Gun Brooke. A dynamic, erotic romance between physiotherapist Lark Mitchell and businesswoman Sheridan Ward set in the scorching hot days and humid, steamy nights of San Antonio. (978-1-933110-88-2)

Rising Storm by JLee Meyer. The sequel to *First Instinct* takes our heroines on a dangerous journey instead of the honeymoon they'd planned. (978-1-933110-86-8)

Not Single Enough by Grace Lennox. A funny, sexy modern romance about two lonely women who bond over the unexpected and fall in love along the way. (978-1-933110-85-1)

Such a Pretty Face by Gabrielle Goldsby. A sexy, sometimes humorous, sometimes biting contemporary romance that gently exposes the damage to heart and soul when we fail to look beneath the surface for what truly matters. (978-1-933110-84-4)

Second Season by Ali Vali. A romance set in New Orleans amidst betrayal, Hurricane Katrina, and the new beginnings hardship and heartbreak sometimes make possible. (978-1-933110-83-7)

Hearts Aflame by Ronica Black. A poignant, erotic romance between a hard-driving businesswoman and a solitary vet. Packed with adventure and set in the harsh beauty of the Arizona countryside. (978-1-933110-82-0)

Red Light by JD Glass. Tori forges her path as an EMT in the New York City 911 system while discovering what matters most to herself and the woman she loves. (978-1-933110-81-3)

Honor Under Siege by Radclyffe. Secret Service agent Cameron Roberts struggles to protect her lover while searching for a traitor who just may be another woman with a claim on her heart. (978-1-933110-80-6)

Dark Valentine by Jennifer Fulton. Danger and desire fuel a high-stakes cat-and-mouse game when an attorney and an endangered witness team up to thwart a killer. (978-1-933110-79-0)

Sequestered Hearts by Erin Dutton. A popular artist suddenly goes into seclusion, a reluctant reporter wants to know why, and a heart locked away yearns to be set free. (978-1-933110-78-3)

Erotic Interludes 5: Road Games, ed. by Radclyffe and Stacia Seaman. Adventure, "sport," and sex on the road—hot stories of travel adventures and games of seduction. (978-1-933110-77-6)

The Spanish Pearl by Catherine Friend. On a trip to Spain, Kate Vincent is accidentally transported back in time—an epic saga spiced with humor, lust, and danger. (978-1-933110-76-9)

Lady Knight by L-J Baker. Loyalty and honor clash with love and ambition in a medieval world of magic when female knight Riannon meets Lady Eleanor. (978-1-933110-75-2)

Dark Dreamer by Jennifer Fulton. Best-selling horror author Rowe Devlin falls under the spell of psychic Phoebe Temple. A Dark Vista romance. (978-1-933110-74-5)

Come and Get Me by Julie Cannon. Elliott Foster isn't used to pursuing women, but alluring attorney Lauren Collier makes her change her mind. (978-1-933110-73-8)

Blind Curves by Diane and Jacob Anderson-Minshall. Private eye Yoshi Yakamota comes to the aid of her ex-lover Velvet Erickson in the first Blind Eye mystery. (978-1-933110-72-1)

Dynasty of Rogues by Jane Fletcher. It's hate at first sight for Ranger Riki Sadiq and her new patrol corporal, Tanya Coppelli—except for their undeniable attraction. (978-1-933110-71-4)

Running With the Wind by Nell Stark. Sailing instructor Corrie Marsten has signed off on love until she meets Quinn Davies—one woman she can't ignore. (978-1-933110-70-7)